Unforgivable

Sharon Robards

Other Books by Sharon Robards

A Woman Transported

*

Australian Flavour – Traditional Australian Cuisine

Unforgivable

Sharon Robards

First Print Edition GMM Press *January 2014*

Cover model image - *Beautiful teen looking through window* © William Moss/ Dreamstime LLC

National Library of Australia Cataloguing-in-Publication entry:

Author: Robards, Sharon Lee, 1966- author.

Title: Unforgivable / Sharon Robards.

ISBN: 9780646910666 (paperback)

Teenage pregnancy—Australia—Fiction.
Unmarried mothers—Australia—Fiction.
Adoption—Australia—Fiction.
Adoption—Religious aspects—Catholic Church—Fiction.
Historical fiction, Australian.

Dewey Number: A823.4

For Mum

Of all the rights of women, the greatest is to be a mother.
Lin Yutang

Melbourne, 1992 _____ *Kim*

WELL, WELL, life can change in an instant in the most unexpected manner. Kim should have known that one day she'd have her past flung at her face harder than any bitter weather Melbourne dished out.

She took the large envelope out of the letterbox, flicked her thumb under the flap and pulled out the top of the letter. A gusty wind ripped the envelope out of her hand, throwing it toward the road. She scrambled to pick up the wayward letter. The wind whipped the envelope backwards, and it clipped the fence and fell into the neighbour's small yard. Kim leaned over the fence, stretched and touched the envelope, but only managed to tug out the letter a little more. She could nearly make out that letterhead, then as if on cue, the neighbour rushed outside.

Mrs Thomson took a couple of quick steps from her front door and snatched the letter right out of the envelope. "Oh, this isn't a bill, is it? That envelope you're holding looks too big for a bill, and I didn't see them read our electricity meters."

"Not sure what it is." Kim glanced inside the envelope. *There's another smaller envelope.*

Stepping closer to Kim, Mrs Thomson looked at the letter as if reading.

Kim grabbed the letter. "Hey! If you don't mind."

Mrs Thomson's face turned into a blend of amusement and spiteful satisfaction. She searched the empty footpath as cars sped past, then looked at Kim and lowered her voice. "I knew a young girl, back when times were different, expectations different, who got herself into a bit of a bother. You know, in the motherly way."

Kim scanned the letter. *Jigsaw, Adoption Agency...St Joseph's Hospital...1966....* If the wind wasn't whipping Kim's hair into her face and keeping her blood flowing, she might have fainted.

"There were lots of girls. Poor souls. Shunned, they were—only one way to escape the shame, apart from marriage, to do the right thing. Perhaps someone is looking for a relative of yours?"

Someone's trying to send me insane. This can't be happening.

"Did you hear me? Perhaps it's for someone you know. Oh, you do look a little queer. Would you like a cuppa, and tell me all about it?"

Now the whole street will know. "It must be for Christine." Kim quickly glanced at the letter, not really looking at it, just hoped pretending to look at it would convince Mrs Thomson. "Christine's doing an assignment—for art—needs to make a jigsaw. I have to go. I'm cooking." She scurried away, trying to shield her face from the wind as much as Mrs Thomson's narrow stare, but unable to deny she had just made a fool of herself.

Kim held a lit smoke in one hand and studied the Polaroid photograph in the other trembling palm, looking into the young woman's brown eyes—the shape and colour identical to her own. *Mine. Oh, God, mine.* The white shift dress suited the thin frame, and Kim heard from some far off place... *For my money, she looks tremendous.* He'd said those words, the first man. *Oh, God. No.*

She allowed herself to drift back to Derby Day in 1965, a few months before she went to *that* other place. Blistering heat smothered the city on Derby Day and all twin-set suits, stockings, pearls, hats and gloves—when the highest paid model in the world stunned Melbourne racing society and the rest of Australia, by making her grand entrance in a white shift dress ending a few inches above her knees. But it wasn't just the short dress, oh, no. No stockings and no hat and no gloves.

"It's disgusting," Kim's mother had said. "They might dress like that in London, but it's not the done thing here."

"She looks like the only one with any sense," Kim had replied. "I'd give anything to get out of these stockings."

Andrew had leaned toward Kim that moment and whispered, "For my money she looks tremendous. I'll take yours off later."

Kim stubbed out the cigarette in the ashtray on the table and pulled herself away from that memory, didn't want to think of Andrew—of loving each other. She ran her finger over the photograph. It was impossible to tell the woman's height. The ocean filled the background of the image cut off at the bare knees. *The top of a cliff.*

She placed the photograph on the kitchen table, not wanting to let it go, but fighting the urge to tear her own likeness into pieces, not because of the one in the snapshot but because of herself, of her memories, of the troubles this would cause. She read the letter again, then folded the piece of paper, careful to keep the same creases the writer formed, each turn of the paper unfolding memories and that shameful secret bit by bit. The burning in her chest deepened. Kim smelt ammonia, despite dragging heavily on the smoke, and threw the piece of paper toward the table. The paper landed beside the photograph as if this was the perfect order of things, that they must lie side by side, neatly and perfectly aligned for all to see.

She studied the woman again, determined it would be the last time. *It's a mistake. These things are for the best.* The matron had said that. *Best to move on and forget. Your secret will be safe.* But Kim couldn't escape the young woman's eyes. *Mine. Oh, God, mine.*

Back then, Kim had stayed silent beside her mother during the plane trip and the short taxi ride between the old terrace houses bordering the narrow streets and lanes, but couldn't stop the words when the taxi parked beside *that* place. "What if I'm making a mistake?"

"Lovey, you're doing the right thing. It'll be over shortly."

Kim dragged herself back to the present, the photograph, and the letter. She lit another smoke and again wanted to throw the letter and the photograph into the bin and block out the words scribbled in the letter. *You gave me no name. How could you give me no name?*

MAYBE HE somehow knew she was leaving. Maybe he stood somewhere by the train tracks in the car park, watching near his panel van. Sylvia opened a train window. But she didn't see him anywhere…he didn't know anything. They didn't let him know…. Then the train moved and the platform disappeared—leaving only metal tracks and gravel and wire fences—wind and heat and dust sweeping through the open doors and windows as the train picked up speed, clanking and rattling and swaying left to right.

The next platform came, then another station, even farther away from him, away from Tommy—to a feeling she hoped she'd never feel again. A mad longing and dispirited heart—limbo—not knowing when she'd see him again. But it wasn't going to last forever. They'd be together again.

She tried not to look at her mother sitting opposite—hat and gloves on and a handbag on her lap, gazing out the window, as if she too, dreamed of being somewhere else.

"You all right, Mum?"

Her mother nodded, but never looked at Sylvia, gave no sign that all would be all right. "It won't be long, and we'll be there."

Sylvia tried to focus on the journey and just looked out the window. A man wearing shorts and a white singlet pushed a Victor mower over a front lawn on the other side of the train tracks—for just a second—the suburbs, a blur of red roofs and flashes of large and green front yards and wide streets and wooden fences.

But the outside couldn't stop her thinking about her mother's silence. People left the train and others stepped on, looking all around—at her, as if they expected to see a friend, or maybe they just looked for a vacant seat, or maybe at all her sins etched across her face.

Before Sylvia fully let her mind wander again to dreams of Tommy, the promises they made a week ago, and her fears of today—the train lurched forward, rocking and clanking closer to the city, and its cluttered terrace house and narrow streets and lanes. In the middle of a road, kids played cricket with metal garbage bins for wickets.

Like a large gravel speedway, the rows of silver-grey tracks of Central Station verged off in different directions toward underground tunnels. In the distance, cranes hung motionlessly over skyscrapers—metal, stone and glass stretching into the summer sky—a deep blue…, then darkness surrounded the train in the underground tunnel. In a burst of light, the train slowed and halted beside the long platform.

Sylvia grabbed the handle of her suitcase, didn't say a word, and followed her mother off the train. They climbed the steps, hit a crowd of people and a small group of soldiers standing near a large clock at the entrance of the country train platforms, and stepped into the street.

The footpaths away from the station went on and on, threading through inner city lanes and streets Sylvia didn't know. Her back hurt too from tugging her suitcase, much heavier than her schoolbag ever was. Rubbish littered the gutters in a lane, and she smelt fish and chips and heard the bells and clinking of a pinball machine. Cardboard boxes of fruit and vegetables sat outside a corner shop.

"You make sure you keep yourself tidy and clean like I've taught you," her mother said. "Keep to yourself, and don't invite any trouble with the other girls."

Sylvia said nothing. In a tiny yard, a boy and girl giggled and splashed under a tap. Kids just being kids. Just being carefree. Not thinking about anything important.

"That's it there," her mother said.

A high wrought iron fence stretched the length of the other side of the street. Hedges hid the grounds beyond the fence. Sylvia and her mother crossed the road and stepped to the iron gate, as high as a door, and like the fence, impossible to climb.

Her mother unhooked the gate latch. "And when you leave, no one is to know about this." She gave Sylvia the briefest of hugs. "In you go. We won't talk about this again."

Pale pinkish-purple flowers, like miniature mountain ranges, lined the side of a gravel path to the old brick mansion. On the other side of the path, a nun pushed a hand grass mower, cutting the lavender spreading from the path across the lawn toward frosted glass doors. A nun, tiny in stature and wearing glasses, stood on the steps, holding a silky terrier under her arm. Sylvia looked up at the windows, four rows of windows, and saw a girl gazing back at her.

"I want to go home." Sylvia gripped her suitcase handle tighter. "This looks like a place people go to die."

Her mother let the gate clang shut and grabbed Sylvia's arm. "Not another word. You will do as you're told until you're twenty-one and of age. Keep on walking."

Sylvia followed her mother along the path, conscious of the crunch of their shoes on the gravel, then up the steps. "Sister Bernard, I'm sorry we're late. Our train was delayed. This is my daughter."

Sister Bernard took Sylvia's hand and gave it a gentle squeeze. "Welcome back to St Joseph's. I remember when you were born." She let go of Sylvia's fingers and patted the terrier. "Come inside."

The Sister smiled as if she forced her lips to be polite. Sylvia imagined the Sister practised smiling so often she probably smiled in her sleep. Her thick black-rimmed glasses magnified her eyes, making her face resemble a black-hooded fish—all eyes and lips.

Sylvia wasn't sure how many doors and corridors they walked through, but the gate shutting out her life seemed far away. Other nuns they passed, some of their faces hard and ridged like bark on an old tree and others solemn and soft as flowers, avoided looking at Sylvia—their eyes downcast at the sight of her.

Sister Bernard led them into a room. Sylvia sat beside her mother. The fireplace was dead, no embers in the hearth. Six brass bells of different sizes sat on the mantelpiece. The open window provided still and warm air. *I need to go to the toilet.* But the way Sister Bernard stepped behind her desk and sat like a school teacher about to give a lecture told Sylvia now was not the time to ask.

"I'm sure you'll enjoy your stay here until the birth of the little one, as thousands of other girls like you and just as many married women have since the hospital's founding," Sister Bernard said. "We only use first names here. As we already have a Sylvia, Susan or Susanna would be nice. Do you understand?"

Sylvia slowly repeated the words in her head. She was used to her own name—didn't like Susan and especially disliked Susanna. Not knowing another way, out of fear, she nodded and smiled. Maybe she hadn't heard right.

Sister Bernard leaned forward. "Pick another name, then."

Sylvia knew all the nuns of St Anthony had men's names. They taught at her school, and Sister Bernard wore the Order's emblem, a little cross and chalice on her habit. Sylvia decided a girl's name was better than Matthew or something, but she didn't want her name changed and was about to say so.

"Susan will be fine," her mother said.

Sylvia gasped. Her mother's face reddened, and she responded to Sylvia's surprise with a look that said *don't say a word.*

Sister Bernard picked up a pen. "Now, you'll need to sign this. Just your initial and surname there." She pushed the paper in front of Sylvia and pointed the pen at words on the bottom of a document, right there, set apart in their own little paragraph. *I hereby relinquish all rights to the child.*

Sylvia studied the words and pretended not to see the pen held toward her. Maybe if she never looked at either woman again, or the pen, this day would disappear. An expectant air filled the room as if everyone, including the dog, held their breath while waiting for something to land on hard tiles and shatter.

Sister Bernard's fingers drummed on the desk, the sound so slight it might not be real. The dog sat next to the fireplace, head cocked to the side moving with the taps. Sylvia sat entranced by the tips of the Sister's fingers twitching and just barely tapping the top of the desk as if she heard a tune that got faster and faster.

Sister Bernard's palm thumped flat on the desk. She cleared her throat and tapped the pen tip on the space for a signature. "You can read, can't you?"

Sylvia studied the words again. A bead of sweat rolled down her nose, dropped onto the paper, and the moisture in her mouth disappeared. "I don't understand what relinquish means." She stole a look at her mother, whose stare shouted, *you've brought this on yourself. Don't embarrass me anymore.* "Does this mean you're going to look after my baby, Mum?"

"It's the consent form, dear, just sign," Sister Bernard said.

"For mum to keep my baby?"

"The consent for adoption. It's the best outcome."

"Just sign it, Sylvia." Tears welled in her mother's eyes. "You need to think of your brother and little sister."

Sylvia leaned toward her mother. "What about my baby?"

"This is the right thing to do," her mother said. "Sign the paper."

"Tommy said he'd help." Sylvia bowed her head and held back tears. "I thought I came here to have the baby and, when it was born, everything would be all right and we could go home together." Sylvia's throat closed up. She bit on her lip to stop crying and felt like slamming her fists on the desk. "You told me—said it was so the neighbours wouldn't see me. You never told me anything about giving away my baby when it was born."

"I didn't think it needed to be spelt out. Just sign it," her mother said, her voice raspy. "Tommy doesn't have a say in this. He's done enough. The sooner you get on with your life the better."

Sister Bernard leaned forward. "It's a loving thing to do, dear. Girls like you give infertile married couples someone to love. I can see you come from a caring home. Don't deny this child that right."

"I must go to the toilet."

SISTER GREGORY stood outside Sister Bernard's office and wiped her fingers under the white band of her wimple, wishing the material repelled heat and had the power to give her more hours in the day. Sister Bernard normally conducted her entry interviews quickly, wasting little time, allowing no emotion, and taking no nonsense from any girls or their mothers. Sister Gregory couldn't help wonder what had stunned Sister Bernard into silence and tapped on the door, hoping the waiting girl was ready to settle into her room.

"What is it?" Sister Bernard's patience wore thinner the older she got, just as that smile she used for every occasion grew more false.

Sister Gregory opened the door. Sister Bernard's dog, Moses, stood at attention next to the fireplace, watchful, his courage larger than his little body. His mistress was also a deceptive opponent—tiny, aged, and frail. At first glance she looked as if she couldn't take a step in her heavy habit, surely weighing twice as much as she did. But she moved around the hospital like her mini terrier. "You asked me to come," Sister Gregory said.

"We're almost finished with the formalities." Sister Bernard tapped her pen on the paper in front of the teenager. "This is Susan. She's about to do what all the clever girls do. Come on now, dear. Sign, then you can go to the toilet."

The girl's dark eyes sparkled like the polished desk, and her lips trembled. *She's about to cry.* She sat with folded arms and her body turned slightly away from her mother. The mother's face was flushed, desolate.

It was difficult to tell the girl's age. Her frame, like the mother's, was petite. *Sixteen? Surely no older than eighteen.* Despite her obvious distress, the girl was lovely, not in a physically beautiful way but in the way young girls often radiate a glow of innocence, of freshness like new flowers in spring. Her dark and sleeveless dress, although close fitting, hid any signs of her sin, and Sister Gregory could not guess how far along the pregnancy.

The girl looked at Sister Bernard. "I'll burst if I don't go to the toilet. I've got to go now."

Sister Bernard dropped her pen. "Sister Gregory, show her where the toilet is. We'll sort this out after." Sister Bernard placed both palms flat on the desk, straightened her back and smiled. "Say goodbye to your mother."

The girl and mother stood at the same time. Sister Gregory noticed the mother's perfectly heeled shoes beside the woman's handbag, and the crisp pale green linen skirt and matching sleeveless top—a woman brought up well, or a woman who knew how to dress like a woman from the right side of the tracks.

The mother and daughter hugged awkwardly until the girl buried her face against her mother's shoulder. Sister Gregory wondered what words they felt unable to say, wondered what they'd say when they next met.

Sister Gregory tapped the girl's arm. "Pick up your suitcase."

The mother pulled away first, her face suddenly as pale as the daughter's. "I'll be back when I can." She avoided looking at the girl, took her gloves and handbag, then stepped toward the door. "Keep your chin up."

"I'm sorry for what I've done, but please don't leave me here."

The mother's voice wavered. "Don't do this."

"Come now, Susan." Sister Gregory held the girl's elbow. "This won't do anyone any good, least of all the child."

The girl shrugged her arm away as the mother escaped along the corridor. "I won't stay. You can't make me."

Sister Bernard stepped from behind the desk. "Oh, yes we can."

SYLVIA WALKED into the corridor outside Sister Bernard's office. She lifted her suitcase and tried not to think of her mother running away.

Sister Gregory's voice held no intimidation, only a slight European accent. "Please follow me."

"I'm not going back in there. I don't want to sign the paper."

"I'll show you where you'll be staying until the child's birth. Now, let's get you settled."

She walked beside Sister Gregory into the stairwell, struck at how mysterious and exotic this Sister sounded and looked with her accent and in her wimple compared to fish-like Sister Bernard. This woman, married to God, stood tall, shoulders back and head high, appearing twice the height of Sister Bernard and strode in a deliberate manner—each step precise and measured.

Singing came from the next floor—"Que Sera, Sera…" *What will be will be*—the same three lines of the song over and over. It didn't sound like Doris Day or Normie Rowe, but a bird squawking.

"Your mother looks like a lovely woman."

Sylvia turned to go up the next level of stairs, into a heat more stifling with each step. The building was as old as any in the city and smelt like a mix of disinfectant and mildew. "How many girls are here?"

"About forty. But they're still working." Sister Gregory stopped. "That's Melissa you can hear singing. She's one of God's special angels despite the voice of a rooster." An expression lit Sister Gregory's eyes as if to say, we think alike but let's keep that to ourselves. "You'll have about fifteen minutes to acquaint yourself with your new surroundings until the other girls come back from work. The rest of today is free time."

Sylvia wondered if her mother would be at the railway station yet or if she'd change her mind, come back and take her home. "I was born here."

"Then you should feel comfortable here. How long ago was that?"

"Almost eighteen years."

Sister Gregory glanced at Sylvia. "I see."

Sylvia searched the nun's face for the contempt she'd seen in Sister Bernard's. "But Mum and Dad were married. They lived in the city when they first got married. Did you work here then?"

Sister Gregory kept climbing the stairs. "I was a novice. Things have changed greatly since then. We have much better equipment. Married mothers still choose St Joseph's to have their children."

"So they had this place back then for unmarried girls too?"

"Yes."

"And you've done the same job all that time?"

Sister Gregory smiled. "A novice, Veronica, supervises the girls in this part of the hospital, but she's not well. I'm filling in for a few days. I assist Sister Bernard in the hospital administration."

The next floor came into view. The ceiling was high. A plywood partition, almost as high as the walls, created two side by side corridors, running the length of the space with rooms on each side. Light flowed into the hallway from the open doors of those rooms overlooking the hospital entrance. No light at all came from the rooms on the parallel corridor. Gloominess shaded that walkway. The wooden floors creaked under the linoleum as Sylvia followed Sister Gregory along the sunlit corridor to the last door.

"There's a recreation room and kitchen at the end of the partition. The shower, toilets, and laundry you're to use for personal items are on the next floor." She pushed open the door. "In you go."

A single bed filled most of the area—a matchbox closed-in-space—and the bed's mattress sagged in the middle. Folded sheets as white and crisp as paper, a grey woollen blanket and a pillow sat on the foot of the mattress. A wardrobe stood against the opposite wall. Under the window a Bible lay on top of a chair, beside a plastic waste basket. Sylvia's mouth dried, and her words caught in her throat.

"There are plenty of girls here who can assist. There's a shop at the front of the hospital, where you can buy personal items you might need such as toiletries or stationary. You're to avoid the reception area until you leave. You can access the shop from the courtyard near the bottom of the dormitory stairs."

"Is there a telephone?"

"Not for you."

Sylvia sat her bag next to the door and stepped to the window—placed her palms on the sun-warmed glass and her face as close as possible to the outside world. The nun had mown most of the lavender, leaving only a little bush near the gate. She thought of her little amethyst ring hidden on a string around her neck and Tommy's last words. *If they take you before I see you again, let me know exactly where you are.* No sound or smell came from the outside world, only the warmth on her hands from the sun on the glass.

The jumble of outbuildings in different courtyards didn't touch the high continuous fence. Two nuns strolled around the perimeter of the entrance area, toward each other, their heads bowed. Although Sylvia couldn't determine what startled the nuns, whether it was a sound from the streets or birds flying overhead, their gazes met then darted in the direction of the frosted glass doors.

"There are to be no unrelated male visitors and no smoking or alcohol. Lights will be turned off at 10pm. Do you understand?"

Sylvia nodded, unable to stop looking at the outside world. The tree-lined streets merged into a tangle of lanes and alleys, terrace houses, and tiny yards. Not the large backyards like the houses in her old street. *Where are you? Tommy, where are you out there?*

A few blocks away, tubes and metal and boards, scaffolding, covered skyscrapers. More cranes hung motionless—construction halted until the work week resumed. Buildings partly hid the Harbour Bridge's coat hanger shape and blotted out the harbour.

Sylvia quickly wiped a tear slipping down her cheek. "If the city keeps growing, there won't be any bush left."

"That might take a while," the Sister said, her accent a little more pronounced.

Sylvia thought of something her father had said often and blurted it out, sounding like him. "Now that Harold Holt's Prime Minister and buddy with the American President, Johnson, the Yanks might as well be running us. We'll end up with as many migrants as they have."

"Many people in other parts of the world like Vietnam, who have nowhere to live, don't have the peace we have, and other Western countries welcome them with open arms."

"Why can't they stay in their country? When they come here, they can't even speak English."

"I couldn't speak English when I arrived here."

Sylvia faced the Sister. "I only meant…. My mum and dad talk like that. I was just thinking of them."

"I know you're upset." Sister Gregory stepped beside Sylvia. "Most are grateful for being allowed into this lucky country."

"Where did you come from?"

Sister Gregory's gaze swept across Sylvia for a moment. "Poland." She turned and looked out the window. "You mustn't ask so many questions. You're not to walk in the area at the front of the hospital. The closed-off courtyard where the chapel is can be used for outside recreation only during specified times, which are different from the visiting hours for married women." The Sister pointed to a small cottage in another yard. Large hedges as high as the fences enclosed the area. "Confession will be held in the chapel tonight at sunset."

The nuns down in the yard walked on, heads bowed again. Sister Bernard's dog ran toward the hedge near the fence. In the dormitory a door opened, releasing the hum of a television. Thumping footsteps made the partition shake. The thumping sound stopped a few feet away. A barefooted girl, dressed in a

14

shapeless floral smock, stood in the doorway. She was taller and older than Sylvia and her stomach the shape of an enormous egg. The girl's gaze looked as if she couldn't rub two thoughts together. A bandage covered one hand, which she cradled in her other hand.

"What have you done to yourself, Melissa?" Sister Gregory asked.

The girl focused for the briefest moment on Sister Gregory's face. "I put a sheet in the roller press thingie, and my hand went in too." She looked at the ceiling and laughed. "It hurts a lot, and was stupid, wasn't it?" she added, as if expecting the ceiling to answer.

Sister Gregory's brows arched. "We all do silly things."

"Sister Bernard said I've gotta stay in the dormitory, so I don't cause any harm to my little one."

Sister Gregory glanced at Sylvia. "Get yourself settled, and have something to eat from the kitchen." She patted Melissa on the arm. "You let Susan be. I can hear the television. I'm sure you don't want more scuffles with the other girls over the chair. If it's vacant, remember what I told you, it's first come, first served."

"But I want to be Susan's friend."

"I'm Sylvia. My name is Sylvia."

"Please give Su—the new girl time alone." Sister Gregory waved Melissa away.

Melissa turned from the door. "I'll go back and watch television." Her thumping steps echoed through the dormitory until a door slammed shut.

Sister Gregory rubbed her brow a couple of times as if to remove an ache. "The best way for you to move on is to avoid mixing with all the girls, unless necessary. It's for the best. Married women are below on the second floor. Under no circumstances are you to go into their ward or communicate with them even if you run into them on the grounds."

"So pregnancy in unmarried girls is like leprosy?"

"Susan, every patient here deserves privacy. That's all I meant."

Sylvia picked up a sheet. "My name is Sylvia."

"The girls take turns cooking breakfast and dinner and keeping the kitchen tidy. Being Sunday tomorrow, after church service in the chapel, you can rest. Monday you'll start work. I'll give you your roster as soon as I can. You'll be rotated between the hospital laundry, kitchen, and the knitting and sewing room."

"I don't know how to knit."

"Now's a good opportunity to learn." Sister Gregory stepped to the door. "Get acquainted with your surroundings. We'll speak tomorrow."

Sister Gregory's footsteps barely made a sound as she walked along the corridor. Sylvia dropped the sheet on the bed and tried to pull the window up. It was nailed shut. Outside, thousands of houses filled up the suburbs stretching into the distance. She patted her stomach. *If I give you to them, where will you live?* She faced her new home—the matchbox space, and her body went rigid. *A box stuffed with dust. We'll die in here without air.*

She ducked her head out of the doorway. The kitchen sat at the end of the dormitory. She stepped past chairs and two enormous elongated tables, but she wasn't hungry. She felt squeamish. The lingering strong and sour smell of cabbage mixed with the fishy stink of cod made it worse. *If cleanliness is holiness, the girls on kitchen duty this morning will get a mouthful from the nuns.* The refuse of food and knives and forks clogged the drain.

A thunder of feet shook the floor. She cranked on the tap, ran her hands under the water, splashed her face and remembered passing the little boy and girl today across from the hospital. It wouldn't be dark for few hours, but she wondered if they were now safe inside.

Missing children feared dead. That was splattered over the front page of this morning's paper. Three children disappeared four days ago. They had been playing at the beach. Sylvia knew the missing children's parents must live in anguish, despair until their children were found and safe. Every afternoon since those kids went missing at the beach, even before it was dark, all the mothers around her neighbourhood called their kids inside. Sylvia tried to imagine the parents' pain—the not knowing where their children were, going over and over whether their children pleaded for mercy or screamed for Mummy, or maybe were dead.

She wiped her forehead with the back of her arm as the first girls dressed in floral smocks ran into the dormitory along each side of the corridors. She cleaned a knife on a cloth. No one seemed to notice her, except for a girl who accidentally elbowed her as they passed. The girl sneered at Sylvia and said, "Watch where you're going."

Sylvia lost hold of the knife, and it fell on the floor. "You're the one who wasn't watching where you were going."

The girl glowed like a light, all sparks and fire, and disappeared into the room beside Sylvia. Sylvia picked up the knife and stepped into her room. The lock on the door didn't work, so she sat her suitcase against it and went to the window.

She worked the knife around the nail head and managed to pry and pull it out. *You have to find me and take me out of this madness.* She tugged up on the window, and it slid open. The first rush of air brought the sweet scent of lavender, then a moist sea breeze tinged with salt and dust and city grime. After the first rush, it gave little relief—did not ease the heat in the room—thick like one more layer of clothing pressing against her skin.

The distant and low rumble of a plane flying away from the city, high over the harbour to another country, was the only sound from outside, and that surprised her. She didn't hear the little boy and girl from across the road. She remembered when she was their age. Back then, the days stretched on forever. Being younger was like that…sunshine and never ending fun filled the days. But now was different. She wasn't a little child anymore—and even though the days were just as long, they seemed much shorter.

The rumble and sight of the plane faded, leaving only the scattered sounds of galahs and magpies from trees lining the street. The Saturday afternoon quiet spread across the city, interrupted now and again by chirping birds, a dog barking far away, the mostly soft hum of traffic, and the occasional tire screeching and horn beeping. Normal life in those streets was now too far away.

Sylvia walked beside Melissa and followed the line of girls toward the chapel for confession. *We look like a herd of fat cows going to slaughter.* The only noise came from moths fluttering around the light above the chapel door as day turned to night.

She thought about how she might avoid revealing her sins in the house of God. *He knows them all anyway... Surely, He doesn't think they should take my baby.*

Melissa tapped Sylvia's arm. "Susan, do you have any brothers and sisters? I don't. Mum says I'm a handful, but I've always wanted a sister."

If I hear Susan one more time, I'm going to scream. "I have a brother and a little sister."

"What's your sister's name?"

"Leanne, but look, let's go quietly inside."

"Mum says God intends us all to be friends."

"I'm not sure I believe in God anymore."

"That's not nice." Melissa rolled her eyes. "Everybody believes in God." She struck a proud pose, her little chin thrust out, hand on her hip as if to say look how perfect I am, but instead looked like a bloated statue. "I'm here because God made me."

"I'm not trying to be nasty, but I really want to be left alone."

"I don't think you're very nice to say that about God."

"Shush! We're almost there. We can speak another time."

Sylvia entered the chapel ahead of Melissa. When she passed the tabernacle, she bent her right knee to the ground. The smell was the same as all chapels—ancient dust and candles and the lingering odour of everybody who ever knelt there.

With little free space apart from the sitting areas, it could have been a second hand shop, cluttered with hundreds of religious statues and pictures—and the nuns could have been kleptomaniacs. One statue of Mother Mary and baby Jesus stood the tallest, but there were lots of her and baby Jesus, and many other statues of saints and martyrs, and even a little Noah's Ark and animals all in pairs. A life-like Jesus on the cross took centre stage above the altar, not far from God's face in the stained glass window.

Sylvia stepped toward a rack of votive candles, placed two pennies in the offertory box, lit a candle, and knelt in a pew. The burning candle flames swayed gently in harmony as if they whispered a hymn, their voices the light flickering around the chapel. The candle flame she lit for her grandmother was larger, brighter than all the other flames around it—prouder. *Oh, Nan, I've sinned. I don't know what to do. I'm going to have a baby.* She bowed her head and imagined what her grandmother would say if alive. *Examine your conscience and ask God's forgiveness.*

Sylvia thought of the Ten Commandments. She hadn't prayed for a long time, had fought about going to church for the past two years, and swore, using God's name with her friends. She had lied to her mother about where she was when she was with Tommy and hadn't been chaste in thoughts or actions. A tremor built in her throat—her sins out of control and confronting. There was no hiding place, where He couldn't see her sins. *Oh, dearest God, please help me not sin again. I'm truly sorry for my sins.*

An older girl stepped out of the confession booth—the same girl that ran into Sylvia and caused her to drop the knife. Her gaze never met Sylvia's, and she rushed out of the church. When no one moved to take the girl's place, Sylvia entered. She closed the door, gulped, and squirmed. She always found confession intimidating—not the confession itself: sometimes the priests didn't sound like they listened to anything. She wondered if they parroted the same thing to everybody—but she hated the booth, the small, dark enclosed place. As she knelt in this one, there seemed to be no air here either, and her breathing tightened.

She waited in the dark, wiped perspiration from her forehead and tried to make sense of the whispering on the other side of the closed wooden window. She wondered what the others confessed—did the priest judge one confessor worse than another? There was silence, then the opening and closing of a door on the other side of the priest. The wooden window opened, leaving a lattice in the wall dividing them. She couldn't see his face, only the darkest of black shades and no hint of any features.

Sylvia crossed herself. "Bless me Father, for I've sinned. It's two years since my last confession. I've—." She couldn't say the words—wasn't sure how to express the worst sin, and blurted out, "When I was little, I used to sneak into the church near our house with my brother and a boy called Tommy and light all the candles without putting money in the offertory box."

"And recently?" The voice was even, comforting, younger than she expected.

She was grateful for the darkness then, wouldn't have been able to look at his face, and even in the darkness looked at the floor, in case he could see the shame in her eyes.

"Place your trust in God. He's your merciful Father, and He wants to forgive you."

Sylvia became aware of someone sitting on the far side of the priest, ears probably pricked, straining to hear, and she lowered her voice. "I don't know how to express my sin."

"Be honest."

"I've fallen pregnant unmarried…I'm sorry." Sylvia held her breath, waited for him to screech about her lost soul, but his voice remained indifferent.

"Do you truly think you have sinned, or are you repenting because you are sorry you are suffering the consequences of your actions?" His voice rose slightly as if he leaned closer to the window—reproach now in the tone. "It's a consequence of your sin that the child will be taken and given to worthy parents."

Sylvia wondered if a heart could break or die. Her heart felt as if it squeezed out of her chest, leaped onto the floor, and the priest stomped it to death.

She bowed her head lower and sat in what she knew appeared reverent silence while searching for a response, for a way to defend herself, anything which might cause them not to think she would be a bad mother. After a time, the truth settled on her. *You're too young…not prepared to be a mum.* "I know I shouldn't have…."

"If you have a contrite heart, God will see."

"I do realise I've done wrong…want to fix it all."

"Then you are contrite."

"So God won't take my baby?"

"God alone knows what penalty remains and the severity and duration of such penalties. Say the Rosary before you leave, three Hail Marys each night and pray for God's forgiveness."

Oh, why the Rosary? Why the Hail Marys? She didn't know either—never bothered to remember them. When she was ten, a nun told her if she didn't say three Hail Marys each night she would go to Purgatory, so she counted to a hundred each night instead of the Hail Mary and avoided the Rosary altogether.

She bowed her head, knew before she mumbled, "I detest my sins. Amen," that she was lost, hadn't really talked to God.

"God, the Father of mercies, through the death and resurrection of his Son, has reconciled the world to Himself and sent the Holy Spirit among us for the forgiveness of sins—through the ministry of the Church may God give you pardon and peace, and I absolve you from your sins in the name of the Father, and of the Son, and of the Holy Ghost."

She heard the priest's earlier words over and over. *It's a consequence of your sin that the child will be taken and given to worthy parents. I'm not being forgiven for anything.* "Amen."

"Give thanks to the Lord for He is good…"

Mmmmmm. Then like a puppet, she said again, "Amen."

"Et ego te absolvo a peccatis tuis in nomine Patris, et Filii, et Spiritus Sancti."

She didn't understand what he'd just said, though it sounded familiar, and had something to do with peace and sinning no more.

Sylvia stumbled out of the booth and to the chapel's exit. Even if she knew how to say her penance, it wouldn't stop them from taking her baby. That was her penance. She caught sight of the large hedges and wondered if they hid a broken fence—big enough that she could slip through and escape from this place.

*

The constant opening and shutting of doors continued through the night, as girls visited the kitchen and the upstairs toilets and showers. The cranking and rumbling pipes made the walls vibrate. But it was the girls arguing, crying and sobbing that kept Sylvia awake—told her she need not worry about going to Hell. She'd already walked through the hospital gate into hell.

She curled up on the bed. She'd never felt lonely before, not like now, despite the noise. She pulled her little transistor radio from under her pillow and turned it on, but the static sounded like ducks quacking and smothered any music struggling to get through. She switched it off and pushed it back under the pillow.

She heard nuns walking on the gravel path. That took her back to gravel crunching under Tommy's car tyres, as they drove into the drive-in theatre, and the delicious buttery smell of popcorn and hotdogs. She thought of where Tommy touched her, and knew she wasn't going to heaven. It was impossible for that now. She couldn't even remember the Hail Mary or the Rosary's other prayers to save herself or her baby from being taken.

She lay there bewildered that all the teachings of her mother and the church had been powerless to stop her sin. Lectures from Mum about keeping her legs shut and Sunday lectures about the importance of matrimony to keep away sin were all sealed up in plastic—didn't make sense to her back then—of no use to anyone caught in that delicious urging for the first time…caught without knowing how to control desire, how to walk away from it.

It started with a kiss. Just a kiss. An innocent kiss. But what a kiss that had been. A kiss she had wanted to never end. A kiss she knew she would never forget. The first time they did it, she thought the devil possessed her. She didn't care that the Lord above saw the brief moment their bodies joined. The naughtiness of it all excited her more, even now, this minute. She hadn't given any thought to what was happening…where it led. She wanted only the warmth of them being one, sharing each other…it to go on forever. Paradise on earth where only sweet, powerful sensations mattered, without a thought or care for later discoveries, later secrets and shame.

"He used you," her mother said, when she'd learned of Sylvia's pregnancy. "Just wait till your father finds out. He'll deal with you both. You can count on that."

"Tommy loves me."

"They all say that, you foolish girl. You've no idea of what you've done, the implications of this. The shame you've brought onto yourself and us. People will wonder what type of mother I am. You're going to the nuns. That's all there is to it. I've spoken to the doctor. He said it's best for you until the birth."

Somewhere in the hospital, maybe on the floor below, a bell rang over and over again. Not the tolling of church bells but a repeated ting-a-ling of a brass bell. Sylvia placed her palms on her stomach, closed her eyes, blocked out all memories turning bitter, dark, disgusting, and all sound.

She touched the slight swelling of her stomach and didn't want to be dreaming, didn't want the flutter in her stomach to disappear. Her sense of loneliness vanished—she wasn't alone. Her tears dried. She lay there, wondering if she imagined the single gentle tap and a slight swishing of her stomach. "Hello, in there. Can you hear me? Who do you look like? Me or him? A mixture of us? I can't wait to see you. See you grow. I won't let anyone take you…promise."

She waited for another tap, her hands pressed gently against her stomach, but nothing came. Maybe she imagined it all, including the bell ringing, dreamt now, and imagined Tommy's words, only a dream, part of the conspiracy to take her baby. Sylvia knew now, her heart had not died earlier today when the priest stomped all over it. Deep inside her heart ached where it was supposed to be.

The door opened a crack. "You awake?" Melissa asked. "I can't sleep. You awake?"

Sylvia kicked the still folded woollen blanket off the end of the mattress. "I'm trying to sleep. You go back to bed." She turned onto her other side, and the breeze coming through the window brushed over her face. The stars sparkled like thousands of minute candle flame tips, and her tears fell harder, even from her nose, soaking the pillow.

"Susan, why are you crying?"

"Didn't you hear me? Go away!"

Melissa's stomps moved along the corridor toward the stairs.

What's wrong with me? It's not Melissa's fault you're here.

The nuns' boots continued to crunch on the gravel path. A guard of nuns circled the entrance, eyes like hawks on the frosted glass doors, and probably holding the giant crosses dangling from sashes at the front of their waists, ready to strike out with them like swords if anyone challenged them.

She was jailed with shunned girls, girls who like her had fallen from grace. She thought of the priest's words during confession. *God alone knows what penalty remains and the severity and duration of such penalties.* Their punishment...to have their babies given to more worthy parents. *Oh, dear God, please don't let them take my baby.*

She looked out the window and tried to count stars, two hundred of them, instead of saying the Hail Mary and Rosary, but like counting sheep when you can't sleep, the sound of the nuns' steps outside hitting the gravel path—one, two...ten...fifty—made her eyelids heavy. The numbers and footsteps blurred into each other and every memory. She strained to stay awake...tried to focus on counting stars, not footsteps. But she knew before she reached a hundred, she wouldn't be able to count to two hundred and mumbled, "I'm sorry. I'll try again tomorrow." The distant bell ringing faded, and everything turned a comforting black.

SISTER BERNARD rang the bell when births were imminent, to ensure on-duty novices and sisters in mid-wife training witnessed the miracle. Cries of agony verging on a scream started soon after the bell rang. Unable to concentrate on mere paperwork, Sister Gregory closed the file on her desk.

Some labouring girls resigned themselves to the pain, enduring their crosses in relative quiet. Others, their fear and anguish that life will end, fought against each wave tearing through them and cried out to God, even more and longer than Jesus cried on the cross.

The chart on the wall showed Sister Dominic and two other sisters trained in midwifery were on duty in the labour rooms. Sister Dominic's reputation said she was the most competent of all midwives. Like many in the church, she believed the way to God lay in self-suffering. She didn't expect others to do all the suffering and often worked sunrise to sunrise, making sure she suffered enough for God's blessing.

Sister Gregory stepped out of her office, past the picture of Pope Paul VI on the wall, and into the corridor. The cries came from the birthing room at the end of the hallway. Nuns walked across the wooden floor, not speaking, accustomed to the screams as much as to the smell of ammonia. *Business as usual.* Except for the girl crying out and the swish-swish of black or white habits, the scene resembled a silent movie—quiet and without colour.

"Please—let me use the mask—I beg of you," the girl pleaded from the birthing room. "I was told I could use the mask...please...help."

"The machine isn't working. Prayer will give you relief. You're almost there," Sister Dominic said. "Push. Now! Ah, push again."

Sister Gregory stood still and took in the girl's words. *O Lord, beloved Lord, preserve the girl and child from danger.*

"Shut it up—you—you get here and push—oh—my God. What are you doing? No. Stop. Please stop."

Sister Gregory ran across the hall into another birthing room. The power cords to the machines were tangled together on the floor like dead snakes dumped out of a basket. She fumbled and searched for the gas machine cord.

The girl screamed again.

Sister Gregory pulled and yanked at the cords, but they knotted further. *Concentrate.* She took a deep breath, thinking of the labouring girl. *Breathe with the pain. Slow down. Breathe with the pain.*

"Sister! Sister!"

"Not now." Sister Gregory realised who said the words. While gripping the cords, she faced Melissa. "What are you doing here? How did you find me? Go—go to your room. Now."

The labouring girl let out a shrill cry, surely reaching heaven.

Melissa walked to the machine. "Everyone is asleep. I can't."

Sister Gregory freed the cord. "You need to go to your room."

The girl's cry petered out into silence.

Sister Gregory put her finger on Melissa's lips. "Shhhh!"

Sister Gregory held her own breath, clenching the freed cable. There wasn't another sound from the birthing room, not a word, not a whisper, and she prayed to the Lord for the child, for the mother, for both to breathe in the first light of day.

The silence stretched on as if a violin string risked snapping while holding a solitary high pitched note.

Melissa moved her mouth away. "I'll suffocate if I keep my lips shut."

A baby cried a healthy little cry.

Sister Gregory kissed the gold cross hanging from her neck. *Dear God, thank you.* "Stay here. I'll be back in a minute."

"I want to come."

"You can't. Don't move." She wheeled the gas machine across the corridor toward the door.

A muffled, hysterical, shout erupted. "Get it away. You must let me see—please, stop. Is it a boy or girl? Get the pillow away from my face. I beg you, let me hold my baby—just once."

"The Lord has chosen parents more worthy of raising the little one," Sister Dominic said. "You need to stay on the bed. The afterbirth is still to come."

Sister Gregory opened the door. Like a woman stealing a precious jewel, a Sister shielding a bundle in a blanket, brushed past and rushed along the corridor.

The girl sat bolt upright on the bed, clutching a bloodied sheet to her. Grief, pain, and fear contorted her face. "Where have they taken my baby? Why can't I nurse my baby?"

Sister Gregory pushed the gas machine past a pillow on the floor toward the other gas machine. "The child has been taken to the nursery. You both need your rest."

"Ah, the cavalry has arrived. Here's the gas," Sister Dominic said.

"I don't want the fucking thing now, you cow. I want to see my baby."

"It will give you relief and help to calm you." Sister Gregory crouched to plug in the new machine and almost smiled at the cow term. Sister Dominic was as large as a Jersey cow.

The other machine was plugged into the power outlet but switched off at the wall. Whether it was sixth sense or instinct, Sister Gregory didn't know, but instead of plugging in the new machine, she flicked on the power.

"Bring my baby, please...."

The machine let out a hum, and the meter showed gas flowed through the mask. Pushing her suspicions aside, despite a slight tremble, Sister Gregory kept her voice neutral. "You said the machine wasn't working."

Sister Dominic picked up the pillow. "Might have been a power surge." She placed the pillow on the bed and frowned. "I'm not sure I like your tone, Sister."

"Why didn't someone get another machine?"

"It's not for you to question me." Sister Dominic stepped toward the girl. "There wasn't time."

"Keep away from me." The girl cowered to the head of the bed and burst into tears again. "She butchered me. Took to me with scissors while they held me down. I heard the snip…snip…snip."

"Stop the nonsense. An anaesthetic was used prior." Sister Dominic said. "You need to lie on your back, so I can massage your lower abdomen to expel the placenta." She glanced at Sister Gregory. "It was an episiotomy. The baby came too quickly, and this one was going to be ripped to shreds."

Sister Gregory handed the mask to the girl. "Please, take it."

The girl grabbed the mask and placed it over her mouth and nose. She took in a big breath…her eyes closed only a second, terror keeping them wide and watchful.

Sister Gregory turned her attention to Sister Dominic. "Why wasn't the doctor summoned?"

"He was, but he's busy in the married women's ward."

*

Attention is the essence of prayer. Sister Gregory stepped through the courtyard toward the chapel, attempting to calm her mind and prepare herself for the sacrifice of Sunday Mass. It was almost six in the morning, but she was tired and running late—so much so, the nuns already sang, "We praise thee, O God…we acknowledge thee to be the Lord…."

She couldn't sing alto or soprano. She didn't have any sense of rhythm, pitch or tone, but loved listening to harmonies made by those God blessed with angelic voices. Before her admission into the Order, she'd often listened to classical music. The tenor voice reminded her of her father, of her old dreams of being like him and teaching music. But that was not her gift.

Right now, she found focussing on the words difficult, conscious of the heaviness of her habit. Some younger sisters whispered about having them shortened, whispered Vatican II now allowed them to experiment with a more modern dress sense.

The older sisters thought it was a conspiracy, couldn't believe the world changed. *What did a few inches have to do with vanity or modesty? Was displaying the ankle likely to place them in moral danger or conflict with their vows? Obedience? Chastity? Apparently so.* They couldn't imagine any other way. Sister Gregory thought since she was inclined to trip on the habit, surely a few less inches would be permitted. As soon as the Order implemented that little change to their habits, she and others would suffer a little less in hot times. Surely, God would not mind.

Melissa trailed the waiting girls funnelling into the chapel. Sister Gregory couldn't see the new girl. Sylvia, who fought being called Susan, wasn't in the crowd. Maybe she had already entered the church.

Melissa waddled toward her. "Sister! Susan isn't coming. She said God won't help her, and she isn't going to church."

"We've all been given free will. She can choose to use it as she pleases. Now, you go back to the other girls."

Sister Gregory waited until Melissa followed the last waiting girl into the chapel, then checked her watch. She was already late. A few more minutes would make little difference. She walked to the hospital and the waiting girl's dormitory. Avoiding Mass compounded the girl's sins. She moved up the stairs, holding her habit up to stop the hem from catching on her shoes. She walked along the partitioned corridor, aware of her steps and how the soles of her shoes stuck to the grime on the linoleum floors. *The girls aren't doing their chores.* Sylvia's door stood ajar, the gap expelling a stream of light.

"Susan, I noticed you haven't gone down for Mass?"

"My name is Sylvia."

"Can I come in?"

"There's no lock on the door."

Sister Gregory opened the door and stopped, taken aback by the sight of Sylvia lying facing the wall in the foetal position. The Bible lay face down sprawled open on the floor as if thrown at the wardrobe. "Why aren't you attending Mass? Are you unwell?"

"Must I go to Mass?"

"Not if you choose not to." Sister Gregory stepped to the wardrobe, picked up the Bible and placed it on the chair. "But I think it might give you some comfort to speak to the Lord. It's also our duty to praise God and give Him thanks on holy Sunday."

Sylvia's body straightened a little, but she stayed facing the wall. "I went to confession last night, but I can't do my penance of saying the Rosary. I don't know the Hail Mary or the other prayers. I woke in the middle of the night and spent a little while ago searching for the Hail Mary in the Bible."

"How long has it been since you went to Church?"

"I just never learnt it properly…never concentrated on it."

"I can help you remember it, if you want? It's not difficult. You would have had it in a little prayer book."

Sylvia rolled over and sat on the end of the bed. "Isn't it in the Bible?"

"Not completely. It's taken partly from Scripture, and the Church added the rest. Remember the Angel Gabriel saluting the Blessed Virgin? 'Hail,' Gabriel said to Mary, 'full of grace, the Lord is with thee.'"

"I don't remember the rest of the prayer."

Sister Gregory sat beside Sylvia. "Hail Mary, full of grace, the Lord is with thee. Blessed art thou among women, and blessed is the fruit of thy womb, Jesus. Holy Mary, mother of God, pray for us sinners now and at the hour of our death."

"Why do we pray to Mary and not God? How will He hear us?"

"You can always pray to God, but by asking Mary to pray for us, we acknowledge we are poor sinners. Mary is Jesus' mother, so we ask Mary for her powerful prayers and intercessions to her son. Do you have any paper and pencils or pens? Writing it down might help you remember."

"Saying penance doesn't mean I can keep my baby."

"Don't block out those who can help you find acceptance of what you have done, of what you must do. Mary and God will hear your prayers. Your prayers will not be ignored, although only Our Lord knows the full plan He has for you. Never make the presumption you can live without God and save yourself. Prayer is all we have to bring God into our life. It's the only way to gain forgiveness from sin."

"Why can't I do something to fix it?"

"God pardons sins through faith in the sacrifice of Jesus rather than works of merit. Prayer is a way to gain forgiveness, not change God's plan for us. Prayer, if you put your heart into it, will give you relief."

Sylvia stood, dragged her suitcase from under the bed. She pulled out a notepad and a pencil-case, then sat back on the bed, paper and pencil held ready.

The singing in the chapel stopped. The little hand on Sister Gregory's watch ticked around. In her mind she heard Sister Bernard screeching and already preparing penance for the mortal sin of missing Sunday Mass. "Hail Mary, full of grace, the Lord is with thee…," Sister Gregory said and finished the prayer. "We'll move onto the other prayers in the Rosary."

*

Sister Gregory was about to enter her office, when Sister Bernard glided toward her in a manner that made Sister Gregory wonder if she had a little high powered scooter under her habit. She carried Moses under her arm, and in the other hand, held the clapper of a brass bell to stop it from ringing.

"In we go." Sister Bernard stepped into the room as if she climbed off the scooter and walked in time to the "oom-pa-pa" beat of the waltz. "I've only got a moment."

Sister Gregory shut the door and prepared herself for a lecture and harsh penance. Sister Bernard was as fluent in the scriptures as she was in running the hospital.

"I noticed you didn't attend Mass today," Sister Bernard said.

Sister Gregory lowered her gaze and nodded. "The new waiting girl wasn't there. I thought she might be ill."

"No need for humble obedience." Sister Bernard carefully placed the bell on the desk, then stroked Moses' back. "We've

known each other a long time. There's no one else in the room."
Sharpness tinged her next words, but impatience, a lack of time
drove it, not antagonism. "Was she ill, or just being wicked?"

"At confession she was given the Rosary as penance and was
distressed she couldn't remember all the prayers."

"I see." Sister Bernard stopped her hand in mid-pat just above
Moses' back. "And…?"

"I would have gone to confession straight away, but had release
papers for a waiting girl to organise."

"No need for Mother Superior Terrance to know. I'll speak of it
no more," she said, her voice as smooth and hard and cold as
marble. "I'm sure you'll seek to rectify offending God and a
rejection of His perfect love and justice."

Sister Gregory's thoughts turned to Sister Dominic. "Have you
heard of any problems with the gas machines?"

"Why do you ask?"

Sister Gregory studied the wall, noticed paint peeling in sections
and recalled what Sister Dominic said, her tone—too brash, no
matter how hard Sister Dominic tried to alter it.

"I don't have all evening," Sister Bernard said.

"Last night Sister Dominic said a machine didn't work, but
when I switched on the power it started."

The Matron sighed. "Probably a power surge at that moment."

"She also interacted with a waiting girl during labour in a
manner, which seemed overly harsh. I wonder if Sister Dominic
might be feeling under the weather."

Sister Bernard didn't blink, not once, as she said, "These girls
come and go, and until now, for the past six years, they've been
only statistics to you on hospital documentation. It's important to
remember our duty is to God first and then to our mission to
protect the little ones. Sister Dominic might be as sanctimonious
as a nun from the dark ages at times, but looked fine this morning
and in good spirits."

"A pillow was placed over the girl's face."

"Over her face or as a shield to stop the girl seeing the child?"

Sister Gregory remembered the girl's muffled, hysterical shout.

Get the pillow away from my face. "I wasn't in the room, just heard the muffled screams."

"Sometimes in our dealings with the waiting girls, we have to be a little cruel to be kind." She patted Moses. "It's routine hospital policy, almost country-wide, to forbid eye contact between the girls and the babies they are relinquishing, to ensure bonding between a mother and child does not take place. You know that, have known it for a long time."

"I'm aware of the policy, but...."

"Do I hear an objection?"

Sister Gregory thought back to what she thought happened in the room with Sister Dominic. It was possible the machine didn't work the moment the sisters tried to use it. Sister Gregory thought about the complexities of eye contact. Sometimes a look overpowers a person. Perhaps if a mother and child did look into each others eyes after birth, the mother would be haunted forever by the image of her child and the child doomed to forever search for its biological mother in their adoptive mother's face. "I'm sure it's only the heat...."

Sister Bernard glanced at the bell. "You'll need that in the morning to wake the girls." She smiled gently. Nothing false in her smile, no strain at all, but the way her eyes focused on Sister Gregory rang a little false, or maybe a little too watchful. "Has Susan resigned herself to her predicament?"

"I believe she has realised prayer can offer her comfort...but already feels a strong attachment to her little one."

"It will pass, once she's accepted what's right and realises the child will be better off with a married couple. Because Susan has taken you into her confidence, you might be more successful in gaining her signature on the papers, especially now she's seeking prayer. They're in my office."

Sister Gregory lowered her gaze to the desk, remembering the day Sylvia arrived at the hospital and the Matron's words. *Susan's about to do what all the clever girls do. Come on now, dear. Sign.*

"Did you hear me?"

"I'll collect them when I have a moment." Sister Gregory picked up papers and shuffled them over her desk, still avoiding the Matron's eyes, trying to think of a way to speak up. A mother wasn't supposed to sign the papers until five days after the birth. "It might be a bit late tonight…when I'm finished what needs to be done."

"Find the time tonight before lights out."

Sister Gregory met blindness she'd never noticed before in Sister Bernard's stare. Not knowing how to reply, how to disobey, Sister Gregory nodded.

Sister Bernard walked to the door, too slowly, clearly not finished, then turned. "After chapel, I noticed Susan's window raised. Organise for it to be nailed down properly."

SYLVIA HEARD the footsteps, slow and precise, over her transistor radio softly playing The Beatles' "*Help*...." The words were mumbled at moments, static fighting for air time, not like earlier when the music blared through her room. The door stood ajar, and she peeped through the gap. The partition shook, but not like when Melissa bounced along the corridor, singing at the top of her lungs, *These Boots are Made for Walking*. Sister Gregory stepped along the hallway, head high, probably saying a prayer. *Maybe she's bringing my roster.* Sylvia smiled, placed her notepad under her pillow, and sat straight, ready to tell the good Sister she'd memorised the Hail Mary.

"Susan, I have the adoption papers."

Sylvia swallowed her guttural moan before it turned into a scream—her jaw tensed, and she crossed her arms. *Please go away.* "My name is Sylvia." She gritted her teeth. "I was going to have a sleep."

"We need to talk about this. I suggest if you want to sleep, you turn off the rocker music. It's the devil's plaything, and you'd be best not to get involved." Sister Gregory pushed open the door and stepped into the room, holding a folder under an arm and a hammer against her thigh. "Your new name is so that no one knows your true identity. It's to ensure your stay here remains a secret."

Sylvia laughed, avoided looking at the hammer and pushed aside the thought the Sister was going to knock sense into her. Her mother had told her, *I should have given you a clip over the ear years ago, but the nuns will knock some sense into you.* "Secret?

We all know why we're here. It's a bit hard not to notice when we end up looking like fat cows. And the music isn't the devil's plaything at all. There's nothing wrong with it. It's rock and roll."

"What's happened since we spoke this morning?"

You standing there, holding the papers and a hammer. "This morning you said only the Lord knows the full plan for me, but you all planned to take my baby before I even arrived. The papers were waiting, needing only for me to sign them."

"For the baby's good."

The song finished, and the radio spluttered and static increased. The announcer's voice croaked, and Sylvia said louder than she intended, "How do you know God wishes this for me?"

"Please turn off the radio, so we can speak without distraction, before I confiscate it and lock it away until you leave."

"My dad gave it to me. You won't be taking it anywhere." But Sylvia switched it off and pushed it under her pillow.

"This isn't about you, but what's best for the baby. Every girl understands why she's here and has already made that choice."

"If they're all so happy with their choices, why do they howl of a night? Why do they all talk about hating their mums and dads and whoever brought them here?"

"You'll make your time here easier on yourself if you resign yourself to your predicament."

Sylvia's shoulders slumped, and her lips trembled. "I don't feel well. I'll sign it tomorrow."

"As soon as you realise delaying the inevitable is only hurting yourself, you'll feel much better. It's time to turn off the lights."

"I can't bear it in the dark in this place. I hate being here alone. I keep having nightmares," Sylvia said, the words catching in her throat, "can't stand hearing everybody crying during the night."

"Tomorrow will be a new day."

"Where I'm locked away as if the sight of me is disgusting. Where no one smiles. It's like a morgue here."

"I wish we had the temperature of a morgue." Sister Gregory shut the door. "Can't you see it's for your own good?"

Sylvia gazed at the window, into the darkness, wishing the slight breeze would turn into a gush of cold wind. *Leave me alone.*

"You're so young." Sister Gregory crouched in front of Sylvia. "You don't know what's for the best. Once you start work tomorrow and your mind is occupied, you'll feel much better."

"I miss him."

"By him, you mean the child's father?"

Sylvia nodded. She didn't want to share her thoughts about Tommy, didn't want them soiled, made dirty, ruined.

"Young love passes. You'll meet someone else one day, marry, and have children…. The way the Lord intended."

"You don't understand how I feel. You've never been in love. I miss him…can't stop thinking about him. This child is my own…too."

Sister Gregory's jaw tightened. She stood and in a very controlled manner, tapped the folder on her thigh. "This isn't about me."

"Ha! You have been in love. Is that why you stay here? Because you were hurt?"

"Listen to me. It's not a sin to fall in love. It's natural, but sharing that love out of marriage is wrong."

"You haven't answered me."

Sister Gregory's lips compressed, her eyebrows almost joined, and she stepped to the window. "It's time to turn off the light."

"I knew it. You've never been in love. You can't understand how I feel. It's all a stupid game to you, a stupid game where me and my baby have to pay for your cold heart, the stone hearts of all of you."

"Why won't you sign the documents instead of playing games?"

"I want something you'll never feel." Sylvia lowered her gaze to the large wooden cross held between the sash and the Sister's stomach on her waist—fixed to the cross, the little metal statue of Christ suffering, sparkled in the light. "I want something you'll never understand."

"Susan," Sister Gregory lowered her voice, "love isn't lust."

Sylvia's entire body tingled. A huge stone formed in her throat that if dislodged would allow a flood of tears. She shuffled her feet, unsure if guilt or shame heated her face, then, determined to regain her composure, met the Sister's stare. "How do you know what lust is? Aren't you a virgin married to Christ? My friend's mother said most nuns are lesbians, and their babies are buried in convent grounds." She pointed at the window. "Dead babies are out there in the ground, Sister."

Sister Gregory tilted her head backwards slightly. Her eyes widened. She froze for a second, looking like she'd never breathe again. "Our bodies are sacred and should only be given in full when vows are taken, whether they're religious or matrimonial." She rubbed her brow and pursed her lips as if she were about to speak another language for the first time. "Lesbians?"

"Women who are inclined to do women."

"I understand what you mean, but two women can't make babies."

"I know how babies are made…so you somehow have sex with Jesus, if not the priests?"

Sister Gregory's grip on the hammer handle tightened. In a measured voice wavering, soft, then loud, then snarling a bit, she said, "I think you already know the answer. Sex isn't something to make a mockery about. It's a sacred thing…. What you suggest…it's blasphemy!"

Sylvia pointed out the window once more. "Can't be too sacred if babies are buried in convent grounds."

"This is a hospital…not our convent." The frown deepened on the Sister's now pale face. "I've never heard such a horrible thing." She stood silent for a moment. The colour returned to her cheeks. "One part of religious life is about physical abstinence, not lustful fantasies about the Holy Spirit or our religious brothers. We seek to be close to God in a spiritual manner through contemplation and prayer."

"Well, it would have been helpful if someone had told me properly what sex was before I did it."

"When did you leave school?"

Sylvia folded her arms across her breasts. "What's that got to do with anything?"

"It's merely a question."

"I left a couple of weeks ago. This was to be my last year, but Mum was mortified the whole neighbourhood would find out."

"Perhaps you can go back to school when this is over."

"I wanted to be a teacher, but Dad doesn't think I need an education."

Sister Gregory sighed. "You'll soon come to your senses about the baby." She placed the folder on the chair under the window, then pulled a nail out of her habit's pocket and banged the nail into the window frame just above the mid-point so the window could not be pulled up again. "When I'm finished, the lights will be turned off."

I'll pull that nail out too.

But another nail, then another, came from the pocket and were banged into the frame.

"Why must it be nailed shut? Suffocating me will kill me and the baby, not make me change my mind."

Sister Gregory hammered in another nail.

Sylvia thought to jump up and grab the hammer and smash it through the window, but then that would get her thrown into jail, or worse—a nut house. "Why are only we imprisoned? What about everybody else having babies?"

Sister Gregory held the hammer mid-air, above one more nail almost pounded into the window frame, then half heartedly let it drop onto the nail—the clang when the hammer head hit the nail a bit of a fizzle. "No one has been imprisoned."

"I've been forbidden to leave without permission. You're nailing shut my window. My mother is pregnant, and she isn't here. Prisoners have more freedom, more visits than we do in this Hell."

Sister Gregory stood still for so long, she could have been a prop. She reached slowly into her deep pocket for another nail. "Your mother is married."

"My dad isn't there anymore."

Sister Gregory hammered in another two nails with as much vigour as a woodcutter chopping down a tree, then without a word flipped off the light and left.

_____ *Sister Gregory*

SISTER GREGORY walked toward the dormitory on the hospital grounds that slept up to thirty nuns. Between twenty and eighty years old, the sisters crammed together in the cubicles separated by curtain walls and doors. Each cell held only enough space for an iron bed, a bedside table with a pottery jug and wash bowl, a locker to hang three habits, and a chair.

Sister Anthony, the oldest of the sisters, sat in a chair on the veranda, her body silhouetted by light from the open window and dormitory screen door. She was eighty and had been the longest serving hospital administrator and Sister Gregory's favourite sister. She pottered around the gardens now, despite her slowness and deteriorating sight, always humming hymns. Sister Anthony refused to retire to the Mother House, despite the privilege and a measure of status, preferring to contribute in minor ways to the hospital's cause.

Sister Gregory stepped onto the veranda. The mumble of prayers and chattering of rosary beads in the dormitory drifted outside. She imagined some sisters bowed their heads and kneeled by their beds, others sitting in chairs and staring at the ceiling, their lips moving slightly, while their fingers travelled around each point of the beads. "God be with you, Sister."

"And with you."

"Why are you still out here?"

"I can't sleep in there like a sardine in a can. It's too hot. Maybe I should ask to have my bed moved out here."

"Or a night light for the grounds, so you can keep working in the gardens."

Sister Anthony laughed. "I wish I had that much energy." She tapped the chair beside her. "It's been a long day for you. Tell me what's wrong."

"There isn't anything wrong."

"You're rubbing your temple. I know you well enough by now."

Sister Gregory slumped into the chair. Each night sleep came easily for most of the sisters from exhaustion, but not to her on this night. "I've been speaking with a waiting girl...have you ever heard...," she lowered her voice, "that babies are buried in convent grounds?"

"The Mother House's grounds?"

"I don't think she meant there."

Sister Anthony frowned and clasped her hands together in her lap. "Everybody, by nature of being born in flesh, are creatures of sin."

"You think it's true?"

"Isn't impossible." She snorted. "Don't look at me like that. I don't mean the Mother House, but for some, the commitment to the vow of chastity comes easily. We promise our body to Him, because He was chaste, and so that we are free from the demands of exclusive human relationships to be able to give all our love to God, and through God to all people. But some struggle with that vow...."

So it, what Sylvia had said might be true. Oh, Father in heaven... "It appears some think we're either lesbians or fooling around with...that the babies' fathers are—."

"Don't be coy. Priests?"

"People think this of us?"

"Some might find it hard to believe we choose Christ and to live as he did, over a flesh and blood groom. Some probably think we hate men or fear relationships, and perhaps some of us do." She paused, considered her next words. "People fear and seek to explain what they do not understand in a manner that makes sense to them, but that's not to say there isn't a nun who has never found comfort in the arms of another woman, a priest, or layperson."

"Have you every heard...in our Order of...?"

"I can't say for certain." Sister Anthony glanced at the door, but did not lower her voice. "But I've suspected it on occasion, and those sisters were separated and dispatched to different locations. Religious authority has always feared and known of lustful relationships forming between…friends."

"That's why they forbid us to visit each other in the cubicles…tell us to avoid friendships?"

"But it has never stopped us huddling in the door recesses of the Mother House or hospital, gossiping, and breaking the rule of silence when we think no one is listening." Sister Anthony leaned forward, but too old to care or too hard of hearing, she refused to lower her voice. "I know of a Sister extremely dedicated to God and the Order…. When a workman came to do repairs, he asked her where the manhole was—well, she told me, she blushed purple—had no idea what he was talking about. She became infatuated with him. Silently watched him every day."

"Here? Recently?"

"Another hospital…years ago." Sister Anthony giggled, her voice rose a little. "She told me…she knew he knew she was watching him, climb up and down the ladder…."

Sister Gregory thought she'd be forced to repeat the words because she said so softly, "She fancied him?"

Sister Anthony nodded. "She couldn't stop herself from trying to see him. Then one day, he stared straight back at her...walked to her with a great and lustful gaze and manoeuvred her into a vacant room…without a word, kissed her—the most passionate kiss ever, and she didn't want him to stop."

Sister Gregory smiled. "Did he?"

"She kept that to herself."

Sister Gregory tried not to giggle and let the older Sister's words sink in. Her thoughts turned to what Sylvia said. "I find this thing about convent babies…."

"I'm sure you're bothered by something other than any lay person's non-belief in our vows."

Sister Gregory moved her chair closer to the older sister and lowered her voice to a whisper. "She asked me how I knew what lust was…."

"Did you tell her you're human?"

Sister Gregory bowed her head. "How can we advise and comfort when…our worldly experience does not match theirs?"

"Regardless of your veil, you're still a young woman."

Seeing, even feeling, are altogether so different from experiencing.

"Look at me…please…," Sister Anthony said.

Sister Gregory glanced at the hospital windows, tried not to let Sister Anthony scrutinize the secrets her face might reveal in the soft light from inside. She had always thought her desire for close human relationships, for a human touch, was locked away, didn't exist beyond those occasional school yard infatuations.

Sister Anthony gently squeezed her hand. "There isn't anything wrong with you."

"Your hand is cold."

"And purple in the light, but we aren't talking about my hands."

"I feel…."

"Sometimes we find it easier to deny the wants and needs women feel outside our walls, because we have no emotional attachment to anyone in particular. That's how life-long abstinence for most of us is attainable."

A strange lingering want and need came and went from time to time. It was not mere lust, but a deeper need to connect at a level forbidden to her. She understood it was partly an urge for physical fulfilment—the tinges and ache of want and need she often felt deep inside. And she often remembered a boy kissing and pushing himself against her, both awakening and confirming that feeling.

At times she was tempted to explore—to feel that delirious sensation that boy had given her, and a few times gave into the impulse to feed and soothe the unbearable desire for release of pleasure—but she knew that wasn't the ecstasy God intended. Those impulses, those desires, she'd sacrificed in her vow of chastity, in her gift to God. The memories, the desires to pleasure herself almost, no not almost, sometimes they did break her vow of chastity.

Sister Gregory's face burned from those memories of self-pleasure, of that boy kissing her. She looked through the door. No one appeared to be listening, but she leaned toward Sister Anthony's ear. "I'm not sure I don't feel what they do—what the girls do."

"Perhaps you should speak to Mother Superior."

Sister Gregory shook her head.

"You're feeling what you're missing. If you weren't here, you'd be like other women your age, feel what they feel. Most are married, have felt a bond with a man who is capable of touching them in both spirit and body."

"I can't miss something I've never had."

"We, every sister here, can imagine. Some of us do feel something."

Sister Gregory's gaze locked with the older woman's, and she wanted to say *I pray most nights for the Lord to take away my ability to imagine and to feel.* Her face burned again, and she stood. "I better go to bed."

"I'll enjoy the night air a bit longer. God be with you."

"Thank you for listening...allowing me to speak."

"We all have wicked thoughts from time to time. Without them, we'd have no doubts, wouldn't be as God intended us to be."

"God intends this?"

"We're all flawed...human with wants, needs and desires. Without our deep desire, we'd have nothing to sacrifice to Him."

Sister Gregory walked into the dormitory, to the far end of the room. She brushed aside the curtain to her cubicle, sat on the chair next to the open window. The mumble of prayers and chattering of rosary beads still filled the room.

She recited the Rosary, beginning with the *Our Father*...then moving into, *I believe in God*...slowly enough to admit an interval of breath between the words and sentences, so she had time to think and take in the meaning of the words. But she knew she mimicked the words—true, deep prayer, not in her this evening.

She understood why so many girls and young women came to be at St Joseph's. They weren't prepared for lust in all its fullness, the overpowering urge of the physical and emotional combined. By joining the convent, she had removed herself from that. Perhaps abstinence was achievable. Prayer gave her the strength to fight her needs and wants, most times—but how could total physical detachment from others, lead to the full understanding of human love—could allow her to help those led astray by love? Perhaps, on this day, that was the hardest question.

Sister Gregory stood, pulled down the window, then took off her wimple and cotton bonnet and faced her own reflection in the glass. She sometimes wondered what it would be like to dress like some women in their form-fitting twin suits, gloves and hats, women of Sylvia's mother's age. If given the choice, she'd happily remove the coifs and her wimple's starched band, but her veil was dear to her—a symbol of consecration to God.

That day of her vows had been so special. With sixteen other girls, she stood as a bride, ready to marry the Lord, in a ceremony fit for a princess, with all the girls' family members watching, and her proud father. St Gregory the Great was the patron saint of teachers, and she had closed her eyes for the briefest moment as the Bishop acknowledge her new name, a masculine name she had chosen without question.

But now she understood the deeper meaning of that name—a man's name, hard as stone even on her tongue, and together with her hair shorn off, any trace of the feminine gone, forbidden when she took her vows. A bride of Christ she had become, but a woman she would never be, and her own child she would never hold.

She opened the window again. Sister Anthony's soft humming of a hymn mingled with the mutterings from the dormitory, and crickets, the distant streets and city sounds—a collective buzz from another world. She wondered how many waiting girls in that other building stood at their windows, dreaming of returning to their old world, thinking about the children they would never hold.

_____ *Sylvia*

THE BELL clanged and clattered at dawn like cymbals before the birds chirped. *The horrendous sound probably killed them all.* Sylvia pulled the pillow over her head, wrapped it around her ears, but the noise went on. She was sure if the noise didn't stop, it was because she'd gone insane in her airless room in the night. The sound was madness, but it had the desired effect. You had to be dead not to wake and sleep impossible for hours once the sound hit your eardrums. The dormitory turned into screeching, screaming, and banging of doors and cupboards.

Sylvia jumped out of bed. *Jesus Christ. What the…*

She and half the girls in the dormitory were doomed to Hell. Their curses and profanities would make the devil clap his hands and probably made the bell ringer, one of those nuns, smash the clapper as hard as she could while calling out, "Praise be to Jesus!"

Sylvia flicked on the light-switch. The horrible sound stopped. *Thank God.* She stepped into the corridor. Girls scuttled and stumbled about, wiping sleep from their eyes, looking around disoriented. Sister Gregory stood at the end of the partition, a hand in the bell, holding the clapper, and a piece of paper in the other hand. *That damn document.*

"Enough!" Sister Gregory shouted. "To use Our Lord's name in vain is blasphemy. Reverence due to Him forbids all profanity and blasphemy of Him."

"If the bell didn't scare the crap out of everyone, no one would blaspheme anybody," Sylvia blurted back, loud enough for many to hear.

"Young ladies don't use improper language."

"You think we're all Mary Magdalenes, not young ladies."

Sister Gregory's eyes glinted, but she didn't blink and moved closer to Sylvia. "Mary Magdalene was a repentant sinner and a special disciple of Jesus. The Sisters of St Anthony hold no malice against anyone."

"Not one sister has looked me in the eyes. They didn't want me to see the hate in their eyes. Apart from Matron Bernard who smiles like the devil."

"Oh you, young Susan. You know so little and are so self-absorbed." Sister Gregory was now on her at full height, looking down on her. "You confuse your own guilt with their humility. I'm looking at you now. I see a girl on the verge of womanhood, angry because a bell ripped her from sleep. Nothing more, nothing less."

"You don't even see my baby...."

"Susan, you're tired." She held out the piece of paper. "Take your work roster. Get dressed and get to breakfast. You're to start work at eight and will work till two."

This place is madness. Sylvia snatched the roster and stomped back to her room. *I'm acting like a child....You want to drive us insane.* She threw the paper onto the pillow, dragged her suitcase from under the bed, and pulled out a dress. Her stomach appeared to have grown over night. A wondrous sight—and she caressed the bulge. *Me and you aren't staying here. I won't let them take you.*

Sister Gregory

SISTER GREGORY placed the cracked bell on the desk, wondering how a flawed bell existed in a world the Matron wanted to run smoothly—a bell, which every morning made a sound that clashed with the beauty of the sunrise. The bell emitted a noise nothing like the joyful sounding Sanctus bells used during Mass to herald the miracle on the Altar of Sacrifice.

Sometimes Sister Gregory struggled to wake up when the sisters' dormitory bell signalled it was time to work or pray. Often the Matron had suggested that a foghorn should be used. Sister Gregory smiled. The Matron still had a sense of humour—the bell today merely a joke.

Documents Sister Gregory needed to sort and file sat beside the bell. A folder lay on top of a pile. It wasn't there earlier. She read the note clipped to the folder. _Deliver to Mother Terrance._ Sister Gregory ran her palm across the folder. If she wanted you to read it, she wouldn't have written, _Private and Confidential. She said there was no need for Mother Terrance to know about missing Mass, but if it is about that, what penance will be chosen for me?_

As a new novice, Sister Gregory once knelt beside the then Mother Superior and asked the Mother Superior to forgive her laughing in Silent Time. Mother Superior ordered her to spend the next day's Silent Time, four hours total, kneeling with hands and arms stretched out in front. If her arms fell, she was to repeat the exercise each Silent Time until she could hold them out, could achieve her penance. The first time Sister Gregory fell on her face after five minutes and laughed at the senseless viciousness of the penance. But after five days, her arms and legs in agony and with calluses sprouting on her swollen and red knees, she prayed to God while tears ran down her cheeks for Him to hear her suffering and help her become a better nun. At the end of ten more days, she did it, her penance done.

She pushed the memory away, picked up Sylvia's folder, and scanned through the notes Sister Bernard obtained from the girl's mother. Sylvia turned seventeen eight months ago and had a brother and sister. The sister was younger and the brother enlisted in the army. Her parents were married. Sylvia's father worked for a bakery and the mother in a factory sewing Hessian bags used for potatoes. Their address was a caravan park.

The only notes of the father of Sylvia's baby said he was twenty, had brown hair and eyes, information to be used in matching the unborn child to potential parents. She picked up a photograph of a smiling Sylvia. She resembled another girl now at the hospital, although that girl was two years older. Sister Gregory shut the folder, remembered Sylvia's mother's perfectly ironed skirt and spotless clothes and shoes. The mother didn't look pregnant. So, the mother's flushed cheeks might have come from the baby growing in her, and not all from Sylvia's predicament, from leaving Sylvia here.

Sister Gregory tapped the top of the folder. Something was missing. Sylvia said her father had left the mother, whether before or after the mother fell pregnant was anyone's guess. Looked like married couples kept secrets too. Divorce was almost impossible. If Sylvia's mother was pregnant with the child of someone other than her husband, well then, one more seemed to give in to, dare she think it, to *enjoy*, lust outside of marriage.

She set Sylvia's folder aside. Tides of people would be flowing into the city on trains and buses from the suburbs to work. Construction and renovations would continue on the buildings of St Joseph's as well. Outside was so noisy, so busy, growing and bursting with new life at a pace faster than ever. Sister Gregory knew she missed all that, missed it profoundly, deeply.

She tapped her fingers on Sister Bernard's folder—played with the corner.

SYLVIA ENTERED the sewing and knitting room from the stairwell on the second floor. It was 8am, but the sun already pressed on the window, throwing heat and light over what looked like a room of beautiful flowers—except for the solemn faces sprouting out of shapeless floral smocks.

Five girls sat in a corner, silently knitting tiny blue, pink or lemon coloured bonnets, mittens, and booties. One of the girls focused on the page of a magazine. Four girls hand-sewed bibs and matinee jackets, while two girls operated machines zipping along floral material.

A barrel of a Sister, her cheeks puffed like glazed pastries, looked down at the clipboard in her hand, then waved Sylvia forward. "You must be Susan."

"And I suppose you're Michelangelo or someone?"

The Sister let out a bellow of a laugh. "I'm Sister Dominic and pleased to make your acquaintance. With wit like that, you could join us and become the convent clown. But for now, save the humour. You'll need it in the birthing room. Sit beside Sylvia. When she's finished you can make yourself a couple of dresses." She pointed to a wire basket holding white material. "Until then, take the basket and mend those."

"I have my own clothes," Sylvia said, "and I don't know how to use a machine."

The Sister laughed. "They won't last long. You're going to end up the size of a house. I'm sure one of the girls will help you with the machine."

"It won't be because of the dormitory food."

"We know why." The Sister stepped to the door. "Work, girls. No chatter. Use the time for contemplation and seeking forgiveness from the Lord." She left the room and closed the door.

The other Sylvia's hair was tinged pink and all teased up on the top of her head a bit like fairy floss, and it probably tasted like it too. If you didn't have the money, sugar and water worked well as hair spray. The girl turned around. She was a year or two older than Sylvia, and her pregnancy looked further advanced. *Oh, the horrid girl from the other night, the same girl who ran out of the chapel yesterday.* The girl looked Sylvia up and down, then with her nose upturned, faced the sewing machine and continued to run stitches along the material's hem.

Sylvia picked up the basket and sat beside the other Sylvia, then held up an enormous pair of white bloomers. "They don't expect us to wear these, do they?"

"Most have the waist elastic snapped." The other Sylvia rolled her eyes as if it was the most stupid question ever. "The nuns wear them under their habits. You do know how to sew, don't you?"

"A little."

"Then thread a needle." She pointed to a bowl of square material on the table beside Sylvia. "Use the patches to cover any holes and strips of elastic to replace the snapped ones."

"My name is Sylvia too. Sister Bernard told me there was another Sylvia here, so they want me to change my name."

"It wasn't me they're talking about. My real name is Kim."

"Who is the other Sylvia?"

A spark of life lit Kim's eyes. "Don't you get it? There is no Sylvia."

"You've signed the adoption papers?"

Kim's chin tilted, and her lips quivered. "It's the best thing for me to do. I have my whole life ahead of me. I'll forget this. I'll get married one day and have my own family."

"I want to keep my baby."

"For goodness sake. Have you any idea of what you're saying?" Kim smiled like Sister Bernard, almost smirked, but her eyes were red and puffy as if she rubbed them or cried too much the night before. "I'm not going to be a fool and let this—this indiscretion ruin my life." She turned around and continued to sew the hem.

Sylvia let the word play in her mind. *Indiscretion.* Yes, oh, yes, she'd been thoughtless, careless, and had no respect for her body. *It can be fixed. It's for the best, dear. Just the stroke of your signature can fix it all.* "I can feel my baby move...can't bear the thought he won't know me."

An older girl, possibly in her early twenties, and heavily pregnant, shook her head without looking up from the blue jumper she was knitting. "You're creating a rod for your back. Without help from your parents, it'll be impossible to raise a baby. How are you going to put a roof over his head, feed and clothe him?"

"I'll find a way."

"And end up a hooker on the streets. That's the only place to go from here if we take our babies with us. No man will want us with a kid. Besides, I don't want my kids raised like I was. I don't want to struggle like my mother did when my father left us. My kid deserves better than I can give it."

"But they'll be strangers. Look nothing like my baby. And how do you know they won't be sickos?"

Kim cut a thread from the machine and took out the floral material from under the needle. "The married couples are screened. They pick people that look like us...happily married and unable to have children. They'll love our babies as if they are their own."

"My boyfriend said he'd help...," Sylvia said. "I keep thinking about what I should do. I want to do the right thing, but it's not only my baby."

"As soon as it's out," the older girl said, "he'll be off like a rabbit in his portable bedroom to the next fool who'll open her legs."

Kim laughed. "Don't they love their panel vans? One boyfriend had little drawers and cupboards beside his mattress in his car."

"They don't care if we get knocked up," the older girl replied. "My mother keeps taking my youngest sister's father to court to get him to pay a pittance a week to help her. The judge only lectures him about his responsibilities. He still doesn't pay."

Kim looked up from the machine. "When this is over, I'm going to try to save enough to go to America or London."

"If we're not careful, we'll all end up back here," Sylvia said.

"Oh, no I won't," Kim said. "There's a drug you can take."

"I have a friend who had an abortion," Sylvia said.

Kim shook her head. "The drug is taken each day…it's a pill, doesn't allow the pregnancy to begin. Abortion is illegal and a sin. It kills the baby."

"You're all stupid to believe in the Catholic dogma," another girl said.

"You're not Catholic?" Sylvia asked.

"My parents can recite the Bible back to front, made me come here, but I'll marry who I want. Not everyone believes what the stupid nuns do. I don't believe there's a friggin' God."

"That's blasphemy!" Kim said.

I'm struggling to believe in God too. "Why didn't they tell us about the medicine if they're so unhappy with us now?"

"A heathen probably invented the pill," Kim replied, as the door opened, "but…."

Sister Dominic stood hands on hips, in the doorway. "I said prayer and work. No chatter."

Sylvia put her head down, holding in a giggle, trying to concentrate on pulling a piece of elastic attached to a safety pin through the waist of the bloomers.

Kim leaned close to Sylvia and whispered, "When I get out of here, I'll be using the pill."

"Last chance." Sister Dominic waved her finger at Kim. "If I come back, find you talking again, I'll separate you all and a few of you can scrub the kitchen floor on your hands and knees before our precious Lord." She left the room and closed the door.

Sylvia laughed. "Is she for real?"

"I think so." Kim said. "But I'd rather be here than scrubbing floors. I reckon she'd probably enjoy seeing us on all fours."

Sylvia shuffled in her seat to unstick her legs from the chair. "Do you think Dominic will come back again?"

"She likes to put the wind up us," Kim said. "She's probably been called to the labour ward. I've heard she's their main midwife. She looks like she's had a few children herself."

Sylvia remembered the missing children. It was on the radio this morning. *Missing children feared dead. Thousands assisting police in search.* They were looking for the children, plus a surfer type teenage boy last seen with them. "Did you hear anything on the television last night about those missing kids?"

"Still searching the rivers and storm drains," Kim said. "Their father spoke, asking whoever took them to bring them back. He was sobbing."

"It must be horrible, the not knowing what happened to them."

"It doesn't make sense how someone could get all three of them. Some people think they might have drowned."

"The two girls they found murdered at Wanda beach last year didn't drown."

Kim shrugged. "Maybe we'll never know what happened to them." It came out as a flippant comment, but when Sylvia met and held Kim's gaze, the girl frowned. "Yes, it must be horrible, the not knowing."

A chill ran down Sylvia's spine. "After we sign those papers, can we see our babies again?"

"Oh, no. Once the adoption is finalised, the files are closed."

"I don't understand."

"Once we sign the papers, that's it. It's all over. We'll never see our babies again."

Sylvia fiddled with the elastic, then threw it and the pair of unmended bloomers back into the basket. "Are you due soon?"

"October. I feel like I'm having a giant." Kim stopped the machine. "I'll measure you. The pattern on the material is pretty. Least it's cool to wear, and no one is going to see us in it."

It didn't take long. Sylvia stood and held the smock against her body. The hem almost reached the ground. "Couldn't we turn it into a mini-dress?"

"The nuns would have heart attacks." Kim laughed. "We buggered up the measurements. We'll cut it off to come just below your knees, otherwise as you get bigger it will be up to your bum."

"Mum isn't too impressed with shorter dresses either." Sylvia wiped the back of her hand across her forehead to remove sweat and stepped to the window—it too nailed down. "Mum thought that pommy model had a nerve turning up to the races on Derby day with her dress so high above her knees." She glanced back at Kim, waited for a response, but Kim seemed to be staring at nothing. "If the nuns don't starve us, they're going to cook us alive. Why do they nail down the windows?"

"A girl tried to jump out of a window." Kim went back to the machine to run over the hem. "Your dress is finished. Now, I'll sew a little tag on the inside for you to write your name."

"From the dormitory window...you'd have to be mad."

"From a birthing room, after her baby was taken to the nursery. She was lucky she wasn't killed."

Two novices, looking like doves in white flowing habits, circled the area at the front of the hospital. Sister Gregory, carrying a folder, stepped toward the gate. She followed the postman, his mailbag thrown over his shoulder.

"How long do they guard the gate of hell?" Sylvia asked.

"There's someone usually there all the time," Kim said. "At mid-afternoon, though, old Sister Anthony potters around there when it's their recreation."

"How do we send mail?"

"They sell stamps and envelopes at the hospital shop," Kim said, "but if friends and relations think you're interstate or visiting another town, you can give your letters to any nun. They'll make sure it's sent from that town or state, so no one knows you've been here."

Sylvia folded her arms across her breasts. Sister Gregory raised the gate latch and followed the postman outside the grounds. The postman walked in the opposite direction from Sister Gregory and disappeared behind the hedge hiding the chapel yard. Sylvia couldn't stop smiling and thought she must look like a goose, smiling for no apparent reason. She stepped away from the window and opened the door. "I'm not staying here."

_____ Sister Gregory

THE AIR was without any breeze, searing and heavy, the sky cloudless, hot for this time of year. And something didn't feel right—as if everything in the universe would somehow change because God already predetermined it to be a certain way, depending on the direction Sister Gregory moved and how many steps she took.

Beside the main hospital building, a crane lowered wooden beams toward a four-storey building. Workmen scuttled over scaffolding on floors. A man, tall and muscular, handsome even from a distance, dressed in shorts and white t-shirt, pounded a big hammer on a line of nails. The motion of his arms striking the nails brought the memory of nailing down Sylvia's window, of denying the girl fresh air and the sound and smells of the outside world. A fleck of sadness, guilt, settled in. *Yes, well, you only did what you were told. What if another girl tried to harm herself?*

The workman looked her way and held the hammer mid-air. *He's smiling.* The sensation of making eye contact flashed over her spine. She bowed her head, gripped the folder for Mother Terrance, and hurried on faster after the postman.

The postman flicked up the latch and held the gate open—his hand large and tanned. *No wedding ring.* "Ladies first, Sister."

She kept her gaze lowered. She had to turn sideways to move through the space he left. *Front or back? No. You'll end up brushing against him.* She grabbed the gate—her fingers tiny and paper white compared to his. "I'll close it. I'm sure the bag is heavy."

He nodded and walked away whistling. Avoiding looking at the workman again, her clammy and shaky hand placed the latch back on the gate. She peeped between the edge of the gate and a hedge. Sylvia watched from the sewing room window.

A man wearing a grey suit, white shirt, thin black tie and hat, walked toward Sister Gregory. She quickly lowered her gaze again, as usual gaining only vague impressions of people in the outside world, avoiding eye contact, not really seeing them, and moved past the man, closer to the little boy and girl chasing a pup in the front yard of their small terrace.

"...satisfaction," blared from a stereo through the open door on the terrace's second floor balcony.

The corner shop was near. The tinkling and chiming of the pinball machine reached her ears, sounding a little better than the horrible dormitory bell. Two teenage boys loitered outside the shop. One puffed on a cigarette. The other dipped his fingers into a paper wrapped bag of hot chips. She passed the door, the vinegar and fish smell lingering, and turned into a lane.

She heard murmuring—moans tinged with pleasure. A teenage boy leaned against his girlfriend positioned with her back on a tin fence. Wrapped around each other, kissing slowly, thoroughly, unaware that she stood wide eyed and transfixed—the noises they made, the lingering, caressing motion of their hands, the supple movements of their hips and thighs pressing against the other, they blended and melted together.

Oh, dear Lord.

She stepped around them, warm and uncomfortable, disgusted at the tremor in herself, depressed, lonely, and envious more than shocked at the closeness they shared, and quickly walked to the end of the lane.

A white Mini Cooper, driven by a woman, flashed past and sprayed gravel and dirt onto the bottom of her habit and over her shoes. The polishing of shoes, the removing of lint from the habit, and the constant round of chores, while sustaining work hours to keep up on all the paperwork, and hours of prayer every day, at times seemed impossible to manage. *What is a bit more dust and dirt?*

In the wider street, brightly painted Kombi vans carried surfboards on top, and polished Mustangs, Holdens, and Fords zoomed along the road. Today the noises seemed louder, as if the entire city shook with noise, with human turbulence. Fashion exploded into an ocean of colours around bare and tanned legs. She couldn't, dared not, focus on just one. The scant summer dresses and shorts, the legs, the bodies all whirled too fast, too intensely, great leaves swirling in the wind of life, of girls and young women giggling, laughing, talking too loudly, hips swaying, breasts barely covered. Pink, yellow, and even silver and gold skirt hemlines rested mid thigh, making them all look cool despite the heat, free and, oh, so lustful.

Older women wore hats and gloves, their glances turning into stares at *those* short skirts. The display of teenage girls and young women, the freedom and individuality in their clothes, in their confident smiles—how they walked, stood, talked, all made it hard for Sister Gregory to look away, to focus on the ground before her. None of the girls and women appeared to have a care about anything except living this life boldly, openly, sexily. She suddenly felt closed in, trapped in her habit—clumsy and large.

She wondered what it would feel like to take off her thick bloomers, allow her hips to sway naturally once again—the novice mistress had shouted that out of her in those early years—to hitch her habit above her knees, to let the sun and the air and dust on her calves, to join the others with her white skin. As a child, she ran without shoes, a sunburnt nose, her hair blowing in the breeze. One time, she sat on a fence beside a boy she liked, his warm palm lightly resting on her bare knee…the instant thrill and fear.

She'd looked down at his hand, trying to decide if she should swipe it away. He leaned toward her looking at her lips, and she jumped off the fence and ran into her house. *I need to do homework,* she called back. *I'll see you tomorrow.* The next day, she allowed him to kiss her, but it was awkward and horrible, their lips touching and their noses bumping, nothing like the young couple shared in the lane.

That infatuation didn't last. It had all been a game to him, a bet...nothing more than a bet and challenge for the boy. She overheard him tell his friends the next day *the wog's a tart...I put me hand there, I did...she let me. You owe me threepence.*

She hurried on, pushed away the pain that had caused...still remained at times.... Against her will, always against her will, the memories of another time rushed into her thoughts, her heart. It was a couple of years after that first kiss. Like her, the second boy to touch her, more a man than a boy, had Polish parents...his English no better than hers. When he kissed her, they melted together, safe from the world they didn't understand, that didn't care about them.

She forced that memory away and concentrated on her dust-covered black boots. *Our Father—Our Father who art in heaven... Our Father... Oh, blessed Lord, please help me to pray without distraction.* But the pain from her good memory hurt too. He'd moved away, and she'd never heard from him again.

Relieved to be outside the brick Victorian building at last, she climbed the few steps and entered the Mother House...the convent. Musky tinged rose incense enveloped her. It was a scent she'd known for seventeen years—told her that she was home. The silence of the Mother House, a little like a funeral parlour but without tears, was broken only by whispers drifting through the hallways and the occasional tap of a walking stick.

The Mother House was home for the old and frail or ill nuns who no longer had the ability to contribute to the Order. Most gave in to the ills of the body, some the ills of the mind, but not sister Sebastian. She was notorious. She refused to stay in the infirmary and spent her days and nights walking the halls. At ninety, her constant displays of piety knew no limit. She ate her meals while kneeling, kissed the ground at the entrance of the church, and often collapsed in apparent ecstasy. She had the bones of an ox to not have broken her hips or back.

Mother Terrance, at fifty-two, was the youngest of any previous Mother Superior but managed the Order without the forced smile of Sister Bernard. She took over from Sister Bernard after the customary secret vote by the sisters. Sister Gregory assumed younger sisters, including herself, who wanted the changes Vatican II proposed, voted in Mother Terrance.

Sister Gregory knocked on Mother Terrance's door. She dreaded a reply. Always did. This private room of every Mother Superior before her, including Sister Bernard, reeked of the dark ages and oppression. She didn't like being reminded of some of her struggles and thought again of that most hated penance. *Please don't ask me to kneel on tiles with my arms outstretched.*

"Come in," came Mother Terrance's soft voice.

Sister Gregory opened the door. "Sister Bernard requested I bring you these reports."

"Sister, please sit." Sister Gregory handed over the folder then placed her hands in her lap. The other woman's long fingers opened the folder and as she read the document, her forefinger trailed down the page. She closed the folder and put it on her desk. "Now, tell me how you are, Sister?"

"I'm well." Sister Gregory's scalp prickled against the cotton bonnet from sweat, and she ran her finger under the starched band of her wimple. She had the biggest urge to take it off and shake her short hair free. She shivered. The rebellious thought frightened her. Missing Mass was enough rebellion for one week, no excuse that her compassion for Susan, or *Sylvia*, made her miss Mass. Had Sister Bernard told Mother about that missed service?

"You look flustered."

Sister Gregory had taken the same journey to the Mother House hundreds of times...always found the sights and sounds in the streets exciting—though a little beyond her world, but today much more so than ever before.... *Bewildered and confused, Mother.* "It's hot outside."

"I understand you've taken on Veronica's duties since she became ill. You must tell me if they're beyond your capabilities."

"Not at this stage.... Have the doctors said when she may be better?"

"No one knows when she'll conquer her delusions, or if she will."

"When I have more time, I'll try to comfort her?"

Mother Terrance nodded. "You must know Dr Dennison, the Matron's brother?"

Sister Gregory's fingers tapped her lap, and she clenched her fingers to stop the motion. "He's the head gynaecologist in the hospital."

"With his contacts, he brings a great deal of charitable funds to the hospital and convent. The new dormitory for the sisters is being built because of his hard work."

Sister Gregory nodded. She knew the new dormitory would make it easier for the nuns who worked at the hospital. They'd even been promised rooms rather than cubicles with cotton walls. But it would mean living enclosed like the waiting girls, separated from the other sisters. "The new dormitories will be a great privilege."

"A just reward for everyone who has worked tirelessly over the years at St Joseph's. Don't you agree?"

"Any sister, young or old, will welcome any providence bestowed upon her."

Mother Terrance stood. "As they should. The current cubicles don't acknowledge each of us is an individual searching for God's grace."

Sister Gregory understood the hint to leave, and left the room a little puzzled. The sisters were never encouraged to indulge in their own personal needs and wants.

*

Sister Gregory placed the latch on the gate. It was recreation time and she glanced toward Sylvia's window. But the girl wasn't there. That familiar creeping feeling of something not right snaked through her body again. Sister Anthony had replaced the two novices in the grounds earlier and knelt pruning bushes near the steps, singing as joyously as her old and croaked voice allowed. The crane above the new dormitory sat motionless, its wire hoist empty. The men on their afternoon break, sat eating, legs dangling over scaffolding, and the construction noised halted.

She crouched beside Sister Anthony. "God be with you, Sister."

"And with you." Sister Anthony stopped clipping the bushes. "Have you heard about Veronica?"

"Apparently suffering delusions."

Sister Anthony sighed. "...or a battle with her vow of obedience?"

"What do you mean?"

"I heard she snapped at Sister Dominic."

"She can be harsh at times."

"Don't let Dominic get on your goat. She means well." She started to prune again. "It will be a shame though, if Veronica doesn't stay. She reminds me of you...when you first came to us."

Sister Gregory wanted to hug Sister Anthony. Instead she stood. "I need to go."

"Visit me tomorrow?"

"I'll try. If there's time."

Sister Gregory walked up the steps, opened the frosted glass doors, and Moses' dog door rattled. The scent of disinfectant hit her with the silence of the Mother House. Three paintings showing the story of St Margaret of Antioch, the patron saint of women in childbirth, hung on the wall. The middle painting slanted sideways as if someone had brushed past and knocked it slightly.

In the form of a dragon, the devil lay at St Margaret's feet—the end of a cross thrust between his teeth. She straightened the painting and moved past the last one. St Margaret was about to be beheaded the day after slaying the dragon, looking up to God at the moment she thanks Him that the end of her travail has arrived. St Margaret prayed that in memory of her miraculous deliverance out of the dragon's womb, women in labour who invoke her might find help through her suffering and their children delivered safely.

Sisters Alexander and Matthew were in the reception area. Sister Alexander, the youngest of the sisters, sat in the office. A male student doctor spoke to her in a soft voice, his words not clear. The young sister noticed Sister Gregory, her face blushed, and she picked up and studied a document. The young doctor's back stiffened. He cleared his throat, slunk away from Sister Alexander, and pretended to look at something on another desk.

Sister Matthew, two years older than Sister Alexander, always spoke in flustered whispers as if out of breath and as if she wanted only the person she was speaking to hear. She handed a cup of tea to a gentleman sitting, his hat on his lap—the same gentleman Sister Gregory passed on the way to the Mother House.

Sister Mathew stepped to Sister Gregory and whispered, "Mr Dawes came to see his daughter, Sylvia, but I can't find her." She pointed at a book sitting open on the counter. "I checked to see what her new name is. There wasn't a Susan in the sewing room. The girls didn't know where she was."

Sister Gregory stood motionless, caught between belief and disbelief, belief that Sylvia would do foolishness, but disbelief Sylvia's foolishness would come so soon. "The girls will be on rest time now."

"I checked the dormitory…told the father I couldn't locate her."

Sister Gregory considered smiling to push away the frown she knew formed on her brow, but instead turned her attention to Sylvia's father. "I'm sure she's still on the grounds. I'll find her."

"That would be nice." Mr Dawes took a sip of his tea. "Sylvia has made a mistake, but she's not stupid."

She can't have left the grounds. No one has ever left them. "I won't be long. She can't be too far away."

_____ *Sylvia*

SYLVIA SAT on the wooden seat behind the chapel, out of view from the hospital, underneath the image of God in the stained glass window. She reread the letter she wrote to Tommy, trying to focus on the words, not on where she expected the nuns to walk from, taking in each word, trying to imagine what he would feel when he read the letter. Then she read again.

Over two weeks had passed since she last saw him, and maybe he didn't care if she was here. He wasn't happy when he found out she was pregnant, well before she told her mother. Not one bit. He asked her before they did it the first time at the drive-in, if she knew about the Pill. She said yes. None of her girlfriends knew about the drug. She was stupid and nodded like an idiot, hoping he would tell her what he meant, but after that nod, the only thing he cared about was peeling off her underwear.

The last time together flooded into her—his body heat, his heart beat, as if then was now, the essence of that moment of him and her—she breathed him in, every part of him, in and out, and reached her hand out to touch him, but he was out there, not here, a triumphant smile on his face as he leaned over her until he laughed and broke the spell. *I've got a goddamn cramp.*

Someone else laughed. Here now, but where? A man sitting on the four-storey building, at the side of the hospital, above the hedge, laughed. She wanted to cower, so they couldn't see her—see the small bulge pushing out her shirt. Those men probably laughed at her, laughed because they knew why she was here, laughed as they jokingly bragged about having put her here.

She placed the folded letter between her writing paper with the letter she wrote to her brother. She rushed into the screen-enclosed veranda surrounding the hospital, through the waiting-girls' meeting room, passed the scattered armchairs, and was about to turn into the hospital shop—the closest wall lined with racks of magazines covered in images of fashion from London, Paris, and New York. Girls in swimwear posed on the covers. She gulped. Their bodies were perfect. She wasn't going to fit into anything like that for a long time—was already wearing a maternity bra, and stretch marks already tracked across her breasts and thighs.

Prince Charles's face smiled from the cover of *The Women's Weekly. The New Boy at Timber Top.* On the side, there was a smaller headline, *Baby Hand Knitted Patterns 20 new designs*—the same patterns the girls in the sewing room were following. The other cluttered shelves and racks held soaps, perfumes, cards, flower arrangements, baby bottles, and bibs, socks, mittens—like the girls knitted and sewed—for strangers to dress their children.

On the counter sat a box. *Outgoing Mail.* She thought about walking to the box, but Sister Gregory marched down the corridor.

"Susan, where have you been?"

"A walk."

"Why didn't you stay in the sewing room?"

"It was too hot."

"Don't leave where you're rostered again. We need to know where you are at all times in case of an emergency."

"I had an emergency, suffocating in that room."

"What do you have in your hands?"

"I was about to send a letter to Mum."

"Your father is here."

"My father?"

Sister Gregory frowned. "Have you turned into a parrot? He's in the reception area."

I don't know what's up your nose. Sylvia walked past the Sister into the shop. "My name is Sylvia, and I don't want to see him."

Sister Gregory blocked Sylvia's way. "He'll be disappointed after waiting for over two hours."

"I didn't ask him to come."

"Go to the dormitory." Sister Gregory walked toward the reception area.

Right beside the mailbox, an elderly nun dusted the counter, and Sylvia said, "I'd like a couple of stamps and envelopes."

"No envelopes in stock to sell at the moment."

"Then how am I supposed to send my letters?"

"Boxes are coming at the end of the week. In the meantime, give me your mail and write the address on a piece of paper. I'll send it using the hospital stock."

Well, that's just great. "Thank you. I might come back later."

Sylvia ran out into the chapel yard. She waited for the crunching sound of footsteps on the gravel path away from the frosted glass doors, but instead heard the gate latch open, then footsteps moving away from the hospital.

She placed her writing paper on the ground and pushed between two hedges, until she met the iron fence reaching higher than her. She gripped the fence grills and looked through them. Her father walked away along the footpath, carrying a brown paper bag in one hand and a cigarette in the other.

She bit down on her lip to stop herself crying. *Let him go.* "Dad! Dad! I'm here."

He turned toward her, his pace quickening. He took a final puff on the cigarette and threw it into the gutter. He was soon in front of her, reaching between the bars to hold her face closer to his, and he kissed her on the forehead. "Why didn't you want to see me?" He held up the bag. "Grapes."

Sylvia took the bag to avoid looking into his eyes. "I didn't know what you'd say when you saw me like this. I'm so sorry."

"I'm not happy, not one bit, but you'll always be my girl."

"Thank you for the grapes, but I don't want to stay here."

"Here's the best place…."

"I hate it."

"You've only been here a few days."

"They want to take my baby away."

He leaned in closer and lowered his voice. "This is the way

things are done."

"I'll look after him."

"I know you'd try. But no man will want you with a baby. They don't want someone who's been around the block."

Sylvia's hands sprung from the fence. "What am I supposed to do? Lie the rest of my life? Pretend this never happened?"

He nodded slightly, his voice so soft Sylvia thought he did not answer, but he did say, "Yes."

"If God made my body old enough to have a baby, surely He thinks I'm old enough to look after it."

"You're only a child."

"It won't be long before I'm eighteen."

"You're not twenty-one…not of age. You will do as we say."

"You left Mum alone…what's the difference?"

"I love your mother."

"No one is making sense. I've made a mistake, which hasn't hurt anyone, and suddenly I'm locked away as if I've murdered someone."

"You've hurt everyone, including yourself. You betrayed the trust and freedom your mother gave you, and shamed your brother by falling pregnant…came between two mates."

"I want to see Tommy."

"Listen to me. I've given him a clip over the ear, a good one, and I'll kill him if he comes near you again. If you leave here and keep the child the entire neighbourhood, wherever you go, will do nothing but gossip and shun you and your child. Your child will be called a bastard, teased and punished because of his mother's lack of respect for her body."

Sylvia felt her face crumble, and backed out of the hedges, would have tripped except the closeness of the two hedges and thickness of the branches held her upright. "I never want to see you again."

"You can only run so far from what needs to be done," he called back. "I'll tell you this much for nothing, once you accept responsibility for what you've done, you'll be able to move on to a decent and proper life."

She fell out of the bushes, almost onto the ground, dropped the bag of grapes and they scattered over the grass. *I don't need any of you.* She snatched up her belongings and gathered the grapes. Moses ran toward her.

Sister Bernard stood by the door leading to the veranda, her arms folded across her chest. "What were you doing?"

"Saying goodbye to my father." Sylvia patted Moses. "I can tell why she loves you. You're beautiful." She reached out her open palm holding a grape. Moses took it and gulped it down.

"What ever that is, don't give him anymore." Sister Bernard stepped toward them. "He's already eaten today."

Sylvia kissed Moses on the head and whispered, "I can't give you any more." She looked toward Sister Bernard. "It was a grape."

Sister Bernard nodded and picked up Moses.

IT WAS almost recreation time, 8pm, and the night air cooler than in many days. A weak breeze drifted through the window into Sister Gregory's office, giving the first hint that autumn wasn't far away. A relieving brush of air, salt and lavender spread over her face. She stood up. The breeze, or was it a yearning for the outside world, calling her to the window?

Sister Anthony's words rang through. *We all have wicked thoughts from time to time.*

In front of the window, Sister Gregory welcomed the onslaught of southern winds that would likely not come tonight. She closed her eyes, savouring the slight relief the breeze gave, the way it dried little beads of sweat on her forehead. Teenagers and young women out there let the air and warmth caress their uncovered skin, dressed as they pleased, let their skirts fly up in gusts of wind—and then giggled. She felt middle-aged, restrained, none of any girlishness part of her.

The door was closed, and like a child, she tugged at the white band of her wimple, wanted more than anything to take off that wimple and habit and lay herself bare to the breeze. Off came the wimple and her bonnet. The breath of freedom's breeze spread over her face into every pore and danced over her shortened hair.

Someone knocked. She didn't have time to return her bonnet and wimple to their rightful place, before Sister Bernard opened the door.

In the instant awkward silence, the Matron reared back as if examining and ugly and strange creature.

Sister Gregory felt as close to naked as she had in seventeen years. She cringed inwardly, fumbling with the wimple and bonnet in her hands and mumbled, "I was—was…."

Sister Bernard smiled. "Oh, please. I know it's hot." Then she laughed. "God is merciless at times. Put it back on. Mother Terrance has called us to a meeting."

She placed the bonnet and wimple on her head. "Mother Terrance never mentioned it this morning."

"God works in strange ways." Sister Bernard said. "Has Susan signed the papers?"

"She refuses."

"Doctor Dennison has found a very influential couple who want to adopt Susan's little one. They've provided a large donation to the hospital and convent. That's what my letter to Mother Terrance was about. I've met the wife and wasn't to recommend a child until I could find a girl with the wife's complexion and features. Susan is a perfect match."

"I think she needs more time."

"The more her baby grows, the harder it will be for her to sign. Then where will she be? Stuck with a child and no way to care for it. Emotion swept her away, not sense, and she now carries a little one she'd like to own and keep. But that's not for her to decide. She must deny the pleasure of holding a little one, at least until married. We must always think of the child's happiness."

"I wonder if the father of Susan's little one, will try to contact her."

"This has nothing to do with him. If I need to, if he dares to contact her, I'll call the police for attempting to place the girl in further moral danger."

The meeting room door lay open. Boisterous voices filled it. Sisters crowded around Mother Terrance, Sister Anthony sitting by her side. Mother Terrance nodded at Sisters Bernard and Gregory—one that said she was satisfied everyone expected had arrived, then put her fingers to her lips for silence. Like a group of children playing Simon Said, Sister Matthew made the same motion as the Sister beside her, then the others followed until the room fell silent.

Mother Terrance smiled. "We've talked a great deal of changes needing to be implemented since Vatican II. We've all heard what Pope John XXIII said, 'It's time to open the windows of the Church and let in some fresh air.'"

Sister Gregory stood stock-still. *What about the waiting girls' windows? What about the oxygen machines not turned on, pillows on the face. What about all this denial of the real world out there?* As she tried to focus straight ahead on Mother Terrance, she couldn't help but look to the left and right, and saw everybody doing the same thing. An undercurrent of anticipation flowed through the room.

Mother Terrance let the anticipation build, met everybody's gaze one by one. "Our stand on this to date has been conservative. But this morning, the Bishop forwarded papers from Rome, based on the *Decree of the Adaptation and Renewal of Religious Life.*" She looked at the three piles of colour paper. "Today you'll be given notes. A different colour for each vow. In the spirit of renewal, we'll ask ourselves what is the purpose of Religious life. All three of our vows will be re-evaluated, especially obedience. We have some serious thinking and debating to do."

Thinking and debating? Ludicrous to many of us, our lives spent in unquestioned obedience.

"This isn't a choice...," Mother Terrance said. "Changes will be implemented. Not doing so will ensure Orders are disbanded."

Most older sisters swayed. Sister Anthony looked amused, while Sister Alexander and some younger nuns bowed their heads to hide smiles.

Sister Dominic frowned. "These whispered changes regarding meat allowed on Friday and altering the habit are bald concessions to human weaknesses. We must resist, be stalwart, preserve our true ideas and customs."

Mother Terrance raised her voice. "They're not whispers but reality. No one will be forced to eat meat on Fridays, but it will be an option, except for Fridays during Lent and Ash Wednesday."

"Lent days no longer days of penance, that's blasphemy!" Sister Gregory said.

"We may substitute another penance, which should involve a level of sacrifice comparable to abstention from meat."

"It does appear we will be repudiating holy traditions," Sister Gregory said, surprised at her own reluctance to change. "Jesus died on Friday. Is the Church diminishing human sins and the need for penance?"

"We are all free to continue to choose to fast and abstain, but as we enter future prayer and abstinence let our spirit generate and herald a new birth of loving faith to become one with Christ and servants of God's people."

"I can't imagine sitting at the table where meat is served on Friday," Sister Gregory said. "I've never eaten meat on a Friday. It will smell so foul on that sacred day." And she was surprised how strongly she felt, how brash her comment. Had the years in here done that to her?

"Nor can I," Sister Dominic said. "I won't sit at the table either."

"I don't care who eats meat," Sister Anthony said, "but the thought doesn't appeal to me, but I can't tell the difference between meat and fish until it's in my mouth."

"I also won't sit where meat is served on Friday," Sister Bernard said.

"I didn't mean I wouldn't sit at the table," Sister Gregory said, "but that I can't imagine such a change. And Sister Anthony, I'll ensure you're not served meat on Fridays."

Sister Anthony smiled and winked. Sister Gregory knew the old sister couldn't be certain she winked at the right person and wiped a finger along the corner of her eyes. "Excuse me, I have something in my eye."

Sister Anthony laughed. "I didn't spit, now stop that."

Mother Terrance looked at Sister Gregory in a manner that said I love Sister Anthony too, but let's get back to business. "There's no reason why we can't begin to implement change after the fasting period of Lent."

Sister Gregory's stomach churned and bounced at the thought of meat on Friday. The older sisters' plaster white faces said they weren't far from becoming physically sick too.

Mother Terrance cleared her throat. "Our beloved founder, Mother Augustine's spirit and special aims will remain faithfully held as will our devotion to prayer. Our search for God's grace will always come first. But in the spirit of renewal we will examine our constitution, customs, book of prayers and ceremonies and ensure they are adapted suitably and re-edited to the decree of the sacred synod."

"What of our habit and wimple?" Sister Alexander asked. "They're ridiculously hot in summer."

"No need to change them," Sister Dominic said. "It is an outward mark of consecration to God. And God sets my policy, not some scrivener at the Vatican."

"They must be changed," Mother Terrance said. "But any change will ensure it remains simple, modest and poor, but becoming as well as meet the requirements of health and suit our working conditions and the world we live in."

"Surely God is not going to judge us on thinner material or a few inches less," Sister Gregory said. And that surprised her too. She had never talked out this boldly, one thought, one sentence contradicting the next.

Mother Terrance nodded. "I agree."

"What will these changes mean to the hospital?" Sister Bernard asked.

"We must become more aware of the world around us to assist effectively those who come into our care. We will look at our hospital policies and procedures and ensure they're in line with those expected by society and government and that our own religious beliefs and practises are not forced on those seeking our care and help." Mother Terrance glanced at her watch. "Any more questions?"

"Will we be able to visit our families?" Sister Mathew asked so quietly, her lips barely moved.

"We will discuss individual needs…how they affect the group as a whole. We've already implemented some changes in the form of respite from duties when needed."

"These outside influences can't be good if they flow into the Order," Sister Dominic said. "Younger novices and sisters have lost their spine. Look what happened to Veronica. At the first instance of a little hardship, a little of God's testing, she's suffering, taken off to the infirmary."

"We can't stop change. It's all around us," Mother Terrance said. "Change must happen in our Order, or our congregation won't survive. Let's discuss next week the opportunity we've been given to visit families. Some of the elderly haven't seen their overseas families for many years. Shouldn't it be an individual choice?"

Sister Dominic bowed her head. Everyone knew she didn't have any living family. Tears filled Sister Gregory's eyes. She also had no family alive. But she wouldn't let herself cry. *Not now. Not here.*

Sister Gregory might not be able to hold and be held by her parents again, but she'd be able to visit their graves. The words, the gratitude, welled up in her, and she let it out. "This is a wonderful thing for us as daughters and a wonderful gift the Church is giving back to our parents."

Sister Terrance nodded. "When you leave this room, think about the seven gifts of the Holy Spirit—wisdom, understanding, counsel, fortitude, knowledge, piety, and fear of the Lord and apply them to future discussions."

Sister Gregory lowered her gaze to the three coloured paper piles on the desk. Everything she believed was turning, piece by piece, upside down—the vows of poverty, chastity, and obedience reduced to different coloured paper. The reality of accepting change to deeply held beliefs piled on top of the torment of Susan, of women and girls out there, of her own body's feelings in ways so new, so unexpected.

*

Sister Gregory closed her office door and sat in the dark. It wasn't uncommon to hear a sister crying gently in the dormitory, but she hadn't cried for years and had no desire for others to know she cried now. Tears wet the back of her hand. She could still cry, and knew she hadn't completely numbed to the world, hadn't withered away to a dry shell of a woman, wasn't just a cold symbol of the Lord. She closed her eyes wishing for some warmth—strong arms to embrace her and tell her all was right, would be fine—that she was loved and needed.

She thought all her past efforts to find the grace of God might have been futile and end in nothingness. *Lord, give me the grace to see beyond what is visible. Help me become more aware of Your Wisdom.* But the prayer brought no relief from the pain and tears for the first time in years. Her mother died when she was a child. Like a distant puff of smoke, her mother's image drifted in and out, but she was unable to see the woman's finer features. She remembered the words her mother whispered in Polish each night when she was tucked into bed. Kocham cie. *I love you.*

Sister Gregory's father put her into the Junior Novitiate as soon as she was old enough, and it was a natural progression to join the Sisters of St Anthony aged sixteen. But after she took her final vows, she had seen her father only seven times, each supervised by those in the convent on Mother Augustine's festival day.

A tap came on the door. Sister Anthony said, "You all right?"

"I have a headache—can't bear the light. But I'll be fine."

"I know you're upset." She opened the door slightly. "There's no need for you to be alone."

"I've never been able to hide anything from you."

The older nun gently closed the door, and darkness returned. Only the building lights in the distance out there fell on the window. "I'm sure you have." A slight wheeze tinged the Sister's voice. "We wouldn't be human if we were perfect. Only our Lord can claim such greatness."

Sister Gregory stood. "I need to turn off the waiting girls' dormitory lights."

"Sister Dominic's off duty. She'll settle the girls." Sister Anthony wrapped her arms around Sister Gregory and smoothed down the back of Sister Gregory's veil as if it were hair. "Let it out...God knows our suffering."

WAITING A week before envelopes arrived was ridiculous. Sylvia was sure she would go crazy before they came. She wished all afternoon that she could take back what she said to her father. But who was he to dictate? He left when her mother found out she was pregnant. No wonder he expected Sylvia to get rid of her own baby. He probably never wanted her mother to have another one. But he said he loved her mother. *Oh, what's going on with them?*

She wanted to scream at the hypocrisy. Her mother had eight brothers and sisters, four of each. Pa had a nervous breakdown during the depression, and Nan struggled to keep them all fed and clothed. But Nan would never have given away any of her children.

Sylvia pulled the radio from under her pillow and turned it on, expecting splutter and static, but a sombre male voice poured into the room. "This coming year, Australia will spend millions on war…this coming year, we will spend two hundred million on peace…." Sylvia turned up the volume. Prime Minister Holt spoke, and the government were going to send thousands of men to Vietnam.

Don't worry about me, Tommy had said. *Just because I've got to register for National Service, doesn't mean I'll be drawn out of the ballot to go to Vietnam.*

"Holt is a bit too friendly with the Yanks," her father said, only a few months ago. "It's not enough the bloody mongrel, if he gets in, is going to let in more migrants. There's enough of the daggos in the street now. Soon they'll override the country. Now he wants to force more of our boys off to fight. I've got no problem with

National Service. It makes men out of boys, but forcing them to join the regular army when they can't even drink or vote, to fight overseas is another thing altogether."

Footsteps moving past Sylvia's room didn't let up at anytime, but one set stopped outside her room. Sylvia put her face into the sheets. *One of them with those damn documents. Go away.* But when she looked up, Melissa peered through the gap between the door and wall.

"You awake." Melissa asked. "I wondered where you were when the other girls came back."

"I took a detour." Sylvia turned over and sat on the bed. "But at the minute, I want to listen to the news."

"I want to listen to music."

"Lights will be turned off in a minute."

Melissa put her hands on her hips. "One song, pretty please?"

"Oh, I've missed the rest of the news now anyway. One song."

Melissa sat on the bed, and her hand crept toward the radio. "I want one, but Mum says they're too much money."

"You can hold it," Sylvia said. "But by any chance do you have envelopes?"

"I can't write—I'm stupid. Though, Mum says I'm a good scribbler."

"We can't be good at everything. I'm horrible at remembering some things."

Melissa tossed her hair behind her shoulders, then placed the radio next to her ear. "Mum says if I'm good while I'm here, I can go back home when the baby is born."

"Your mum is going to help you look after your baby?"

"Don't be silly. The best thing for me to do, after it's born, is to forget the whole sorry episode. Sister Bernard has found nice parents for it. Mum says looking after me is enough, and she can't have another child running around. Besides, it's a bastard. Everyone will hate it."

Sylvia felt her eyebrows rise. "How old are you?"

"Twenty, going on twelve, Mum says."

"Does your boyfriend know you're here?"

"I'm not allowed to speak about its daddy. It'll get him into lots of trouble."

"Who told you that, the nuns?"

"Mum said I'm to keep my gob shut, or the police will lock him up, and we'll be destitute."

Sylvia sighed, letting the reply sink in. "You told anyone this?"

"I told Sister Veronica." She pointed at the chair. "What's that there?"

"Grapes. You can have some, but wipe them first. There's dirt on a few."

"I don't like them. The seeds get caught in my throat." She placed her forefinger on her lips. "That's probably Sister Gregory coming up the stairs."

But Sister Dominic stood in the doorway, her puffy-face reddening like a large beetroot. "You dirty, dirty girls. Melissa, back to your room. Right now! Matron will hear about this disgusting behaviour."

Melissa put the radio on the bed and ran out of the room.

Sylvia stood. "We weren't doing anything."

Sister Dominic's nose crinkled. "If the Matron catches any girl smoking in here, they'll find themselves on the street."

"Then I should take up smoking."

"There are hundreds of girls waiting in line to get in here, all the way from Ayres Rock at the moment. Now lights out."

"What difference does it matter if the lights stay on?"

Sister Dominic flicked off the light. "While in our care, you'll do as we say."

Sylvia waited until the Sister completed her rounds and flicked off all the lights in the dormitory. She flicked on the light switch, but the light didn't come on, so she stepped out of her room. The corridor was black, that deep scary blackness, like when you go camping and the clouds hide the stars. *It's a blackout.* The scent of tobacco whiffed past—*Cravens*—the same cigarettes her father smoked. The hallway light came back on, as did the light in the kitchen. The door beside her opened. Kim walked out with curlers in her hair and holding a little torch.

"Were you smoking in there?" Sylvia whispered.

Kim nodded. "I thought I blew all the smoke out through the wall vent."

"I'll bet my socks Dominic's gone straight to the Matron's office, and it's going to be on for young and old."

"They're all bark and no bite. They get satisfaction watching our suffering, that's all."

"They don't even have envelopes in the shop."

"I've got some envelopes if you want them."

Sylvia threw her arms around Kim and hugged her. "Thank you." Then jumped back as if the other girl were a hot potato. "I'm sorry."

"Don't be." Kim's face reddened. "If you hadn't moved away so quick, I would have hugged you also."

Sylvia smiled. "The curlers spiked me in the forehead. Don't know how you sleep with them."

"Used to it."

"One of those nuns will come back. Sister Dominic knows I wasn't smoking. I could mind your fags and give them back to you tomorrow."

"Where are you rostered?"

"The laundry."

"It's like I imagine Hell, hot and stinking, and you'll pray to get out of there."

"It can't be that bad."

"It's worse than a pig pen."

*

Sister Gregory called out, "Praise be to Jesus!"

Sylvia was in bed and covered her ears, waiting for the horrid bell to start ringing, but a knock came on the door. "Time for dressing, breakfast, then work."

Sylvia jumped off the bed. *I'll be able to send my letters today.* She moved the chair next to the wardrobe, climbed onto the seat, and pulled Kim's packet of cigarettes and matches off the top. She placed a cigarette and the matches into her pocket and put the rest back on top of the wardrobe. She stepped out of the room and bumped into Sister Gregory, holding up a floral smock.

"Sister Dominic found this in the sewing room. It has your name on it."

"It's like a tent."

"It will keep you a little cooler than your other clothes and be more comfortable."

Sylvia grabbed the dress.

"Were you smoking last night?"

"I hate the things."

"Do you know who was?"

Sylvia shook her head.

"I need to check your room."

Sylvia remembered her letters sitting on top of her bag under the bed. "You have no right to do that."

"We have every right if you have brought contraband into the hospital."

"Since when is smoking a sin?"

Like storm troopers out of a movie, a flurry of nuns entered the rooms along the corridor. Sister Gregory stepped past Sylvia and opened her wardrobe. "It isn't allowed on the grounds."

Sylvia put her hands on her hips.

"I'm not going to touch anything, unless it needs removing."

"Sister Bernard is picking on me because I haven't signed the papers."

"The Matron is concerned someone might go to sleep with a cigarette and the hospital burn down."

"I don't have any smokes."

"Then you shouldn't be concerned."

"Do what you want." Sylvia rushed back into the room and picked up the letters and envelopes from the top of her suitcase.

Sister Gregory snatched the letters from Sylvia's hand. "What do we have here?"

In an instant, Sylvia snatched part of them back. The letters ripped in half. She and the Sister both held half the letters. "Is it a sin to send letters to my mother?"

Sister Gregory frowned, still holding the paper at a distance as if it smelt putrid. "Why were you afraid I would find them?"

"I wasn't. I was going to send them this afternoon."

"To your mother."

Sylvia held her breath, could see the doubt and confusion in the Sister's eyes—a temptation to read what was in her hands, and Sylvia nodded. "And one to my brother."

Sister Gregory held the pieces of paper toward Sylvia. "Sorry…."

Sylvia reached for the paper, met the Sister's stare and touched the torn surface. "Thanks."

Kim's voice rang through the dormitory. "Give them back."

Sylvia stepped to the door as a nun came out of the next room, a gentle sway in her hips as if she'd won first prize in a competition. "When you leave."

Sylvia turned to Sister Gregory. "You don't need to search my room now."

"We'll be searching them all."

"I'm going to have breakfast. You won't find anything here."

Sister Gregory pulled the chair closer to the wardrobe and climbed on its seat. "What's this?" Sister Gregory sounded more dismayed than Sylvia felt. "You said you didn't smoke." She pulled the smokes off the top of the wardrobe. "Are you deaf? What's this?"

Sylvia crossed her arms. "I've never seen them before."

"Sister Bernard won't be pleased."

"If she wants to put me out onto the street, my mum or dad will have to come and get me."

Sister Gregory put the cigarettes and matches in her pocket, big enough to hold a whole drawer of knives and forks, and climbed off the chair. "Are the cigarettes yours?"

Sylvia nodded. "I'll pack my bags."

"You said you didn't smoke."

"My father gave them to me."

"I think we might keep this between ourselves."

"Pardon?"

"I consider taking the blame for someone else rather foolish, but it's also a commendable quality. I don't think Sister Bernard needs to know about this."

"But they are my smokes."

"Sister Dominic said she thought the smell came from Sylvia's room."

Sylvia gritted her teeth. "I am Sylvia."

"Are you in the laundry today?"

"And tomorrow."

"We'll make it all week."

"But everyone hates it there."

"Then the punishment is fitting. Or would you prefer two weeks?"

ALTHOUGH THERE was still half an hour to go before 2pm, Sister Gregory reminded herself she started work well before the sun rose. She couldn't stand the thought of staying at her desk for another moment, couldn't concentrate with all the banging, sawing, and crashing noises from the new dormitory.

Sister Anthony pruned near the gate, just off the path, a bucket beside her and an unused pair of gloves. The older sister didn't turn, didn't hear the footstep along the gravel.

Sister Gregory knelt and shouted over the construction noise, "I'll join you today." She rolled up her sleeves, put on the gloves and pulled out weeds.

"I can't hear a thing," Sister Anthony said, and as if God heard, the noise died. "Lucky the workmen eat. What's bothering you?"

"Nothing."

"There is if you're weeding."

Sister Gregory met the older woman's questioning gaze. "One waiting girl doesn't want to sign the papers."

"She isn't the first.... We can only advise them of the situation they'll find themselves in if they leave with their little ones. The world isn't a kind place for a single mother. People are cruel."

"Interfering in the relationship between mother and child when they have yet to sign the papers is a cruel practice."

Sister Anthony sighed. "Don't lose sight of the real issue. If a mother doesn't have the capability of providing and caring for her child, adoption is really the only alternative."

"I can't help feeling like...." Sister Gregory pulled out more weeds and dumped them into a bucket, "a jailing nun."

"You're not failing anyone."

"I feel like a prison warden."

"This isn't jail."

"Most girls probably wouldn't agree—allowed to go nowhere, only their rooms, chapel or chores."

"Sounds like our life."

"We chose this life."

"We can't change the world. Their choices brought them here...each of them has free will...knows what's right and wrong."

The hospital gate opened, and Sister Bernard entered the grounds. "You'll both need an extra long shower."

Sister Anthony held the clippers toward the Matron. "Join us."

Sister Bernard laughed. "I'm struggling to kneel in church these days. The knees are like floorboards, but the back is like a tree about to collapse."

"How is novice Veronica?" Sister Anthony asked.

"Hopefully...more rest and she'll be all right." Sister Bernard checked her watch and frowned. "It's a little early for recreation."

Sister Gregory stood. "I thought Sister Anthony might provide some insight into why our records show a great rise in admissions to the hospital by unwed girls since the fifties. This year, if the current trend continues, we'll have organised the largest number of adoptions ever."

"I see...don't stop your conversation," Sister Bernard said. "Enjoy the sunshine."

"I was going to speak to you too."

"I'm sure you were."

A girl's voice rang out. "That's not fair, and you know it's not."

"Who on earth is that?" Sister Bernard asked. "Where's it coming from?"

Sister Gregory took off the gloves. "The side of the hospital...near the laundry."

"You let me go," Sylvia, who did not want to be known as Susan, shrieked. "You can't do that."

"I'll find out what's wrong." Sister Gregory threw the gloves into the bucket.

"Mother Terrance wants your summary by the end of the week," Sister Bernard said. "I'll fix this. This girl will be the death of us."

###

Sylvia had left the laundry from the metal doors at the side of the hospital. It was like a sauna except for the stink of a butcher's shop, the humming of driers, and the swishing of machines, and steam from the iron presses. A continuous flow of dirty nappies and bed linen were crammed into the wire mesh trolleys along the back wall.

She'd only moved a few feet away, when Sister Dominic appeared around the corner of the hospital. Sylva had checked the area before and only found a little cemented courtyard out of view from any dormitory windows.

Sylvia resisted the urge to pat down her pocket holding her letters and Kim's cigarette and matches and walked away from the puffy-faced sister. Unlike most other sisters, who humbly lowered their gazes when they passed, Sister Dominic stared straight at Sylvia. "Where are you off to, petal?"

"The toilet."

"It's not time yet. You go back. You don't stay here for free."

"I need to go, and it's almost recreation time."

"Ah, but you've got your hands at the side of your pretty dress. You afraid I'm going to snatch something from your pocket?"

"It's like a tent, but least it's cool."

"You hiding cigarettes?"

"Later, I'm going to send a letter to my mum."

"I can put it in the post for today."

"I'd rather send it myself."

"Have it your way, but you need to go back to the laundry."

"I really need to go to the toilet."

"The discomfort you're feeling is the Lord's way of telling you that you should have saved yourself for matrimony."

Sylvia put her hands on her hips. "You can't stop me going to the toilet."

The Sister's nostrils flared, and she looked a bit like a bull. "If you don't turn around and go and finish your shift like the other girls, I'll make sure you're in the laundry every day until you leave."

"That's not fair, and you know it's not."

Sister Dominic grabbed Sylvia's earlobe. "Back that way."

"You let me go," Sylvia shrieked. "You can't do this."

"It's my job to keep you in line. Turn around."

"Sister!" Sister Bernard called from a window on the ground floor.

Sister Dominic's grip increased on Sylvia's ear. "This one is attempting to skip chores."

"I'm not." Sylvia pushed the Sister's hand away. "I told her I need to go to the toilet, and she tried to rip my ear off."

Sister Bernard gripped the wooden window sill. "Go to the toilet."

You beauty. "Thank you, Sister."

"And Sister Dominic, there's an electrician due at reception. You take him to the birthing rooms. He's coming to check the machines and power outlets."

THE CAR horn had jammed, or someone had died and collapsed on the steering wheel. Kim looked out her bedroom window, clipping in her gold earring. A handful of neighbours rushed outside into their front yards and kind of crept to the car, as if they expected to find a dead body.

Andrew sat in the car, his fingers tapping the steering wheel. He'd pressed on the horn a couple of times, she knew that now, then continuously while watching her window. As soon as she appeared there, he jumped out of the driver's seat, and the horn blaring stopped.

"I'm ready," she said from the open window, taking in his scowl. "Come and have a look at the baby clothes your mother brought over with the wedding list."

"We're running late. Why do you think I'm down here?"

"Has he lost his manners?" Kim's mother asked. "It doesn't hurt to come in for a few moments."

Kim concentrated on the clock on the wall, couldn't meet her mother's gaze. "Our reservation is for six."

"That's no excuse for rudeness."

"Mum, please don't. He doesn't mean any harm."

"Oh, go, I'll sort out the clothes."

The toys and clothes were so small, some lemon, others white. Little chubby hands and feet would fit the woollen mittens and booties. "I won't be late, but don't stay up."

Her mother nodded and folded a baby jacket. "He's a typical man, but…. You look lovely. Go! Don't worry about me."

Kim picked up her handbag, slipped into her red shoes, and

walked outside, the bounce she had in her step all day, now gone. He opened the car door, looked her up and down and stopped at her already showing bulge. A look of distaste creased his face. He rattled off his words and questions without a breath. "You look tremendous. How was your day? Hungry?"

"Thanks." *Good and no, not really.* "Why were you late?"

"Got caught at the office."

She smiled and climbed into the car. *Everything's fine.* "It was such a great day, and your mother was wonderful."

He looked sideways at her. "Want to skip dinner? Come back to my place."

"You just carried on like a lunatic with the horn because we were late."

"We need to talk."

"Your mum brought over your family's side, so we can prepare the invitations."

"Did you hear me?"

"What's wrong?"

"I just…don't feel like dinner out."

"You're not making sense."

"I want to be alone…talk alone." He put his hand on her knee, but there was no warmth in his caress. "Is that so bad?"

She shook her head, crossed her arms, and sat back in the seat silent for a long time, conscious his hand moved away from her knee the second after he placed it there. "Are you going to tell me what's wrong?"

SYLVIA STOOD under the lukewarm water, enjoying the water gently spray her skin, the tension leaving her neck, her face, and the clean scent of lavender soap washing away the stink from the laundry and the heat of the day. The soap was smooth, soothing, sliding over her skin, sensuous. She closed her eyes and slowed down the movement of her hand over her tender breasts, where Tommy's little amethyst ring hung, craving Tommy—a hunger for his arms to wrap around her, to take away the ache, to tell her everything was going to be all right. She wanted him to feel the warmth of her skin, her body that carried their child, and him to hold her.

The letters she wrote were sent. She'd gotten lost, passed the reception area, and wanted to run through the frosted glass doors and walk out the gate. She'd seen the paintings on the wall, briefly noticed them the day she came to the hospital, caught sight of the woman holding a sword thrust into the dragon's throat. *St Margaret slaying the devil.* She'd glanced at the frosted glass doors again, then pulled herself back toward the dormitory. *Even if you could get past the nuns, where would you go?*

She'd remembered Sister Dominic appearing from the little courtyard near the laundry, had wondered what the Sister had been doing there. The area was only a few metres square and squeezed between two brick walls and a wooden fence. She had gone out there again, then had almost left the little yard for good but noticed the fence uneven at the top. A wooden gate hanging in the fence made it uneven, though it seemed to be part of the fence, no locks but hard to see. She pushed on the gate, and it opened into a lane leading to a street. Garbage bins lined a wall. She'd stood there for so long, taunted, freedom so close.

What her mother said, what they all said flooded in, and she closed the gate. *Give up your baby, and you can leave here free.* But that would mean having nothing to show of her love, no proof she had loved, and her child would not know she loved him. *Maybe you're selfish. Maybe you're a fool. Everybody is only trying to help, do the best thing for you. Why not leave him here? Why ignore the advice of everybody? Because I'm not bad. I can be a good mother.* Then she wondered if she heard the voice of God. *Leave the baby. Why be stubborn? How will you manage? Do the best thing.* Sylvia sighed. *Do the right thing.*

A melody of voices rang through. *I'll tell you something for nothing. Your child will be called a bastard because its mother has no respect for her body. You've brought this all on yourself. Why have you done this? Cause I love Tommy. You have no idea what love is, neither does Tommy, and now look at what you've done. Listen to me, you're going to the nuns. It's the only way. It's for the best. You listen to me. You dirty, dirty girl.*

She turned the water on faster, placed her back against the spray, trying not to think of how her body was changing, turning into a rounded woman's body with wider hips and fuller breasts—that she never thought she'd have. She placed her face under the spray and tried to wash away the image of Tommy's face, his voice, his touch. *Sign the papers. Just sign them. It's for the best.*

Sylvia, is that you in there?" Kim asked. "Are you crying?"

Sylvia turned the water off and grabbed a towel. "I couldn't find you today. I managed to save a fag." She wiped her hands and pulled the cigarette and matches out of the dress pocket, knelt, and held them under the door.

Kim struck a match. "You all right?"

"Do you really think we should adopt our children out?"

A cloud of smoke floated above the shower door. "Yes." The longest silence passed before Kim said, "I keep hoping a miracle will happen, and I'll somehow keep my baby. That somehow the bastard stigma will be gone, that I could see the future and be sure

I could look after him as good as a mother and father."

"I hate this." Sylvia patted her face and body dry. "… hate being here."

"I think we all do."

"But you've signed those papers."

"…through my tears. Cried so hard I doubt anyone can tell it's my name."

"I wish it was over."

"It'll never be over." Kim blew another mouthful of smoke above the shower door. "A part of us will always stay here."

"It's so unfair."

"When we leave no one will know we've sinned." Kim took another puff. "Will it be so bad for a couple who really want a child and can give it everything it will need?" Kim put her hand under the door. "Have the rest."

"Thanks, but I don't like them."

Kim handed Sylvia the matches. "Keep them until I work out a way I can get more smokes."

"There's a little gate in the fence near the laundry that opens onto a lane on the other side of the hospital. No lock on it."

"Show me tomorrow, but I think the smokes make me feel sick sometimes anyways."

"Why are you so sure this is the right thing to do?"

Kim walked across the room, opened the Modess pad incinerator, and threw the smoke butt into the furnace. "I'm not." Kim concentrated on the floor, and her voice wavered. "I thought I was doing the right thing, but it was all wrong. I should never have slept with him."

"Do you still see him?"

Kim laughed, but it was to stop tears running down her face. "No… I fell head-over-heels in love, and he said he loved me too…but I felt ashamed after the first time, when I'd realised what we'd done…thought everyone could see what we'd been doing…that it showed on my face. Andrew kept saying it was all right because we loved each other…we were engaged…already making wedding plans."

"He dumped you when he found out you were pregnant?"

"Not straight away. He tagged me along."

"What about your parents?"

"There's only Mum…I was too frightened to tell her at first. I knew it was going to hurt her badly, but when I told her, she never showed it. Just said we needed to think long and hard before rushing into marriage. In the end she left the decision to us."

"My parents have been impossible since I told them. Mum went into hysterics and kept ranting about what people will think in between taking Vincent powders."

"How old is your Tommy?"

"Twenty."

"Then he'd be registered for National Service."

"He doesn't want to go to Vietnam. And it's unfair a little wooden marble with birthdates, drawn out of a barrel in a lottery, chooses who goes and who doesn't."

"If he really doesn't want to go, they won't make him. My uncle is an instructor in the army. He says those who really don't want to go aren't forced. He says they only want the best men to go, not anyone who doesn't have the courage."

"It's not about courage with Tommy. He just wants to build his business. He's a car spray painter."

"One of my brothers doesn't want to go either and won't have to because he's at university studying to become a lawyer, but my younger brother is enlisted."

"My brother joined the Regular Army last year. He was excited the last time I saw him, thinks it will be an adventure. My mum and dad are proud of him, but they think conscription is wrong."

"So does the army, that's why they don't force anyone to go. You don't know if Tommy's going to stay around. His mates will be on his back…telling him he's foolish, and while you're here, he's likely to be bonking someone else. What if he doesn't love you as much as you think he does and when you leave here with your baby, he isn't waiting?"

"He loves me."

"I thought Andrew loved me too. After we'd finished all our

wedding plans, paid for some of it even, he told me he couldn't go through with it—that he didn't love me enough." Kim breathed in deeply and turned her head away. "All the things we'd dreamed of...talked about for hours...were just smoke like from that fag, and my baby wasn't going to have a father."

"If I give my baby away, I'll never know what I could have given him, if I could have done it."

"I want mine so much...if I keep him, one day he'll want to know why he hasn't a father, and when I say I wasn't married, he'll hate me."

"Have you heard from him since you've been here?"

"I don't want to see him again. I love him still...but we're too young." Kim stopped again, and they both stood in silence, in the steam of the bathroom, waiting for others to come in and end the talk. At last Kim finished her thought, "My greatest wish is that my son or daughter will have loving parents like mine were."

"My friend's parents never married, just lived together, and she's been teased for ever at school. Some of the kids wouldn't even sit beside her in class." Sylvia bundled her clothes. "Maybe you're right. Maybe it's the best thing to do. I don't want the world to hate my baby. I wish I could talk it over with Tommy. I wish they'd given us the chance to talk about it before they sent me here. I feel like I don't know what's right, what to do, like I'm in some kind of cruel limbo."

"You are until you decide. You're the mother. You need to decide." Kim laughed and motioned at her large belly. "Look at me giving you advice. It's all so mad."

"Tommy said we might stay with his sister and her husband at Tamworth. They don't have kids. I don't know her well though. She's older than Tommy, but I never really liked her. Used to ignore me. When we lived next to Tommy's family, she'd get out the front of their house in her bikini washing her car. She had tickets on herself."

"Doesn't sound too good, staying with her, if you don't like her."

"If you were in my place, what would you do?"

"I don't know, Sylvia. I really don't know. But you're the one who is here, not your Tommy."

"I'm being selfish, aren't I?"

"Wanting to keep our babies doesn't make us selfish, but it'll be horribly hard to make do on our own with a baby. I wish I had your nerve."

Sylvia rubbed her temples. "I want to do the best thing for my baby, and if it is giving it to someone else…. I will. But if I was doing the right thing, wouldn't I feel it in my gut?"

"Our gut will feel off no matter what we do. That's the way mothers are, they say."

"I have to…just have to wait until I hear from Tommy."

Kim held her lips together, then muttered, "If I felt my baby's father loved me, I would wait until I knew for certain what had happened to him."

SISTER GREGORY sat behind her desk and took the letters from the outgoing cardboard mailbox. Novice Veronica normally checked the waiting girls' mail coming in and going out of the hospital. Nothing was lost, if the letters were harmless. They were simply placed into another envelope and re-addressed, and no one was any wiser.

Sister Gregory searched all the letters until she found Sylvia's name above the return address. All the letters would be checked later, but Sylvia had a defiance she never noticed in the other girls. She seemed more at risk of further damaging her baby, her life, her soul.

She pulled her letter opener out of a drawer and slit open the first envelope. She read the short page and felt an enormous sense of guilt for spying. The letter appeared to be addressed to Sylvia's brother at an army base. It was signed, your loving sister. Sylvia wrote that she hoped he forgave her and would visit her at some stage.

Hopefully, the other letter was as innocent, but from the opening paragraph she knew it wasn't. The other letter was written to Sylvia's young man, Tommy. She scanned the pages until the letter's end, unable to let it go, the passion seeping from the letter like blood. Then as if her fingers were burned, she threw the letter into the bin. Her mind was scorched worse than her fingers, and she let out a long sigh. Sylvia would never be able to live with God alone. The girl clearly craved damnation.

How the Lord must be calling out Sylvia's name with an aching agony in His heart for her to return to Him. The letter was full of angst and pain and lust, written by a poet capable of deception and seduction. According to the letter, the girl had been kidnapped, jailed by Satan's nuns who tried to smother and starve her, and the whole time her flesh ached for sinful pleasures. *I crave the touch of your lips...one more kiss.*

Just after the celebration of Lent during Easter week, was to be their meeting time—a meeting that wouldn't take place. During Lent when extra prayer, fasting and abstinence, went for forty days, Sister Gregory would join many in her spiritual struggle and self-denial—to prepare to die spiritually with Christ on Good Friday. But Sylvia was alone now, and her plan to run off with her young man would never get to him.

A knock came at the door, and Sister Bernard stepped into the room. "Good. I see you're going through the mail. I saw it building up."

"Susan tried to send a letter to her young man."

The Matron's pace slowed. "Do you still have it? Are you sure the girl wrote it?"

"She signed it." Sister Gregory pulled the letter from the bin. "I don't think she's going to sign the papers as easily as you think."

"Easily or not, she'll sign them." Sister Bernard scanned the letter. "My, I see, but this Tommy won't see this. I'll speak to her mother about it, then rip it to shreds."

"I saw an electrician checking power-points."

"All points are fine, although he found a fault in the gas machine cable."

"I see."

"Surely, you never believed Dominic deliberately denied the girl relief?"

Sister Gregory rubbed her brow. "It was odd...strange...the machine worked when I just flipped the switch."

Sister Bernard sat. "If you look for evil you'll see it." She adjusted her glasses. "How are the reports for Mother Terrance going?"

"I can't locate the first adoption legislation to compare it with the current one."

"Will be somewhere in the archives...but was introduced to provide for children who didn't have parents to care for them. Give me what you've done. I'll have a quick look."

Sister Gregory pushed a folder across the desk. "Sister Anthony said before the war the poor would put their children in institutions until they were better placed to care for them, and sometimes that never happened."

"Adoption was in the child's best interest...the preferred option to becoming a state ward."

"Yet, adoptions were low."

The Matron nodded. "Slow to be accepted...illegitimate children and children of the poor were believed to inherit evil tendencies, passed on from mother to child."

"What changed?"

"Shame of the Holocaust...society rethought...decided a child's environment had more to do with the quality of the child than who he was born to." Sister Bernard drummed her fingers on top of the folder. "And infertility...soldiers bringing home sexually transmitted illnesses. Welfare departments put great pressure on hospitals like ours, have for years...infertile couples demand newborn infants, and change won't come soon—so many girls come here two or three times."

Sister Gregory imagined the Pope would fall off the wall, if she said what she wanted to. She played with the folds of her dress, before finding the courage to look into the Matron's eyes. "Can't we advise...these girls of the new contraception?"

"The Pope's stance is clear." Sister Bernard drummed her fingers again. "As ours must be."

"Surely, since Vatican II, the possibility is there for the future. How can the Catholic Church move forward in a new world, if it doesn't look at advancements? The Anglican Church has acknowledged contraception in various forms and allowed its use for thirty years."

"We are not Anglicans.... Contraception in any form is a violation of natural law and scripture." Sister Bernard started to read the report. "Concentrate on the problem at hand?"

"I wonder how many hospitals run by Anglicans are filled with waiting girls."

Sister Bernard turned over a page, took her time, appeared to study the text. "We shouldn't concern ourselves with their moral struggles with the Lord." She sighed, sat back in her chair, and placed her hands in her lap. "What we are seeing with these girls isn't a religious issue but a social one."

Sister Gregory looked at her own hands, rubbed them, and almost whispered, "Can we separate society and religion? Can we help society without understanding it, all of it?"

"Religion hasn't driven the younger generation to dress alike, dance to music in a vulgar manner, or to rebel in tens of thousands against society's good expectations."

Sister Gregory walked to the window, struggling to keep her tone neutral. A nun pushed a Victor mower beside the gravel path, the grass cuttings spurting from the blades. "We only need to look at the fashions and magazines in the hospital shop, or outside…in our own front yard or over our fences to see and hear the great changes. How could this generation not develop their own culture and identity in a world bursting to amuse, to capture them? And what can we offer against that?"

"We all have the power to reject what is not God's will." Sister Bernard stood. "That's the issue."

"Sweeping things under the carpet…pretending they don't exist, will not let us reach them, help them when they need help."

Sister Bernard stepped to the door. "Perhaps you should ask yourself why you're asking these questions, then seek the answer from the Lord. Perhaps the problem lies with you. Should He fail to respond, as He sometimes does, maybe Mother Terrance can help resolve what is truly bothering you."

Sister Gregory turned around, was about to say *nothing is bothering me*, but the door had been gently closed.

*

Sister Gregory carried two handfuls of the waiting girl's mail, plus her report for Mother Terrance, as she ran after the postman. "Excuse me!" she called. "I have mail."

He stopped at the gate and held the latch. "I thought the box was unusually light the past week."

"I needed to...we ran out of envelopes." She glanced at the sky. *Dear Lord, forgive the partial truth.* "Take these." Two letters fell to the ground. She and the postman bent at the same time, brushed hands as they reached for the envelopes, and almost bumped heads. She jumped up and fiddled with Mother Terrance's report, warmth lingering from their hands touching.

The postman gathered the letters. "What about that in your hand?"

"Only those. This isn't mail. I'm about to take it—this report to the Mother House."

"I don't know your name, Sister. You all look alike."

"Gregory, Sister Gregory," she said, and had an ache suddenly in her stomach and a desire to escape his smile. "That's all—you have all the mail."

He placed the letters in his bag, flung the sack back over his shoulder and opened the gate. "Ladies first."

She slipped outside the hospital grounds, not looking back, and marched, until she reached the Mother House. She carefully closed the door behind her, then stepped along the hallway, past the cedar shelving, some as old as the house, her black shoes tapping across the floor, hoping she'd get past Mother Terrance's door to the stairs without interruption.

Sister Sebastian appeared at the top of the steps, her thin frame flanked by a habit too large for her frail body. "God be with you." The woman's hands clung onto the railing, and she descended the stairs, her balance uncertain. "Where are you off to?"

Sister Gregory lowered her voice. "Is Sister Veronica still in the infirmary?"

"No. Not with us old fuddies. She's in the room at the end of the hall."

Sister Gregory went to the landing.

Sister Sebastian pulled a handkerchief from her habit and

mumbled the *Our Father…* as she shuffled her feet along the hallway, wiping the cedar shelves.

Sister Gregory passed the infirmary and two sisters mopping the corridor. She reached the last door, gently tapped, then opened the door. The room was sparsely furnished like the cubicles in the dormitory, with only a closet, a small reading table and chair. Veronica lay on her side, her back to the door.

Sister Gregory pulled the curtains aside and opened the window. Two toddlers played together in the yard, while a nun sat on the steps of one of the cottages watching them. The three small cottages made up St Joseph's House. Women with young children stayed there usually to escape abusive relationships and occasionally single mothers with nowhere else to go.

"Are you awake?"

Veronica nodded. Sister Gregory walked around the side of the bed. The young woman's eyes were almost as vacant and lost as Melissa's. "I've come to see Mother Terrance, but it's recreation time. I thought you might like some company."

"…to convince me that I'm delusional?"

"To sit and listen…or we could pray to end what bothers you."

"I want to be set free from this place."

"Why?"

"You won't listen either. You don't see what I have in the wards. You're always in your office."

"What did you see?"

"Babies stolen."

Sister Gregory took in the words and plunked into the chair, else she might have slumped to the floor. "The waiting girl's babies are to be adopted."

"But they aren't even allowed to nurse them, not once."

"To avoid the attachment, the bond if allowed. Their hearts will only break further if they see their child's eyes. They won't want to let their little ones go."

"Their hearts break even more if they don't see their child. I've read the reports."

"Where?"

100

"In the archives. Even in America, they've done studies that say it's harmful for the mother to be parted from her child the way we do it."

Sister Gregory shook her head. "These mothers have no means of caring for their little ones."

"Should their babies be stolen from them?"

Sister Gregory stood.

"You think I've gone insane too?"

"Something given can't be stolen."

"Last month I was in a room...a waiting girl's little boy was born. Before I reached the nursery, Dr Dennison asked me whose child it was. When I told him, he said to follow him. He walked into the married ward. A woman was crying. Her son was stillborn. He handed her the waiting girl's child, told the woman to take it to her breast and allow the child to suckle as if it was her own, because now it was. He leaned in then and whispered to me, 'That's adoption. Policies and procedures are irrelevant. We need not bother with the law when dealing with unwed mothers.'"

"This is why you have blocked out the rest of the world?"

The younger Sister's eyes watered, and she shook her head. "No, Sister. I've blocked out this world. I'm not suited to this life. It's madness, cold, harsh."

"You haven't been thinking of hurting yourself."

"I only want to leave the Order, but they keep telling me I need to rest. Search hard for the Lord, that my suffering is normal—all part of seeking grace, you all say."

"If it was easy to become a Sister, if it was easy to find the Lord, we wouldn't spend our life searching, studying the Lord's word, seeking to please him." Sister Gregory sat on the end of the bed. "I have felt as you do...no Sister could claim to have found Christ without a great sacrifice of their own wants and needs."

"I'm not rejecting Christ. I pray night and day, for him to help, but I can't bear this life—that we can't hold our own views, right and proper views."

Sister Gregory answered slowly, measuring every word, as if talking to herself—because she knew she was. "The vow of obedience is the hardest vow of all to bend to. Don't be too hard on yourself for struggling with the concept it is God's will we must follow, not our own. Maybe if you continue your studies away from the hospital, perhaps a teaching environment, you might find a desire to serve God's people again."

"The expression on their faces when their baby is taken, breaks my heart every time."

"Speak to Mother Terrance. Have her move you to another vocation. I'm sure she'll oblige. I think you're coming to the realisation of the compassion within yourself." Sister Gregory held Veronica's hand and squeezed it gently. "It's that empathy you feel towards the waiting girls, and the helplessness their situation places in ourselves, which makes us question not only God's word, but our world, while we search for the grace of God."

I do every day, every moment, still.

OH, THE nuns are wicked though not as clever as they thought. Sylvia saw Sister Gregory, the day after she placed the letter for Tommy into the mailbox, chase after the postman and hand him a pile of letters. Sylvia didn't think anything odd about it at the time, thinking they were letters the nuns or hospital needed to send, until a week later when she received a letter from her mother, but not Tommy or her brother. It wasn't her mother's writing on the envelope Sylvia received.

Sylvia knew then Tommy would never get her letter. Sister Gregory probably shredded that letter, and her brother couldn't be bothered to respond. Sylvia wrote another letter to Tommy, this time with a better plan. She stood at the sewing room window, mending bloomers, until the postman walked up the street, then excused herself to go to the toilet. She ran down the stairs, into the chapel yard just as a bell rang signalling recreation.

She squeezed through the hedge where she had spoken to her father and gripped the fence rails. Sister Anthony hummed in the gated courtyard. The gate latch clicked, but it wasn't the postman. A man walked to his car parked beside the curb.

She slipped back between the bushes to hide and wait for the postman's whistling. Moses sprung through the bushes—sniffed her shoes. She covered her mouth to stop her muffled shriek. "Go!" she whispered. "We can play another time."

"Moses!" Sister Bernard called.

"Shoo! Go."

Moses barked, and Sylvia froze.

Sister Bernard was closer. "Moses, you come out."

But Moses wanted to play. Sylvia put her arms out, and he

jumped into them as the gate clicked. She held Moses close, tried to hold his mouth shut, but he kept licking her hand. "You're gorgeous, but please don't bark." She patted his forehead. "Please be quiet."

The hedge rustled. There was nowhere else to go—the bushes on either side too dense to push through. Sylvia closed her eyes. Any second now, she would be face to face with Sister Bernard and the postman about to walk past.

"What are you doing?" Sister Gregory asked.

Sylvia jumped, the voice sounding so close. Moses barked, jumped out of her arms and ran through the bushes to the nuns.

"Moses was playing hide and seek," Sister Bernard said.

Sylvia held her breath. The postman moved closer.

"I'm looking for Susan," Sister Gregory said. "I have an article for her to read."

"Probably in the toilet." Sister Bernard's voice drifted further away. "Seems to be her favourite place."

"I'll leave it on her bed."

"I need to get back inside too," Sister Bernard said.

Just at that moment, the postman passed Sylvia. She lunged toward the fence.

The postman jumped back. "You almost gave me a heart attack."

"I missed the mailbox," Sylvia whispered and held the letter toward him.

"As long as it has a stamp." He examined the envelope, then dropped it into his bag. "You have a nice afternoon, miss."

"If you get any mail for me, please hold it until I can meet you here. I'm Sylvia Dawes."

"I'm sure the nuns will pass it on."

Should I tell him? He might tell the sisters. What do you have to lose? He looks kind. "I think they read our letters and only send and give us what they want."

"They don't look like people who would spy and, besides, that's illegal—to obstruct the mail."

"Please…keep them for me."

"All right, and I'm not meaning to be rude, but what if the baby is born and you can't get down here?"

"Sister Gregory tries to be kind, but I think she never sent a letter I wrote."

The postman walked off. "I'm not promising anything. Must deliver the mail to where I'm supposed to."

Sylvia stayed there for a long time, not wanting to move out of the hedge, thinking Sister Bernard and Gregory heard everything. When she finally moved out of the bushes, a girl sat on the grass reading a book, and two other girls sat near the steps to the veranda, whispering as if in a library. Two women looked down from a window on the second floor. *The married women's ward.* One woman pointed at Sylvia. The other covered her mouth, and they giggled. At Sylvia. At her shame. She looked away.

In Sylvia's room, a cut out page from a magazine with a small note lay on her pillow. *Read with an open mind.* She kicked off her shoes and sat on the bed. *Unmarried Mother* was the headline. *He said he didn't love me enough* was almost in a font as big as the headline. *This girl will have her baby adopted* was in the smallest print. The article was from a previous *Women's Weekly.* She placed the page back on her pillow and stepped to the window.

"I was wondering where you were." Sister Gregory stood by the door. "May I come in?"

Sylvia watched the cars on the streets. "I was in the toilet."

"Have you read the article?"

Sylvia faced the Sister. "I have before."

"Oh."

"I also read the other articles from the same issue months ago, where the large headline read something like *He hasn't the courage to marry me.* And the smaller headline *Girl plans to raise her baby herself.* I wonder why they have the most important headlines in the smallest print."

Sister Gregory frowned, and Sylvia thought she was about to say one thing, but chose to say another. "The reason might be the plight of the mother is the most important part of the article."

"You gave me only one of those articles, chose the one you wanted me to read."

"I gave you the most relevant and helpful one."

Sylvia picked up the page and shook it. "The fathers of these babies deserted them. I haven't been deserted."

"It's only a matter of time."

"You don't know Tommy."

"I'm trying to help you make the right choice."

"Lots of people wrote into that magazine the month later about those two girls, and they all said different things. Lots of women said mothers should stand by their daughters—not throw them into homes, homes which would make most people cringe."

"If you read all those articles you would also have read the most important one."

"Oh, which one?"

"From the child kept by her unmarried mother. She and others like her all said their mothers should have adopted them out. They all suffered from taunts and rejection and loneliness because of their illegitimate status."

"That was years ago, and her father never stayed to support the mother."

"You're not old enough to get married."

Sylvia handed the article to the Sister. "Give it to someone else."

"Would you want Tommy to resent you? To feel trapped into a forever after relationship?"

"I don't want that, but he loves me. I love him."

"Then think of him, if you don't want to think of yourself or the child."

"I don't know why I can't make my own decision without everyone forcing it down my throat…everyone who doesn't know me, know Tommy."

"We are trying to help you reach the right decision."

"Why is everyone so certain we can't stay in love? My mum and dad met when they were teenagers and already married at my age."

Sister Gregory moved next to her. "You told me they broke up."

"They did." Sylvia started to cry.

Sister Gregory looked away, stood awkwardly, her hands clasped together, and said very softly, "Getting upset is no good for you or the child. Speak to the Lord. God knows our suffering."

SYLVIA, DRESSED in a floral smock, sat on a lounge in the crowded waiting girls' meeting room, hands in lap, her face growing more radiant every day. One would expect the glow on her face came from grace within—if they didn't know about the letter Sylvia wrote to her young lover. She had been a perfect display of humility for the past month, attended church without issue, finished her chores, and walked with an air of contentment.

Sister Gregory hadn't given Sylvia the papers to sign again. The girl was right. It had to be her choice, but Sister Gregory didn't tell the Matron she had stopped trying to get the girl to sign. God would judge Sister Gregory's disobedience how He chose. She prayed to Him every day to forgive her. The law of men said the documents should not be signed until five days after the birth of the child. With an aching heart, Sister Gregory decided to follow the law and not what her superiors demanded. And she knew that this one time, she had passed a point of no return in breaking her vow of obedience to the Church.

Sylvia never sent any other letters and no letters, except from her mother, came back to her. *She thinks Tommy received her letter. She's waiting for him. How quickly the glow on her face will disappear by day's end.* Sister Gregory was about to leave the room for the main reception area. There was no need to stay and watch the girl. No one would come to see her. Moses' dog door rattled in the hallway. Sister Gregory glanced at Sylvia, and Sylvia's gaze flashed back, then her face turned pale and they both looked at the door. A woman walked into the room, making eye contact with another girl. Within seconds they embraced.

Sister Gregory avoided looking at Sylvia. No need to rub salt into a wound. Then she heard heavy footsteps in the hallway—slow, cautious, as if they stopped at each picture of St Margaret. Someone followed the woman through the frosted glass doors and stood in the hallway. Sister Gregory was about to go and see who it was, when Sister Bernard burst into the room.

"I've been looking for you everywhere," Sister Bernard said.

"Today, she was going to meet him here."

"I've destroyed the letter. No more have been sent or came into the hospital, have they?"

"I've checked every letter."

"Melissa has gone into labour, and Sister Dominic is at the Mother House. Thank God, we're Jack of all trades."

The heavy footsteps made their way toward the reception area. Sister Gregory turned around as a young man in an army uniform entered the room, his face lighting up at the sight of Sylvia. A frown of disbelief crossed Sylvia's face, and she ran to him and they hugged.

Sister Gregory took a step toward the couple, but the Matron held her elbow. "That'll be her brother. Her mother told me yesterday, her brother was going to visit today. He's on leave for two weeks before being deployed to Vietnam."

"But she was going to meet the father of her child today."

The man pulled away, held Sylvia by her shoulders at arms length. Sylvia wiped away tears, before they embraced again and he kissed her forehead.

Sister Gregory could not stop looking. Their embrace could be one of young lovers, no longer sure they know each other.

The Matron clicked her fingers. "I need you in the birthing room."

Sylvia and the young man exited toward the enclosed veranda leading to the chapel yard.

Sister Gregory frowned. "What if it isn't her brother?"

"I doubt the girl's mother would be involved in such a deception...they clearly resemble each other."

Sister Gregory knew many young couples did strangely

resemble each other, without knowing, as if they sought out a part of themselves in their partner. "It seems too much a coincidence."

"The girl is taking up too much of your time. Come now."

###

Sylvia led him into the yard, toward the seat behind the chapel. "You must be excited."

"There's not much point joining if we don't see action." He studied the image of God in the stained glass window. "Nervous and excited." His gaze flashed over her, but he avoided looking at her stomach bulge. "You look good."

"I'm glad you came." She sat beside him and placed her hands on her stomach. "I'm going to turn into a fat cow."

"You'll be right, just eat properly. It'll go. What's the food like here?"

"I miss Mum's cooking. I even miss arguing with Leanne. Mum didn't bring her to visit, said she'd tell the whole world where I was."

"What about the nuns?"

"Same as school. Some sour and bitter cows, but most of them don't look at you."

He pulled coins and notes out of his pocket and counted a few. "Buy yourself something from the shop. A magazine or something. The shop up the road sells fish and chips."

"I'm not allowed to leave the grounds." Sylvia turned a silver coin over in her hand. "I got coins in change from the hospital shop. It looks like monopoly money, but I don't understand it."

"Get used to it. It's the new currency, and it's staying. The silver five cent is like a sixpence, the cent like a penny, and that note, that's a dollar. Same as a pound."

"I won't ever get used to it. It feels strange."

"Put it away."

"What was training like?"

"The officers were pricks." His face lit up. "All they did was shout and bark like loud speakers, as if we're deaf and treated us like dumbass bastards. Kept calling us girls. Made us parade at dawn in underwear." He laughed, and as he spoke his hands moved through the air—talking with his hands just like a bloody daggo, Dad used to say. "They told us pets weren't allowed, and when a Sergent saw an ant crossing the floor, he charged us all with harbouring pets. One hundred push-ups each. A mate got a cramp and didn't complete the set and the bloody Sergent shouted, 'Let's fucking try it again, shall we, girls?'"

"Doesn't sound like fun." She met her brother's gaze. "It must have been hard."

"It was at times, but they were only trying to get us to work together, teach us how to survive." He smiled, but sadly. "I'm sorry I didn't write back."

"This doesn't hurt you."

He shoved his hands in his pockets. "You're my little sister. Mates don't do that."

"Have you spoken to him?"

"I don't want to talk about him."

"Anyone would think he raped me by the way everyone is carrying on."

"He took advantage of you."

"You're sounding like Dad."

"Maybe because we both care."

"He doesn't care too much about Mum anymore."

"They'll work it out."

"He's probably got another sheila."

"He's just as cut up as Mum."

"Then why did he leave?"

"I don't know." He tapped the tip of his boot on the bin. "But I know they still care about each other."

"If everyone really cared about me, they'd try to help me do what I want."

He lowered his voice. "You can't still be considering keeping the baby?"

"Tommy said he'd help."

"If he really wanted to help, he'd keep away."

"If you had a girlfriend and she fell pregnant, would you dump her?"

"That's what you're not getting. You don't get a girl pregnant in the first place if you care for her."

"So you've never had sex?"

"I'm old enough to get married. You're not."

"So it's all right for you to have sex because you're old enough to get married, even if you're not?"

"It's different for men than women."

"Apparently not for Catholics. Do you know about the Pill and French Letters?"

He lowered his gaze to his polished boots. "You're my sister."

"And I have feelings like every girl you've been with."

"Just because some fellow says 'Getyagearoff!' doesn't mean you should."

"He's the only person I did it with."

"And now every other man you meet will think you're easy."

Sylvia walked away. "You're just as much as a hypocrite as the rest of them."

THE BIRTH of Melissa's little girl was quick. The doctor in training gave Melissa an injection to dry up her milk and bandaged her breasts to stop further milk production. She hadn't asked to see her child, only when she could go home.

"All in good time," Sister Gregory said. "You'll be taken to a ward to rest." Sister Gregory attached a tag to the bottom of Melissa's notes on the clipboard at the foot of her bed, near another tag marked *BFA* in thick black print.

Sister Bernard said from the door. "I'll call her mother and the adoptive parents. They'll all be glad their waiting is over."

Sister Gregory went to her office and caught sight of him, Sylvia's brother, striding toward the gate, hands in his pockets, his pace quickening. He unhooked the latch, stepped outside, and without looking at the hospital, walked quickly down the street.

Sister Bernard came into her room, face pale. "Bad news from Doctor Dennison. The child has a cleft palate. Speak to Melissa's mother. I'm wanted at the Mother House. We were always going to have difficulty placing Melissa's little one because of her poor family situation, but now it will be impossible to place the child. The child will have to go home with Melissa."

This was not the first time…. She knew the answer but hated it, pretended she didn't know. "What am I to tell the mother?"

"That no one will adopt the child."

She felt like shouting. *Cleft palates are easily fixed, seldom left any mark.* "It's only a minor deformity, repaired straight away. We all know it. Surely, such a child is in more need of a loving family."

"I agree, but I'm not the one adopting."

SYLVIA STOOD at the window and watched every car go past, every person walk down the street. But she didn't see him and if it got too much later, it would be dark. Then she wouldn't see anything, would be flashing Kim's torch hoping he'd see the beam. *He'll be here. Your daddy will come. Oh, Tommy, please come.*

She couldn't stop replaying the last day they were together, replaying him stepping toward her and saying, "I think you look cute. Beautiful. I just want to hold you."

She'd kissed him then, and they kissed for a long time, slowly, his hand entwined in her hair, unable to stop. She could smell the fresh sweet wildflowers and the damp grass around her. Hear the water rushing along the river. People's voices. Children laughing. His thighs pressed against her and wanting to be closer to him.

"Mum said I have to go to the nuns."

"Why?"

"She said it's till I have the baby."

"If something happens and they send you away before I see you again, tell me where they take you." He'd reached into his pocket, pulled out a little piece of tissue paper and handed it to her.

She had unwrapped the paper and found a little ring made up of three very small pinky-purple stones. "I love it. Love the colour. They're lavender."

"They're chips from amethyst stones. One for each of us."

She patted her stomach, not removing her gaze from the outside world. *He won't let us down.* She didn't hear the knock on the door or Kim walk beside her.

"Is he here yet?"

Sylvia shook her head.

"Take this." Kim handed her a torch.

"What if he doesn't come?"

Kim put her arm around Sylvia's waist. "Then it's meant to be, and you'll be better off without him."

"The letter might have gotten lost in the post."

A white panel van crawled along the street. Sylvia held her breath, moved closer to the window and put her palms on the warm glass. The panel van stopped near where the little children lived. He got out then, closed the door, lit a smoke, and leaned against his bonnet, staring, searching, counting the windows. *From left to right. Count them from let to right. One to ten. I'm here. Right where I said I'd be.*

"Is that him?"

Sylvia nodded, all words lost. *You came. I can't believe you're here. Oh, God, how I love you.*

"He's a bit of a sort. Do you think he saw you?"

"I don't know. I feel like jelly. I don't know if I'm going to be able to walk down there."

"You must go.... Hear what he has to say."

"Hope he still wants me."

"Don't guess. Go, get, get down there."

"It'll be dark soon." She turned and faced Kim. "Why do I feel so scared?"

*

Sylvia walked along the corridor toward the veranda leading to the laundry area. It was dark, but she knew the way well. She stepped outside, closed her eyes, praying Sister Bernard wasn't looking out of her office window. She reached the little courtyard. A light on the side of the hospital lit up the area, and she pushed on the gate. It didn't move, seemed jammed. She shoved it, and it flung open—so hard, it crashed against the brick building and now leaned a little off the hinge.

She was torn between crying and laughing. He stood there, waiting beside his van, his face all quizzled, as if she were some type of puzzle, and she became self-conscious, turned and put the gate back as best she could. "I know…Tommy…I look like a fat cow."

He smiled and walked to her and took her in his arms. "It'll be all right. It's okay. I'm here."

"I thought…you wouldn't come…hadn't gotten my letter, that I'd never see you again."

He took her hand. "Come and get in the back, least if someone comes they won't see you. I'll move away from the gate."

Sylvia knew that moment, he wasn't going to kidnap her, take her out of this place, this night. He'd leave her here, and her stomach dropped a little. She climbed into the back of the van and sat on the mattress as he drove slowly along the lane. She looked for clues whether someone else had been here and pushed away the thought. He was here. She was with him. She looked out of the side windows. "Remember when we all used to go camping with our dads? How dark it used to be out in the middle of nowhere? It's like that outside now."

His car stopped, and he climbed over the seat into the back, but he sat away a little, his legs spread out, almost touching hers. "Yeah, I remember."

She struggled to meet his gaze. "I'd convinced myself you weren't coming."

He kneeled on the mattress and pulled her toward him. "I told you I would. I can't believe they've done this."

"I hate it here."

"My birth date has been called out."

Sylvia looked away from him.

He held her hand, his touch firm and warm. "It doesn't mean I'm going to have to go."

"But what if you do?"

"Part of me thinks I should go. Most of my mates are signed up. What if the communists ever get here? What chance would we have?"

Sylvia sat and cradled her knees against her stomach. "Do you think I should give away our baby?"

He waited a long time, looked off, then back at her and smiled in the dark. "I told you then, and I mean it now. I don't want that to happen." He ran his hand through his hair. "But I wish I had known you didn't know what the Pill was. I wish…I had the sense to be more careful."

"You're avoiding the question."

"I love you…." He leaned over and kissed her. "I really do."

The instant their lips touched she was lost, didn't want to move, didn't want to stop, didn't want to return to the place they now were, but she pulled away from him. "I want to keep our baby."

"Dad said he'd sign the papers, so we could get married, but…."

"I'm sorry my dad belted you."

"I deserved it. He trusted me." He stroked her cheek. "Everyone keeps telling me this is the best thing to do. That we're too young."

"So we just stop loving each other, because we're too young, let them take our baby?"

"I can't stop thinking about you, thinking about my child inside of you. I tried to get your mum to tell me where you were, but she wouldn't talk to me, just said let things be."

"Maybe they're right. If I wasn't pregnant, things could just go on like this didn't happen."

He lay back on the mattress. "Nothing will be the same again, no matter what we do, either way."

"I'm scared, really scared…." He cradled her in his arms, and she cried—couldn't stop for a moment. "I wasn't going to cry."

"I don't feel the best either."

"What are we going to do?"

"I spoke to my sister and her husband. She said she'd think about us going to stay there. I'd take you with me now, if I thought I could look after us all. Had a job up there, or knew I could get spray painting work there. I'd have to start all again to get customers."

"What if you go to Vietnam?"

He put both palms over his face, and rubbed them downward, as if wiping away exhaustion. "I don't know."

"I'm going."

He grabbed her hand. "…I've missed you…but maybe it would be best if we…."

Sylvia pulled her hand away and moved to open the door. "Weren't together anymore? You're just like the rest of them."

He shook his head. "Don't go yet. I didn't mean it like….I just want to do the right thing."

"Then what do you mean?"

"I'll find a way to be together."

Sylvia moved toward him, and the world turned to slow motion, but her heart beat so hard. The more he kissed her, the more he touched her, the more she melted and wanted everything to disappear but them, three of them now—three of them being one.

"I love you," she said. "I've missed you so much."

"They can't keep us apart for ever….I won't let them…."

###

Sister Gregory dragged the bin toward the fence. The gate was open slightly. When she pushed on it, the wooden fence hung from the hinge. She pulled the bin next to three others. In the shadows along the lane, she heard murmurs, whispers—a man and woman talking, their voices hushed, from a panel van parked at the end of the lane.

She remembered the light streaming from a window in the hospital across the road to a panel van near where the little children lived. *It's the same car.* She took a couple of steps toward the van. The voices stopped. *Can it be one of our girls? Not possible. It's only two lovers moved off the main street.*

She stepped back to the gate, closed it, and made a mental note to have the gate's hinge fixed and the gate bolted, but not tonight, tonight might force someone out onto the street, deny them entry back into the hospital. *Oh, Lord.* She opened the gate again, strained to hear the voices from the car.

Nothing. They're silent. They know I'm here. Watching. Waiting. What are you waiting for? Go inside. Go now.

But when she shut the gate again, she leaned her back against the wood, closed her eyes, and heard them once more.

They are lovers. Making the sounds of loving each other—enjoying each other.

She thought of her own small and white hand on the gate and the postman's large and tanned hand beside it. She rubbed her temples, wanting to remove the ache in her conscience, but it wouldn't go—the panel van squeaked, moved in a rhythmic motion—provoking disgust and longing and confusion and inadequacy, and she rushed toward the sisters' dormitory.

SISTER GREGORY stood outside Sister Bernard's office and was about to knock, but in the room, a man spoke softly, his words unclear.

"I do understand," the Matron said. "But...."

Booted footsteps came down the hallway. As Sister Gregory turned, two police officers swaggered toward her.

"We're after the Matron. A Sister rang us about an hour ago."

Sister Gregory knocked on the Matron's door and opened it slightly. Sister Bernard's dog, Moses, stood at attention next to the fireplace, just as watchful as always, but the Matron looked smaller and more tired than she normally did, sitting opposite a young man.

"The police," Sister Gregory said.

"About time." Sister Bernard stood and glared at the young man. "I gave you the opportunity to leave."

The young man swung around, confusion and fear widened his large eyes, heavy with long lashes—*lovely eyes.* He jumped to his feet as a police officer entered. The young man's face flushed, and he quickly glanced toward the Matron's window as if he thought he might make his escape.

Sister Gregory wasn't sure of his age, perhaps twenty, perhaps older. His build was tall and strong, his brown and wavy hair slicked with grease back off his face, and as his eyes darted around the room from the Matron's face to the police officer's and Sister Gregory's—he swallowed, his Adam's apple pulsing, and the dimples in his cheeks creased deeper as he gave a final desperate look at the window.

"You'll be coming with us," a police officer said.

"You can't do this," the young man said. "I haven't done anything wrong."

"We'll talk about that at the police station."

"I only want to see her for a few moments."

An officer stepped toward the young man. "You want the cuffs?"

The young man walked toward the door and stepped past the police officer.

The officers followed him down the hallway, and Sister Gregory turned to the Matron. "Who did he want to see?"

"That's not important." Sister Bernard took off her glasses and sat them on the desk. "Why do you want me?"

"Just to say…the wooden fence…the workman just replaced it with a metal fence like our front gate but with a big padlock."

The Matron nodded, put on her glasses, but didn't look up. "Is that all?"

Sister Gregory walked away, her pace faster with each step, and climbed the stairs two at a time, then quickly made her way to her office window. The police car was parked outside the gate. They lowered the young man into the back seat, and as they did, an officer banged the young man's head against the car's doorframe.

THE HOSPITAL was probably colder than the place called Siberia. Despite the cold, Sylvia craved, needed fresh air and stood as close to the window as her stomach allowed. She felt whale-like and wondered how the giant baby would exit her body. She held a knife, trying to remove another nail, one in the seam of nails Sister Gregory had pounded into the window frame.

Earlier, five sisters had jumped into a battered and pale blue Kombi van, including Sister Gregory and the Matron. Now not many were left to watch, to stand guard. The postman was running late, and part of Sylvia hoped he didn't come, so she wouldn't look like an idiot asking him again if he had any letters for her. None had come from Tommy, not yet, but she'd sent him one every month. *Something must be wrong.* He had said *I'll find a way for us to be together.*

Maybe he changed his mind. Maybe he decided he couldn't stand the sight of her growing body. Maybe Kim was right, and he'd met someone else. *Maybe he's gone to Vietnam. You're an idiot. He's not coming. He would have sent a message by now. What are you going to do?*

The postman came into view. He lifted the gate latch, looked toward the windows, and she waved but knew he probably didn't see her very clearly—only an impression of a girl standing by the window, just like she'd seen Melissa that first day. Sylvia threw the knife onto the top of the wardrobe with the other nails she'd removed. She rushed to the chapel yard and squeezed through the hedge. She waited for the postman to return—found it unbearable and decided if there was no letter today, she wouldn't wait again.

The gate latch sounded, but the postman wasn't whistling and seemed to walk a little quicker when he saw her. She held her breath, trying to determine the expression on his face. He was usually happy, but a bit of a sigh came from him the last few times he told her there was no mail for her. "Sorry," he'd say, then tilt his hat and walk on.

He stopped and smiled, opened the bag, and handed her a letter. "I hope it's what you've been waiting for."

Sylvia gripped the Tamworth postmarked letter. *Tommy must be there. He hasn't forgotten us. He's coming to get us.* "Thank you. So do I."

THE FESTIVAL of Mother Augustine, the founder of the Sisters of St Anthony, was just about over. At sunset it would be officially finished. It started the evening before, to mark her passing at sunset over a hundred years ago. Much of the Mother House was open these two days every year after early morning prayers. The Mother House's clinging scent of age left for a few days, replaced by home-made breads, cinnamon cakes, biscuits and boiled sugar lollies, with lots of prayers and reflection.

The clonk of walking sticks were smothered by the sounds of the local priests laughing and mingling with the nuns and guests and family members. Novice Veronica wasn't among them. She left the order a month ago. There were no goodbyes, just a hasty exit from the Mother House early one foggy morning, with only a few sets of clothes and no compensation of any kind for two years in the Order as a novice.

No one would have known Veronica had even left, but Sister Gregory made an early morning trip to the Mother House that day. Veronica walked slowly down the steps like a child abandoned, looking around as if trying to locate something to grasp onto. She was dressed in a skirt and blouse, covered with an old coat, and carried a suitcase.

"You're leaving?" Sister Gregory asked, trying to sound kind, not surprised, not hurt.

"Mother Terrance said I could leave last night."

"Where will you go?"

"With my grandmother until I find work."

"Oh, that's good. There's plenty around."

"I hope so. They've made it clear I can't come back."

"Then walk away. Head up. Don't look back. You'll always have God. He'll look after you."

Veronica stepped away down the corridor, the steps and out the gate, head high now. Sister Gregory watched until the young woman disappeared around a corner. No one mentioned Veronica. It was as if she had never been there.

New rumours said Sister Alexander wanted to leave the Order, that she had a flesh and blood groom in mind, but it was harder for Sister Alexander. She'd taken final vows, and only the Pope could release her from them.

The nuns fluttered around the room laughing, relieved from all work and chores, turning their usual sombre and humble expressions into bright smiles and nodding heads. Sister Sebastian walked into the room, and they quietened. Sister Sebastian smiled and nodded at everyone and went straight to the table, beside Sister Anthony, cut herself a piece of chocolate cake, put it on a plate, knelt at the side of the table and proceeded to eat a little like a sparrow.

"What else would you like?" Mother Terrance asked the elderly sister.

"I'll get this down first." Sister Sebastian put another piece of cake into her mouth and chewed as if savouring every morsel and savouring everyone watching her.

Sister Anthony grinned. "There's a bit of the devil in that cake."

Sister Sebastian laughed, chocolate on her teeth and lips. "It's heaven."

Sister Gregory slipped out of the room.

Sister Bernard followed holding a cup of tea. "I also think the day's run its course. If you wait, I'll get Sister Anthony and the others. We can all go back in the bus."

"I'd like to walk." Sister Gregory said, as two priests said goodbye to Mother Terrance. "Sister Sebastian knows how to clear a room."

Sister Bernard laughed. "People known to collapse in ecstasy will do that every time. Don't forget we need the dormitory in perfect order by Wednesday, before the reporters come. Sister Dominic said the dormitory is a disgrace to each of the girls."

"I can't be in three places at once."

"You need to learn how to delegate, Sister. Sitting on their backsides in their rooms, won't help them one little bit. Tell them the showers are to be done too, otherwise their television and radio will be removed."

Sister Gregory heard the sudden sharpness in the Matron's tone. "What's wrong?"

"What a stupid question. A novice and a couple of sisters leave, and our senior sisters can't control these girls."

Sister Gregory found the four-door minibus parked next to the curb—a recent addition to the sisters' assets. As she stepped closer, she mumbled, "Oh, Dear Lord."

Someone had painted graffiti on the Kombi van in bright red. *Peace.* She walked around to the other side and passed a large pink flower painted on the rear window. *Well! It could be worse.*

Sister Bernard and Mother Terrance helped Sister Anthony down the Mother House's steps. Sister Bernard took off her glasses and stepped closer to read the painted words.

"It gets better." Sister Gregory waved them to the other side of the bus. "Australian art appears alive and well."

"Make love, not war." Mother Terrance folded her arms, reading the green painted words on the bus again as if she struggled to comprehend the words, as if she didn't know what they meant. "This wouldn't have surprised me so much parked outside the hospital, but here? What's going on with the youth of today?"

Sister Gregory moved beside Mother Terrance. "Someone doesn't like that Vietnam war."

"Most of the country agrees with it at the moment." Sister Bernard pulled open a door and helped Sister Anthony into the van. "I don't agree with conscription, sending our national service boys overseas, but if it keeps the louts off the street, who are we to argue?"

MEN AND women formed a small crowd over the past hour and stood near the hospital gate. A woman cradled a baby wrapped in a blue shawl, surrounded by Sister Gregory and two Sisters of St Anthony. A man in a suit took notes while speaking to Sister Gregory and the woman holding the baby. Another man held a camera. All the nuns walked back towards the hospital, and with Sister Gregory, they disappeared near the frosted glass doors.

The cameraman motioned for the woman holding the baby to stand closer to the open gate. Then he knelt in front of the woman, aiming his lens upwards as if he searched beyond the woman—searched the dormitory windows. The odd sensation, the realisation, an understanding you've met someone's gaze, crept through Sylvia.

Sylvia glared at the photographer, knowing he took her picture. She envied the woman standing and nursing a baby on the other side of the gate, and watched until the little camera crew and the woman and the baby left.

Sylvia put more bending pressure on the blade, on one of the last nails, one of the hardest. The knife snapped, the blade flying under the wardrobe. She threw the knife's handle to the floor. *These are never going to work.*

It didn't matter anyway. It was so close now, only a few days to go, and she would be with Tommy again and their baby safe, the constant nightmares over, and hope growing that they wouldn't give her child to strangers. There was a flicker of movement in her stomach, and she smiled. The sensation stopped. *We'll be with your daddy soon.*

She imagined the window open, thought of Tommy's words again. *I'll be waiting. I promise.* She daydreamed she was the woman standing on the other side of the gate, leaving with her baby, leaving behind the haze of bells ringing, chores and church, imagined the wind of the outside world brushing over her face.

THE NEWLY added television sat in a corner of the sisters' recreation room, switched off, and scattered newspapers lay on the tables for the very first time. Changes had started, but still most sisters avoided touching or tuning into anything of the outside world. But some younger sisters embraced the changes, watching the television well after 10pm lights out.

Sister Gregory had been guilty too, had watched *The Sound of Music* well past the time she was supposed to. A glorious movie, a guilty pleasure that never made her feel particularly guilty, despite a woman joining the convent only to be booted out and become a governess who then teaches a widower's children to sing and dance, and even falls in love with the widower. The star was as spectacular as the stunning alpine scenery. The movie would stay with her forever, with that yearning to see, to know, the outside world.

She turned over the front page of a newspaper and read a headline. *Adopt Unwanted Children*. A photograph showed a young woman holding a baby, standing in front of St Joseph's open gate, with two Sisters of St Anthony standing near the frosted glass doors. The article featured an infertile married couple, blessed by adopting a little one of their own. Whose fate, so the article said, would be one of abuse and neglect had the child remained with his biological mother.

Sister Gregory crossed her arms. She explicitly told the reporter and photographer the waiting girls were not to be spoken to nor photographed in any manner. The angle of the shot, the picture suggested the photographer knelt and aimed his camera so he captured the waiting girls' windows. And several girls, smeared images of them, appeared in the windows. You couldn't tell one from the other, but they looked as if incarcerated—now stared out at freedom. The whole world would see faceless girls caged like criminals.

She flicked through a few pages and came to the editorial section. Readers wrote in with their thoughts on adoption. One quoted a Chinese proverb. *To understand a mother's love, bear your own children.* Sister Gregory realised not one sister could understand how the waiting girls felt. *Imagining and actually feeling are two different things.*

Twigs and dried leaves from the hedges whirled in the air just above the ground, scampering like living things around a woman walking toward the gate. She studied the woman's form, shapely from behind and wearing an ankle length coat, suitcase in hand, a few feet away from the gate, almost about to pass Sister Anthony pruning a bush, the clippers snipping in the name of God's glory.

She thought of Sylvia and her brother leaving the reception area for the chapel yard, the car in the alley, and having locks put on the gate the next day, and the young man in the Matron's office saying *I only want to see her for a few minutes.*

It wasn't your brother at all who came to visit the day of Melissa's little one's birth. It was him. But that's impossible. How did you arrange it? Or was it the young man in the Matron's office that day? Your Tommy has come for you, or you're escaping alone. How will you survive? How will you feed yourself and your child?

Passion seeped through the pages of Sylvia's letter to her young lover and angst from a broken heart. She thought of the sound of those lovers in the panel van that night when she put the bins in the lane. *If he's going to meet you somewhere, if he hasn't deserted you, what is the worst that can happen if you cling together and refuse to separate?*

"What are you doing?" Sister Bernard asked.

Why haven't you moved? Sister Gregory spun around. "I just saw...."

Sister Bernard, holding Moses under her arm, scuttled to the window. "Oh, the devil lives in that girl." She glared at Sister Gregory. "You were going to watch her leave?"

"Of course not. It only just registered what I'm seeing. I thought Sister Anthony would...."

"Get down there before the girl passes through the gate. Sister Anthony might be keen on singing and pruning, but isn't on hearing and seeing. If the other girls find out they can simply stroll through the gate, they're all likely to run. Then where will we be?" Sister Bernard straightened, her brows arched as if her own words surprised her, and she cleared her throat. "These girls are put into our care. It's our job to ensure they make the right choices for them and their little ones. And they can't do that if they leave too soon." She stepped to the window and looked below. "How did she get past the reception area?"

"I don't know." But as Sister Gregory spoke, a thin line of smoke rose toward the sky. "Is the chapel on fire?"

Sister Bernard pushed up the window, letting in a gust of wind, and leaned outside. "It appears so. I'll sort it out. There are enough of us here. Oh, go after her, go now."

Sister Gregory as if talking to herself, as if thinking aloud, said, "By the time I get to the gate, she'll have disappeared into the streets. I've no idea where she's going?"

"There's nowhere she can hide where God won't see her. He will guide you."

As Sylvia moved closer to the gate, a little boy and girl chased a pup on the opposite side of the street. Moses barked, jumped out of Sister Bernard's arms and ran out of the room.

###

Sylvia kept pushing herself toward the gate into the wind, the hospital smell disappearing, each step closer to Tommy. She didn't look back. Only a few feet more and she'd reach the gate. Only a few steps and she'd be free, out of the mad house, and gone for good, her baby safe. *Don't stop. Don't Stop. Not now.*

She opened the gate latch—the clippers still snipping, the nun still humming, escape so close. She stepped through the gate, pulled back the latch. She picked up her suitcase and ran as fast as her swollen and bursting body allowed toward the street corner, toward the little shop. She passed the little girl and boy, laughing and playing with a barking pup, as carefree as the day she came to the hospital. She looked down the lanes, trying to remember the one she came through.

Another dog now barked. She looked back toward the hospital gate. Moses barked through the gate's rails. *The Matron will be close behind. Keep going.* The little boy and girl chased their pup toward the road. A car sped toward them, closer. *Oh, Dear God.*

"No!" Sylvia dropped her bag and ran toward the gate. "Stop! Don't run across the road."

###

Sister Gregory ran after Moses, against the wind, toward the gate as if a magical gust blown by the Lord accompanied her pace and blew her forward. She was glad that moment for her heavy habit, because the cold wind attacked every bit of showing flesh, her stinging nose and hands.

Something burned. *Leaves and bark.* She glanced back at the hedge hiding the chapel. No smoke rose.

Moses stood by the gate, yapping away.

Sister Anthony, clippers in hands, looked up from pruning and smiled. "God be with you, Sister."

"And with you." Sister Gregory opened the gate as a car sped down the road.

The pup ran across the road toward Moses.

Tyres screeched.

Sylvia stood near the alley, dropped her bag and ran toward the children. "Stop! Don't run across the road."

The boy and girl chased their pup in front of the car.

The car skidded to a stop. The pup and children ran toward Moses. Sister Gregory swung around to grab the pub as it ran into the hospital yard. Sister Anthony dropped the clippers and collapsed. Sister Gregory's heart stopped, and she could see in her mind's eye Sister Anthony falling again. She ran to her, knelt, cradling the older sister's head in her arms. "Sister Anthony, can you hear? Please answer."

"Don't hold me back." Sister Anthony opened her eyes. "I can see through the gate. It's wonderful."

Sister Gregory held tightly to Sister Anthony's hand and glanced at the gate. *Sylvia's gone.* When she turned back, Sister Anthony's eyes stared transfixed at nothing—no emotion, no light, no feeling in them, pale as if the colour had drained away. Sister Gregory gently touched the elderly woman's clammy forehead, searching for light in her eyes, a twitch in her body, a sound from her lips, but the elderly woman was without breath. *Oh, dear Lord...God bless you, dear Sister Anthony.*

"She's gone, hasn't she?" Sister Bernard said.

Sister Gregory nodded and patted Sister Anthony's cold hands, hands turning from purple to white under her touch, hands she wanted to warm, hands she'd always remember having held her, stroking her veil as if hair. She became acutely aware of the clouds building, of her own breathing against the old woman's motionless and bony chest, the hedges rustling in the breeze, until the cold silence of Sister Anthony hammered in her ears, and the breeze turned into a hideous howl. She gently closed Sister Anthony's eyes and tightened her grip around the old sister. "Our Father...."

Sister Bernard picked up Moses, shut her eyes, crossed her heart, and mumbled a prayer. "I'll go and get someone to assist. She'll need to be moved. As soon as I get back, take the children and their pup home. Tell the mother the road is not safe. I'll get the police to come, then you must find Susan. It was only rubbish and leaves on fire in the bin behind the chapel."

_____ Sylvia

THE LAST train, like all the rest, hooted and tooted from the platform above the steps, then screeched stopping, followed by the brakes hissing and panting. Sylvia sat opposite the steps, under a large and vaulted roof, enclosed in walls of sandstone near the country train indicator board and a large clock. There was no wind down here, but it was cold and smelt of dampness, metal, and dust.

It had been easier than she thought to walk out of the hospital. Someone locked the gate in the fence leading to the lane after that night she spent with Tommy. A big padlock blocked the way.

So today, Sylvia waited until Sister Anthony replaced the novices guarding the front gate, left her suitcase in the stairwell and went into the chapel yard, gathered up leaves, threw them into the bin, then lit them with Kim's matches. Then she went into the reception area and told the two sisters that the chapel was on fire. They bolted from their posts.

But she became lost in the tangle of alleys and lanes and arrived at the station after Tommy's train was due. She'd sat here for an hour. He probably thought she wasn't coming and had already left. The crowds thinned coming down the steps after the last train arrived.

In the late afternoon quiet, a tall woman as attractive as any magazine model and dressed like one too, came down the stairs in red high heels. Closer, she looked weary, her brows creased and her lips thinned. The woman searched the crowds, looked up at the clock, then at her watch. The woman's searching gaze met Sylvia's. Then like the Matron, the woman smiled.

Sylvia imagined many men had shouted out of their car windows 'Getyagearoff' at Tommy's sister. "Where's Tommy?"

"He isn't coming, and I've been looking for you the past hour."

"Why?"

"He got his brown envelope. He's gone to Vietnam and asked me to speak to you."

At the sound of the words, there was a pulse of fear—a jab of panic, and Sylvia was speechless for a moment. "He said he didn't want to go."

"Well, he has."

Sylvia shook her head. "Why didn't you come to the hospital and tell me this? Why write and pretend you're Tommy?"

"I didn't think you'd come if you knew it was me. I spoke to your mother. She thought this was the best way. She didn't want me to tell you what the plan was."

It didn't sound right. Tommy would have found a way to tell her himself, would have at least given his sister a letter or note for her. Sylvia, too tired and frightened for small talk, blurted, "You're lying."

"I know you've never liked me, but I'm here trying to help."

"By taking our baby away from us because you can't have your own."

"I'm trying to help you and my brother. Would you prefer strangers to raise the child?"

"It's my child, and it might as well be strangers. I know nothing of you. You couldn't give me the time of day when you lived at home."

"I'm Tommy's sister."

"This is my baby."

"You're being silly."

"Tommy said you might help us, but...not this way."

"He isn't here, and how far are you now? By my calculations, you're due this month or next. I think if he were going to come and save you, he'd be here by now. This is one way you can keep the baby in our family."

"Your family."

"What's so drastically wrong with that? Hundreds of people do it all the time. Not everyone goes to the homes. Wouldn't you prefer to stay with family than be at the hospital alone?"

Sylvia wished a train would pull into the platform, bring a great gush of wind, to cool her face. "The result is the same."

"You're being childish."

"How am I supposed to act like an adult, when everybody keeps treating me as if I'm twelve years old? Anyone would think you're all taking about a doll I've outgrown and needs to be discarded."

"My brother asked me to come here and bring you back until the birth of the child."

"I don't believe he wanted me to give you our baby."

"Sylvia, if he wanted to, he could have got out of going to Vietnam. He told me himself, they asked him to sign a paper during training if they wanted to go."

"He told me he wouldn't let anyone take our baby."

"He's young, and he's realised the best thing to do is to move on in life, and I'm not anybody."

"When did you speak to my mother?"

"A couple of months ago, but Frank's been a bit ill, and I couldn't get here until now."

"Frank could drop dead, then you'll be in the same place I am."

"He had the flu. He's not likely to drop dead. Besides, we're married."

Sylvia sat silent, head bowed, taking in all she'd heard, the words, the way they rolled out, the lack of emotion, of caring, behind them.

"Your mother can't support you."

"I'll get work. I don't care if I've got to clean toilets."

"You won't be able to work the first few months. You'll need someone to care for the child, and your mother can't do it if she's working to look after you and your sister. The train back to Tamworth leaves in half an hour."

"Then you best go to the toilet and be ready."

"We don't have all day to argue. Come with me and think about it."

THE POLICE officer opened the hospital gate. "I'll keep several feet behind. If you see the girl, nod in her direction. I'll take over from there."

Sister Gregory felt the weight of purpose lost. It had to be impossible to find Sylvia. Two hours had passed. The narrow lanes and streets led into the wider road. She scurried through the parting crowds, reminding her of Moses holding his hand over the Red Sea and God parting the sea for the children of Israel to escape. Did God deliberately create a path for Sylvia to escape? Had He reached out His hand to block her path to Sylvia? If Sylvia managed to escape for good, perhaps a miracle had happened. No waiting girl had ever left the hospital without signing adoption papers.

There was only one way out of the city unless you fled to an adjacent suburb or Timbucktoo. She must have caught a train to meet him somewhere else. Maybe she had caught a bus, but Central station was only a brisk ten minute walk. If Sylvia caught a bus or train, she'd be long gone. Sister Gregory again pictured the panel van across the road late that afternoon, then again in the lane that night, then the young man escorted from the Matron's office. *If he came to collect you in his van, you could be part way to Melbourne.*

Six young men stumbled out a pub's door. "Come on, let's get out of here. Jagger's cover band is starting shortly."

She stepped into the gutter to evade them. Another young man laughed. "Sister, you ever thought about his big tongue and lips on you?"

The words startled her. She had no idea who this Jagger was, and for an instant envisioned a large serpent coiling toward her, aiming a large hissing and jagged tongue at the very thing making her different from man. Revulsion made her tremble. There was no indication this young man understood she did God's work, that she was needed somewhere. She put her head down and scuttled past them. *Forgive them. The devil in the form of alcohol has taken their good sense.*

"Hey, you don't do that, you dick," another man said. "After that, you'll go to Hell for sure."

"I ain't no Catholic, so don't tell me they aren't all lesbians."

The sound of *that* word stopped her. *Lesbians.* She thought of saying *I'm more inclined to do a priest*, but kept going.

"Move on," the police officer shouted. "If I hear or see you accosting anyone else, you'll be locked in the slammer. Understand?"

Sister Gregory chided herself for the sinful thought about a priest. She didn't intend to tell Father Angus at confession about that—instead she decided her penance was no dinner tonight. *Perhaps three nights.* She glanced at the sky. *Blessed Lord, forgive me.*

She turned a corner into crowds of people and had no choice but to slow her pace. Sylvia was nowhere in sight. God closed the path. She thought of ripping off her wimple, the weight of its meaning not wanted, and screaming, *Sylvia, don't do this. Come back before it's too late.* Instead, she walked into the thick traffic of Central Station's entrance and hoped she wouldn't return to the hospital with nothing.

She brushed through the crowds, climbed the steps, and walked up and down the first platform between crowds, then the next platform and more after that, until she lost count of how many platforms. The police officer followed at a distance. She couldn't see Sylvia anywhere—never expected to see her. *She's long gone.*

The steam trains came and went, and a couple of electric red rattlers screeched to a halt. She sat on a bench on the last platform and bowed her head. *I should have left as soon as I saw you leave, and if I had, would I have caught up to you? But we don't have choices in the crosses we bear. Where did you go?*

She remembered the young man in the army uniform embracing Sylvia. The army bases were in the country. A large clock hung above the entrance of the country platforms, but Sylvia wouldn't be still there. No trains were scheduled to leave from those platforms for a long time. Only arrivals came in there now. But she had to look. At least then, she could go back to Sister Bernard and say she'd tried everything.

Sister Gregory stepped under the vaulted sandstone ceiling. Crowds of people stood waiting for arrivals. But a pregnant teenager, looking very much like a young woman, sat on a seat, a suitcase beside her legs. Sylvia wearily scanned the steps leading to the platforms. Sister Gregory stood still, not knowing how to move or what to say. More than three hours had passed since Sylvia left the hospital. Sylvia wiped a tear from the corner of her eye. *She's waiting for him, and he's not coming.*

Sister Gregory remembered the police officer stood somewhere behind, watching, waiting to take over. *What if I turn away? What if I pretend not to see her? What if he's about to walk down those stairs? You need to do the right thing. You need to do what's best for the child.*

The policeman tapped Sister Gregory's arm. "Is that the girl?"

She nodded. He went to step forward, and she put her hand out to stop him. "Let me speak to her."

###

A copper stood behind Sister Gregory in a crowd, his arms crossed over his chest. Sylvia thought of running, waddling in the opposite direction but where to? With a tired certainty, she knew it was too late to escape. *Even Tommy has forsaken me.*

"Sylvia, what are you doing here?"

"Waiting for him." She struggled to say the words, felt the tremble in her voice, and the words came out softly. "I received a letter saying he'd meet me here, but—."

"You foolish girl." Sister Gregory's words flowed out with anger and fury, surprising herself. "Did you really think he would come? Stop this nonsense. Good parents are waiting, people who will give the child all it will ever need. You'll never be able to provide for it."

"I'm to be arrested if I don't return?"

A sadness and disappointment lurked behind Sister Gregory's eyes. "You can't stay here all night."

"I can't bear the thought of another night there."

"Please get up."

"What if I don't?"

"Do you want to be dragged back in handcuffs?"

_____ Sylvia

SISTER GREGORY tapped on the Matron's door, then pushed it open. No fire burned in the hearth, although it was cold enough to light a bonfire. A box of matches sat on the mantelpiece, but it wasn't *that* box of matches. They burned with the leaves.

Sister Bernard smiled, but the ice in her glare sent a shiver down Sylvia's spine. "Come in, dear, take a seat. I'm glad you came to your senses."

Sister Gregory closed the door—entombed Sylvia alone with Sister Bernard. Sylvia sat, crossed her arms, stared back at the Matron, tried to match the coldness in the Matron's eyes, tried to hold on to her defiance—but even it deserted Sylvia, and she looked at the fireplace, her face as hot as if on fire.

The Matron's face creased into a strange expression as if she searched for words. "You made a wise decision, dear, now let's move on. I haven't had a chance to tell you until now, but a wealthy couple in Sydney has chosen you as the mother of their baby."

"They know nothing of me. Why would they choose my baby?"

"They know you come from a loving family and want to help you." Sister Bernard pushed a piece of paper across the desk and placed a pen on top. "All you need to do is sign the paper."

"I can't yet."

"By now you should have realised you have no say in this matter. Sign the papers and you can go back to your life, and no one will know about this."

"I will."

"You'll forget it."

Sylvia clasped her hands together to stop herself picking up the piece of paper and ripping it to shreds. "Can I meet them...just once?"

"You need not be concerned with their character. We wouldn't allow anyone who is not worthy to be given the gift of a child."

Help me understand. "Didn't God bestow this gift on me?"

Sister Bernard sighed, tapping her fingers across the desk as if she played a piano, then glared at Sylvia. "I'm not going to continue this battle of wills, feed your desire for constant attention. You've left me no choice but to end this ridiculous game you persist in playing. I've spoken to your mother and told her of your intention to fly off into the sunset with him at the risk of bringing further shame on not only yourself but your parents."

"It was Tommy's sister I met, and my mother knew who I was meeting."

Sister Bernard laughed, an easy laugh, as if she were truly enjoying herself. "You need to stop this now."

"It's the truth."

"Your mother has had this young man charged with carnal knowledge. When they catch up with him, he'll be jailed."

A sharp pain scraped down the middle of Sylvia's forehead splitting her head in half. She was going mad. Her mind couldn't be tearing into two, but the throbbing pain twisted tighter. She wanted to scream but knew if she did, she would scream herself into madness. Not an ounce of emotion flickered in the Sister's eyes, only a blank expression as if Sylvia was nothing, no one, only a baby incubator. "I was already sixteen. He wouldn't touch me before then. He said I was jail bait. It wasn't a crime. He never murdered me or did anything I didn't want to do."

Sister Bernard smirked. "Your mother believes it was going on before you were of age. It only matters you weren't sixteen at the time of the crime."

"I'm almost eighteen, and we were only friends before. I've known him since I was little."

"Some girls your age need to be protected from their own wicked desires, from young men who take advantage of girls like you. Now, sign the paper." She pushed the document closer. "You've destroyed this young man's life. Don't do the same to the baby. You must sign the papers, Susan. With this young man out of the picture, you have no choice."

Sylvia snatched the piece of paper and pen and signed the paper above the words: *I hereby relinquish all rights to the child*, then pushed the paper into the middle of the desk and placed the pen on top.

Sister Bernard's smile grew wider than Sylvia had seen. She picked up the paper, read the signature, frowned, then the smile disappeared as if she'd eaten lemon and she threw the paper back onto the desk. "You're a stupid girl."

Sylvia despised Sister Bernard, her false poise and false smile. For a maddening instant, she imagined a blaze in the fireplace, jumping over the desk and pushing the Sister into the flames. "And you're a nasty old woman. What's wrong with signing the paper as Susan? Isn't that my name?"

"I don't think you know who you're talking to."

"I'm sure you think you're Christ's favourite bride, but you're nothing but a sour faced, self righteous, bitter old woman who gets her jollies from taking our babies away, because you'll never have one because no real man has ever wanted you."

Sister Bernard's expression never changed, but she swallowed once and then again. "You're a selfish girl. You want to deprive a good infertile couple their only chance of having a child of their own. How disappointed they will be when they have their hearts set on your child."

"How would you like it if someone took Moses off you and gave him to someone they thought would look after him better?"

"How are you going to look after this child?"

Sylvia bowed her head, afraid she was about to dissolve into a crying puddle. "How can you be so sure…they will love my baby as I do?"

"You can't answer. You don't know. But I do know exactly what is going to happen. You're obviously a bad mother. If you don't sign the papers, the child will be taken and given to the welfare."

NOVICES' BOOTS crunched on the gravel path, each step slow and precise, allowing them to walk and pray. Moses ran toward Sister Gregory. She knelt and patted him, knowing that when she stood, Sister Bernard would be close. The Matron said nothing. Just folded her arms and walked in the opposite direction around the chapel yard.

They met again the next morning, when Sister Bernard summoned her. Sister Bernard frowned, her face aged more today, the fine wrinkles now crevices. "Answer me honestly. It need go no further than here. If I hadn't walked behind you in the recreation room, would you have gone after her?"

Sister Gregory knew she admired Sylvia's courage, that Sylvia fought for something she could only imagine. "I was shocked motionless by the audacity of the girl."

"Were you secretly hoping she would escape?"

"I was trying to understand why she was leaving."

Sister Bernard sighed. "Fortunately, she didn't get too far. It would have been a disaster. Can you imagine the bad light this would have put the convent and hospital under—the scandal of it all?"

Sister Gregory stilled herself, hesitated, then said very softly, "Why do you think he never turned up? Why did he give her hope when there is none?"

Sister Bernard picked up Moses. "I don't know. I tried to contact her mother today. She doesn't have a telephone, and I've only a friend's number, but no one answered. It must be the Lord's doing. If Susan was meant to leave, He would have created a path for her to do so. Her young man obviously doesn't care about her as much as she thought he did. But even if he did turn up, what difference would it have made in the long term? Would he have stayed with her? I doubt it. He gained too easily what she appears to have given freely."

A muffled crash came from the hospital. Sister Gregory searched the dormitory windows and caught a flash of Sylvia passing a window. "What's she doing?"

"I think she's thrown something at the window."

*

Banging, crashing, and ranting came from the dormitory. Sister Gregory climbed the stairs two at a time, wondering how Sylvia would emerge through this chaos. Four girls surrounded Sylvia's door.

Kim ran up to Sister Gregory. "She's won't talk to me and is throwing everything around the room."

"Back to your rooms. Everybody…. Now!"

Sister Gregory pushed open Sylvia's door. She didn't believe in the nonsense of being possessed by the devil, although she'd never admit it aloud. But if one could be possessed, the girl in front of her had the eyes of madness, of being possessed. The mattress, sheets, and blankets lay strewn across the floor. Sylvia stood in the corner, sweat soaked hair plastered across her forehead, holding the chair by two legs, caught in half motion, about to fling the chair through the window, panting as if she'd already thrown the chair a hundred times.

"Don't do something you're going to regret. You smash the window—I'll call the police, and they can look after you."

"It's sweltering in here. It's driving me crazy."

"It's winter…your temper is making you warm."

"It was friggin' nailed down when I first came here, and it wasn't winter."

"This is no good for you or the baby."

Sylvia took a step forward, the chair legs still held as if any moment, when she gained the energy, she would fling it at the window or Sister Gregory. "You don't care about me."

"Put down the chair."

"I want to speak to my parents—find out what's happened to Tommy."

"It shouldn't be too hard to guess he's come to his senses and realised this will ruin both your lives. He obviously doesn't love you like you thought."

Sylvia slowly placed the chair on the floor as if suddenly defeated by the words and the chairs weight. "You all tricked me."

"He was the one who never turned up."

"This has to stop now." Sister Bernard came into the room, followed by Sister Dominic. "Give it to her to stop this nonsense, before all the girls in the dormitory become hysterical. This madness can be heard down in the married ward."

Sister Dominic stepped forward holding a needle.

"You're not going to drug me."

"You need something to calm yourself." Sister Gregory reached for Sylvia's arm. "All you're going to do is make yourself sick and cause harm to the baby."

The back of Sylvia's hand flung outwards to push Sister Gregory's hand away, but instead cracked across Sister Gregory's cheek, the stinging slap knocking her backwards. "I'm sorry, I didn't mean to hit your face, but get away from me. Don't you dare touch me with anything."

"Ah! There's always one fly in the ointment, isn't there?" Sister Dominic grabbed Sylvia's hands and pushed the struggling girl against the wall. "That's enough. I'm a lot bigger than you."

Sister Gregory took the needle out of Sister Dominic's hand, and while the larger Sister held Sylvia against the wall, Sister Gregory raised the girl's nightdress to her thigh.

"No!" Sylvia shouted and made a final fling to free herself out of Sister Dominic's arms.

Sister Gregory jabbed the needle into Sylvia's thigh. "You'll feel better in a moment."

An expression of astonishment came into Sylvia's face, then she burst into tears of pain and despair. "I knew you were going to kill me."

"No one is hurting you," Sister Gregory said. "You'll sleep, and in the morning you'll feel much better."

In less than a minute, Sylvia collapsed against Sister Dominic.

*

The night had been long, and the day would probably be longer for Sylvia. How would the girl wake today? How much fury could her body and baby take? Sister Gregory opened Sylvia's door. The girl lay on her side on the bed, staring blankly, looking as young, lost, fragile and disillusioned as Veronica.

"Do you feel better?"

"Please, go away."

"I'm not going anywhere."

"Ha! Kim was right. Because you're all so miserable, you enjoy watching us suffer."

"My entire life has been aimed at helping others. You're the only girl having such difficulty with the process."

"You haven't heard them all cry of a night."

"Do they cry for their children or for themselves?"

"I cry because I might not get to know my baby, and my baby might never know me...won't never know my love for him."

"You can't miss something you've never had."

"He's in my belly, been there for months. It breaks my heart to think he won't know I did love him. That I didn't want to do this."

"Your baby's parents will one day tell them what you've done because it was the best thing to do, and you did so because you loved the child."

Sylvia clenched her teeth. "It won't be the same as me telling them I love them."

Sister Gregory sat on the bed. "I don't understand why you're fighting something inevitable."

Sylvia bowed her head. "I don't know anymore either. Part of me, a big part, wants to give up."

"We can't all be wrong, can we?"

"I know I've sinned. But by taking my baby away, isn't it punishing him by taking his mother away?"

"You need support to keep this child, and your parents aren't giving it."

"But I've helped Mum. I've minded my sister every afternoon because Mum works, and Nan would have helped me."

"Where's your grandmother now?"

"She died last year. I wasn't even allowed to go to her funeral. I had to stay home and mind my sister. I loved Nan more than anything. Since I've been little, I knew when I had children, I would love them as much as she loved me."

"You must miss her greatly?"

"She wouldn't let them do this. She told me only good girls get into trouble."

"Listen to me, you have so many other options open to you."

"Like a husband and family?" Sylvia turned away, laid on her side. "Everyone's forgotten Tommy. What about what he wants? It's his baby too, and he didn't want it to be taken away."

"It appears he has left you to fend for yourself. Sometimes we discover someone we care for, really doesn't care for us the way we thought they did."

"I know he cared for me. Something must have happened to him. He told me that he'd come for me. Why hasn't he? I can't believe he went to Vietnam."

"Why do you think he went to Vietnam?"

"His sister told me he went. He wouldn't have left without telling me that he was going."

"What does his sister have to do with anything...he wouldn't have been allowed to visit you here."

"He could have at least written to me." Sylvia's eyes narrowed. "Tell me...please tell me if he wrote to me...even if you tore the letter up. At least tell me he wrote to me."

Sister Gregory heard the words the young man in the Matron's office said that day. *I just want to see her for a few moments—Not a letter...but we might have kept him, in the flesh, from seeing you, the love of his young life...the love of yours.* She glanced toward the door and lowered her voice, "We haven't kept any letters sent to you."

"I don't believe you."

Deep inside, Sister Gregory was relieved Sylvia did not believe her. *But what if it wasn't her Tommy that tried to see her?* "At some stage you're going to have to face the truth."

"Why wouldn't he have at least written to me?"

"Maybe he didn't have the heart to tell you, what he knew you didn't want to hear."

"Why is everyone trying to force me to stuff my feelings away as if I can put them in a wardrobe, pretend I don't have them?"

"I know you can't just let them go."

"I feel betrayed by everybody. Have you ever felt like this?"

"I've never been in love."

Sylvia laughed and cried at the same time and used the sheet to wipe her eyes. "I don't think I'll love ever again. It's horrible. I feel sick like I'm going to die."

Sister Gregory cautiously reached toward Sylvia and pulled a strand of hair away from the girl's eyes. "I hear first love passes—the pain, the anguish."

"Does your love for God give you so much trouble?"

Sister Gregory smiled, a forced smile in her guilt and anguish. "I don't think the love I feel for Christ is quite the same."

Sylvia hid her face in the pillow. "I'm tired."

"I don't want to leave you like this."

"Please go."

Sister Gregory stood and placed a bottle on the chair. "It will help you relax. There's only one sleeping tablet in there."

"You came to drug me again."

"If you sleep well, like you did last night, you'll feel better and see things in a more logical manner. Take it fifteen minutes before you want to go to bed tonight, and you'll hit the pillow and find peace."

*

Sister Gregory entered the chapel and genuflected, saluting the presence of the blessed sacrament, the real presence of Jesus, after the last waiting girls and took her place in the pre-dieus beside the other nuns lining one side of the chapel. She knelt and tried to pray, tried to say the *Our Father*, but she couldn't concentrate, couldn't take away the sight of Sylvia on the other side of the pews, standing beside a large statue of Mother Mary and baby Jesus, her head bowed as if she listened to nothing.

It was impossible to pray while distracted, unable to hear the words, to feel them. She tried to stop her mind wandering, bowed her head and repeated the prayer over and over.

An altar boy, carrying a cross, led the procession of people into the church, followed by other altar boys carrying candles, the book of gospels, with the priest last. Reaching the altar, the servers and the priest bowed. The cross and the candles were placed in positions on the altar. The priest stepped to the altar, kissed it, sat and waited for the hymn to finish.

God's face in the stained glass window was blackened—blackened by smoke that had poured out of the bin beside the seat outside the chapel. A fire Sylvia probably started, but the novice given the task of cleaning the glass would need to be spoken to.

Standing at the side of a sea of waiting girls, Sylvia swayed, her face pale. Her hand brushed across her forehead, wiping sweat away. Sylvia glanced around the room, looked toward the back door, took a tiny step toward the side-isle and swayed again.

###

Sylvia was hot one second and cold the next. *You never loved me, never wanted our baby. You lied to me. You used me.*…She patted her stomach. *They're going to take you. I have to give you to them. I can't let them put you in a home…you'll never be loved there.*

There wasn't an ounce of space in the chapel and almost no breath of air. If she was any wider, her hip would touch the large Mother Mary and baby Jesus statue in the side-isle.

She looked away from God's face in the stained glass, blackened and blurred, his eyes not visible, as if he'd been punched and they'd swelled so much, bruises hid his eyes. Jesus on the cross above the altar appeared to gaze on her suffering. She glanced back at God in the glass. He didn't even spare his own son, but gave him up for all mankind for her. She wondered what plan He had for her and the baby after blackening His face. *You need to be strong like God. Sacrifice yourself to make another parent happy.*

She avoided Jesus' gaze. The path along the centre isle to the closed back door was blurred, swelled like waves, closer, then away. She swayed, couldn't bear the dizziness any longer and stumbled into the aisle. As she turned to walk to the back of the chapel, her elbow knocked Mother Mary holding baby Jesus. The statue fell and was about to crash into the saint staring at the ceiling, and in her mind, Sylvia saw a line of statues topple like dominos.

She lunged to stop Mother Mary and baby Jesus falling, but was too late. The statue fell into a saint, which hit a table where a smaller statue of Mary and baby Jesus sat. The smaller statue fell too, knocking Noah's Ark beside it, crashed onto the floor, and side swiped another baby Jesus—when the crashing statues, sounding like a truck load of smashing crockery stopped, everyone gawked at Sylvia.

Sister Gregory stepped toward her.

Sister Bernard's voice screeched from the other side of the chapel. "You clumsy, useless girl!"

Surrounded by broken statues of Mother Mary and baby Jesus, Sylvia pushed and shoved her way through a row of girls. "I'm sorry—so sorry about the statues." She ran out of the chapel, bent over, wanted to be sick on the lawn, but only gagged.

An arm wrapped around her waist. "Calm down. It's all right. Don't worry about the statues."

"Please leave me alone."

"I can't leave you by yourself," Sister Gregory said. "I'll take you to the dormitory."

Kim's voice was close. "I'll take her...let me take her."

Sister Gregory nodded. "Stay with her, and I'll come shortly."

Sylvia and Kim walked to the dormitory. "I want to lie down," Sylvia said. "I've got cramps."

"Maybe your baby is coming."

"It's not due for a couple of weeks. I'll be fine. If I need you, I'll call out."

"Have you decided...?"

"One day I think I should adopt him out, the next I can't bear the thought. I wish I could speak to Tommy."

"I don't think you're going to."

"Neither do I...."

Sylvia threw herself on the bed. *If you sleep, you'll feel better.* But she couldn't stop thinking about Tommy that last night they were together, replaying him taking her in his arms. *It'll be all right. I'm here.* Replaying that night was like watching a movie, which could be stopped and started at certain moments. Repeatedly she thought about the touch of his lips—that hesitant moment when gazes lock, then drift downward toward the lips and heads lower toward each other.

Her mother's words *he used you* almost drove her from the memory, but thinking about that last time they loved each other, him kissing her stomach, envisioning and feeling it all again and again made her happy and sad at the same time. *I love you.* He said that over and over, loving her as if he needed to drink her all in, taste and feel every part of her flesh as they teased, played, touched, and fulfilled each other until exhausted and her lips were swollen, her face flushed. While he lay between her thighs, she wanted to hold him against her forever and sleep, but then they heard one of those nuns come through that hospital gate.

Sylvia pulled herself off the bed. *I'm suffocating in here.* She patted her stomach. *I wish I could choose who you went to. I wish I knew for certain what's happened to your daddy. I wish someone could tell me there is hope.* She pulled the chair in front of the wardrobe, climbed onto the seat, and ran her hands across the top of the wardrobe, but the knife wasn't there.

THE PAIN ebbed and flowed. Sister Gregory envisioned her head opening and closing with each wave of pressure on her temples. She stepped down the corridor toward Sylvia's room while the most beautiful melody of music played before a harmony of male tenor voices reverberated around the dormitory. The lyrics were of someone pining for a lover he hadn't seen in a long, lonely time. He hungered for his lover's touch. Needed her touch. Needed her love. The song could have been expressing the most human of hungers—the hunger for God, but it was about the hunger of mortal love between a man and woman.

She tapped on Sylvia's door, holding her breath, straining to hear movement in the room. "Are you all right?" She waited a few seconds. "If you're ignoring me, you need to stop this behaviour." She tapped on the door again, realising her voice didn't reach the fierceness she intended. "Susan, staying in here won't help. You need to keep doing something to take your mind off all this. These feelings will pass. It isn't the end of the world. It will be over shortly, and you can leave as if none of this happened."

A sigh rose in her throat. She had to open the door, and she feared it. *If you're not here, where are you?* Her own words from last week slammed against her temples. *He obviously doesn't love you....* With the memory of her words, she imagined Christ's crown of thorns cutting into her scalp.

She gently pushed open the door. Sylvia's transistor radio sat on the foot of the bed. A nail and broken knife lay on the floor near the plastic waste basket. *She's been trying to open the window again.* Two small handprints, as if stencilled on the window, gleamed clearly on the glass, their borders smeared as if the palms and fingers were placed there repeatedly each afternoon and night. Those small hands, Sylvia's hands, had pressed on the glass as she peered at the streets below—watching the outside world while she waited to be freed from this place.

Sylvia's dresses and shirts hung in the wardrobe. In the drawers sat folded jumpers and underwear. *With no one to save you, where did you go?* She turned the radio off. Part of Sylvia's notepad stuck out from under the pillow. She read the scribbled words *I just want to die* and ran from the room.

"Susan!" She opened Kim's door. "Where is she?"

Kim stirred from sleep. "Who?"

"I told you to stay with her." Sister Gregory pushed open every door in that side of the dormitory, moving from room to room. "Susan, it isn't that bad." But as she said the words, she heard the ludicrousness of them compared to Sylvia's desperate cry. *I just want to die.*

The pipes in the walls rumbled and vibrated as if they were about to explode. Water ran from the showers above. She ran to the stairs, each pounding of her boots on the floorboards vibrating the pain in her head. *She's only having a shower.*

She raced up the stairs, reached the top, and took in the six shower stalls and toilets on the opposite side of the room. All the doors were closed, but only one shower-head spurted water. She let out a sigh of relief and stepped closer. "Susan, are you all right?"

"I am Sylvia. Sylvia." But there was no force or resonance in the words. "I can't stand the sight of any of you."

"I read your note. Finish your shower and we'll talk."

Through the sound of water running came a solitary sob—one wanting to be kept inside, not meant to be heard. No movement of feet splashing, no sounds of anything but running water and gentle crying. Sister Gregory stepped back near the Modess pad incinerator. She bent slightly to look under the foot wide gap at the bottom of the shower door, expecting to see feet and ankles, but the soles of Sylvia's feet faced outwards.

Someone was coming up the stairs. Sister Gregory glanced that way and saw drops of blood leading from the stairwell to the shower. She opened Sylvia's door. The girl sat leaning against the wall, in only pants and bra, while cold water splattered over her face and body. Her trousers and bloodied shirt sat in a pile next to her legs on the floor, and blood flowed from her hand resting on top of her stomach.

"Oh, Sylvia, what did you do?" Sister Gregory turned off the water, then fell to her knees and held the girl's hand with its deep gash in the wrist. *I should have watched you more closely.*

Sylvia closed her eyes, and her words flowed into the next. "I just—only wanted to sleep and let air into the room—but the devil must have seen my scribbles. He's come to take me because I'm bad—don't let my baby die."

Sister Gregory untied the sash holding the cross around her waist. "I'm not going to let you or your baby go anywhere. You're both too precious."

"You only care about taking my baby."

"That isn't true," she said, but the girl seemed woozy, drowsy, and she shook Sylvia's shoulders. "What did you take?"

"It is true. Everyone says—I've sinned...an unforgettable sin."

Sister Gregory wrapped the sash around Sylvia's hand. "Our sins can be forgiven, because Jesus Christ paid for human sin by dying on the cross, paid for the redemption of humanity, but you must tell me what you've taken."

Sylvia slumped sideways.

"Someone help!" Sister Gregory tied the sash in place on the wrist. "You'll be fine." But she wondered if too much life already flowed out of Sylvia and her baby in the blood washing down the drain. She held Sylvia in her arms, thankfully could still feel Sylvia's breathing while she stroked her wet hair, praying to feel the baby's movements in the girl's stomach pressed against her own. "Forgive us. There is a way, and we should have told you." She looked up that moment as Kim, holding her stomach and out of breath, reached the top of the stairs. "Go and find a sister as quick as you can."

_____ *Sylvia*

A SCREAMING A screaming train sped through her mind. *Dead souls through darkness, her soul, toward an incinerator—red, tossing and turning, burning, in a tunnel, unable to escape, unable to see light, only the red of Hell. Darkness exploded into the red, turned to black, cold—grey and white, shapes, shadows, a haze of blended blacks and whites. Light—streaming through wooden beams. A window light. Sunshine flowing through glass and between wooden beams. A crib. A wooden crib. Oh, the nursery. The babies. My baby. Who's that in the room? Shadows. Strangers hovering over the cribs. A stranger in the nursery.*

"Sign the paper, and I'll let you out of this room," a woman whispered.

Sylvia's heavy eyelids could barely stay open in the blackness. The stranger was close, breathing so close, then a blinding white light shone, and no matter how she tried to see the stranger's face, her eyes couldn't adjust. She shied away and closed her eyes. *I've gone blind or insane.*

"You'll never get out of this room unless you sign the papers."

Sylvia clutched the bed covers around her neck, while her other hand hugged her stomach. You're still there. They don't have you. Sylvia moaned *go away*, but the words never formed into sound. She couldn't speak—her tongue thick and lifeless, her voice frozen, and she tried to turn to escape the light and words.

A hand held her shoulder firmly, making her stay on her back, while light continued to shine into her eyes. "You need to sign them before the baby's born."

The light and words too painful, she willed herself back to sleep.

When she woke again, her back ached, and her stomach cramped. She turned her head, searched for the window—the light of stars. There were none, only dense blackness. Her heart pounded as if a sledgehammer slammed inside her chest. *I'm not in my room.*

She pushed away the images of strangers hovering over babies in the nursery, shut her eyes, tried to slow the pumping of her heart, but the darkness was heavy, pushing tightly on her chest. She remembered the tone of the woman's voice—not the Matron, another woman, soothing words, faraway words, words that now flowed into her mind, a whisper, words spoken before this room, another day.... *We should... I can...* She remembered the warmth of the woman holding her. Her habit pressed against her skin—the woman's breasts touching her own, heat seeping through and reminding her of....

Oh, my God. You never came. You never cared. They were right.

She lay very still, then patted her stomach, listening, concentrating on what she could hear. *It'll be all right.* There was sound, voices, coming from outside the room. Then the smell, oh the smell. *Disinfectant. Amnionia. The hospital smell.*

Sylvia looked toward the sounds. "Is someone there?"

She pushed the sheets and blanket aside and sat on the edge of the mattress. Several feet away a strip of light streamed under a door. She stepped off the bed, but the ground wasn't where she expected. She slipped, fell onto the cold floor, and let out a cry that turned into a shout. "Let me out of this God damn room." But no one came, only footsteps, shadows, past the door. "Someone! Come on. Let me out of here."

She crawled across the floor, holding her stomach, and reached the door. Pushing her hands against the door for support, she stood, felt, searched for the light switch, then flicked the button on.

Whiteness, painful for her eyes, a fluorescent glow, exploded into the room. She flung her arms over her eyes, wondering if God struck her blind. She squinted, found the doorknob. It was locked. She faced the hospital bed and four white walls. *They've put me in a nut house.*

SISTER GREGORY balanced the food tray against her hip, while her other hand unlocked the door. She didn't know what to expect, but thought Sylvia would be subdued. But the girl sitting on the bed, who jumped to her feet, looked wild and about to kill.

Sister Gregory placed the tray on the foot of the bed. "You must be hungry."

"You've locked me up as if I'm a nutcase."

"I think you're probably grateful for the light of day."

"It's against the law to kidnap."

"It's also against the law to attempt suicide."

"That's horrible. I wouldn't hurt my baby."

"What were you doing?"

"The knives kept breaking when I tried to remove the nails from my window, so I used a spoon. It broke too, and the broken bit flung into my wrist. I had a cramp in my back and felt hot and had blood over everything, but when I got to the shower I felt dizzy."

"I only saw a knife."

"Part of the spoon flew under the bed, and I threw the other bit into the rubbish basket."

"You also took tablets. Where did you get them from?"

"You gave me the tablet. I took it before I tried to open the window. I've been suffocating and feeling enclosed in a box for months."

"Do you really think we're Satan's nuns?" As soon as she let the words out, she realised her mistake and sighed. "Sylvia, you might as well accept your predicament."

"You had no right to read my letters."

"It's our job to save you from yourself."

"I didn't ask to be saved." Sylvia crossed her arms. "Why do you stay? Why do you let yourself wither away like all the others here?"

Sister Gregory had been thinking this question for months now, had her answer ready, for anyone who asked, for herself. "I gave a life-long gift of myself to Christ."

"Haven't you ever wanted a family?"

"I want God more." She pointed to the tray. "You need to eat."

"How long have I been in here?"

"Since this morning. I've been here all day except the past ten minutes."

"So you were flashing the light in my face."

Sister Gregory shook her head. "I think you were dreaming."

"When my parents find out about you giving me needles and locking me in here, they'll take me out of this hell hole."

"When Sister Bernard comes, ask to use the telephone."

"I have to stay in this room?"

"Yes."

"I will not. I'll suffocate in here. It's worse than the other room. There's not even a window. I'll scream the place down day and night. I want to speak to my parents."

Sister Bernard appeared in the doorway. "No, you won't. You're not fit to care for a child. Your behaviour over the past week proves it. If you try to leave with the baby, it will be taken and made a ward of the state and put into an institution. If you can't be civilised, I'll have you transferred to St Peter's asylum until the baby is due. Would you prefer that?"

"I want to speak to my parents."

"Your mother was told what you've done," Sister Bernard said. "She doesn't think she can cope with you. She can't have your younger sister seeing such behaviour. She's left to my discretion whether to report you to the police for attempting suicide or have you committed into a home for the insane."

"I never tried to kill myself. I've been trying to remove those nails since I came here."

The Matron considered the words. "Combined with the scene in your room, it doesn't look like an accident that you'd have a large gash in your wrist."

"I want to speak to my mother, or you get my father on the telephone. He won't let you do this to me. The only thing I'm guilty of being is suffocating in these rooms."

Sister Bernard closed the door, stepped to the bed, sat beside the food tray and sighed. "You may be a little too strong willed for your own good, but I feel for you. I realise this young man has given you false hope." She looked up at Sister Gregory. "You too can understand, can you not?"

Sister Gregory nodded. "You will make yourself terribly sick, if you hold on to the hope that he is still coming for you."

"You don't want your child to suffer," Sister Bernard said. "Put the little one's needs above your own. You must sacrifice yourself, so your child will have a better life."

"What do I have to do to get out of here?" Sylvia asked. "I can't breathe in small enclosed places without windows. It makes me sick."

"You need to prove to us," Sister Gregory said, "that we can trust you in the dormitory and hospital. We need to know you won't cause further disturbances to the other girls."

Sister Bernard stood. "Even if you don't care about yourself, you might have some thought for them and their babies."

"I'll do anything to get out of here."

Sister Bernard didn't hesitate. "Sign the paper, then."

Sylvia's eyes shut. Sister Gregory knew it was to stop her anger and fear and tears.

"I can't help you then." Sister Bernard walked to the door. "If you dare scream or carry on, I will transfer you to St Peter's. If you're clever, you'll behave until you need to go to the birthing room."

Sister Gregory followed Sister Bernard along the corridor. She remembered the broken knife blades the past months and nails she'd removed from the top of Sylvia's wardrobe. The knives were blunt, only useful for buttering, and the cut in Sylvia's wrist wasn't like she had sliced her wrist, but a deep gash away from her vein, as if a rugged edge of broken metal jabbed her wrist.

Sister Bernard stopped and smiled. "A lack of opinion doesn't suit you."

"I don't believe Sylvia tried to kill herself."

"Looks like it to me, and there won't be a doctor who will think otherwise."

"I'm mortified and disgusted too about her attempting suicide. But I don't think she tried to kill herself. The gash is nowhere near her vein." Sister Gregory met the Matron's stare. "You've told me that if I look for evil I will find it."

"Your point is?"

"I found a broken knife on the floor, and several on top of her wardrobe before this, but she said she then used a spoon to try to remove the nails from her window, and the spoon broke also. I assume she tried to use the bowl of the spoon to lever out a nail in the window frame. She said part of the spoon flew under her bed, and the other part that gashed her wrist is in her bin. If the broken spoon is where she says it is, common sense needs to prevail. No one tries to slit their wrist with a spoon and avoids the vein."

"That doesn't explain the note."

"I see that as an expression of suffering, not intent to do self harm."

*

Kim stood in the doorway of Sister Gregory's office, her face tear stained. "Is Susan going to have to stay in that room?"

"For the time being."

"She's got a phobia about small spaces...on that side of the dormitory there isn't any windows."

"Have you really come to speak about Susan?"

"I'm worried about her."

"Come, close the door." Sister Gregory leaned toward the young woman, who although a few years older than Sylvia, was like her a little in appearance and nature. "I'm glad you came."

Kim closed the door and sat on an opposite chair, but she didn't look at Sister Gregory's face and strained to keep tears from falling. She said very softly, "I was thinking...what if I want to keep my baby?"

"Oh, Kim."

Tears fell then, and she wiped them away. "I don't care if everyone thinks I'm a tart."

"What do your parents think?"

"There's only Mum. Dad passed away last year."

"What of the father?"

Kim clasped her hands together.

"Every child deserves a father."

"We were engaged...our wedding all set."

"You can tell by all the girls here that you're not the only one jilted."

"I can't believe I was such a fool."

"We all make mistakes."

"Why does it have to be so painful?"

"I can't imagine how you feel."

"I've been thinking the life of a nun has an attraction."

Sister Gregory smiled. "I have a different pain to deal with."

"This pain is horrible...the wondering where he will go and if they will be kind to him...I can go back to my old job, dress making...or maybe start my own business—my mum said she'd help mind the child."

"Is that fair to your mother? That she should raise her grandchild?"

"Minding and raising a child are different things."

"This isn't a choice I can make, but something you need to think about really hard."

A knock came on the door, and Sister Bernard stood in the doorway. "Sylvia, what are you doing here?"

"I think...I want to keep my baby. I think I can manage."

The Matron stepped into the room and closed the door. "You're the most clear-sighted and sensible girl we have here."

"I don't feel it...feel as though I'm doing him an injustice...that he should know me—know I love him."

"Oh, I don't think so. I don't think you've thought it through, dear." The Matron pulled another chair from under the desk and sat beside Kim. "You've made the right choice when you came here. Don't make your child suffer by not having a father. You have an entire life ahead of you. You're young and very attractive and will meet another young man, marry and have more children…the way God intended."

Kim bowed her head and wiped away tears streaming down her cheeks.

The Matron handed her a tissue. "It is unused. Cry. It will make you feel better."

Kim took the tissue and wiped her face but looked at the desk. "I'm being selfish, aren't I?"

The Matron lowered her voice. "You need to stay focused on what's best for the little one. For what's best for everyone. The father has his whole life ahead of him, as you do. Both of you can continue as if none of this happened. It will remain a secret, and no one need know."

"I really don't care who knows, any more…." She cried then hard, her shoulders shaking. When the sobs subsided, a desperate, pleading expression came on her face, and her lips trembled, "I feel my baby move…."

"In a month or two or year after the little one is born, you'll be trapped with a child you will struggle to support. You won't be able to go out and enjoy time with your friends as a young woman your age should. You'll be strapped to a child needing your attention every moment of the day and night. These things are for the best. You wouldn't want the welfare to take the child." The Matron tapped Kim on the arm. "Best to move on and forget. You'll never need to bother yourself over it again. Your shame will disappear. Your secret will be safe."

SISTER GREGORY stood near the lavender where Sister Anthony had collapsed, and just like that day, the breeze blew but not hard and stinging those parts uncovered by her veil and habit. The wimple, bonnet, and bloomers were no longer required. There was a great sense of freedom with a habit shortened to mid-calf and without the heaviness of the wimple and the fullness of the bloomers—but she still wore her veil, treasured it.

The leaves on the trees and hedges rustled like the moment after Sister Anthony passed over to the Lord, but today there was no hideous howl, only a glorious sunny autumn day. Sister Anthony's tunes seeming to be part of the breeze. There was nothing hideous about the breeze that day, but she had felt and heard her own grief.

A novice unchained the gate. The postman stepped into the grounds, his mailbag swung over his shoulder. He nodded at Sister Gregory as he passed, then stopped and scratched his head as if he had forgotten something.

"You having a good day, Sister Gregory? It's a great day for this time of year."

"That it is." She turned away, self-conscious of the way the thinner fabric pressed against her thighs and breasts under the postman's gaze, and pretended to wipe something from her shoes, feeling uncomfortable that she liked the way he said her name, and part of her had the urge to say *call me Sister Ann. Ann's my name.*

"Has Sylvia left?"

She might have escaped to the reception area, if he had not said that. "Who?"

"Sylvia Dawes. She's been waiting for me for months, and giving me letters to send." He pointed to the chapel yard. "Waits between the hedges."

"Do you have mail for her?"

"I've held onto a letter the past week. She told me to hold on to them if she wasn't waiting, not to give them to anyone."

"Then why are you telling me?"

"She said you try to be kind."

Sister Gregory lowered her voice. "She is still here."

"So you will give her the letter?"

She nodded. "But please don't give it to me until we get into the reception area." Sister Gregory walked ahead, and stepped into the hallway beside the paintings of St Margaret, as the faint sound of a bell rang on the floor above. She took hold of the letter and placed it in her pocket. "Thank you."

"It sounds like a fire bell."

She smiled. "It's an announcement that a little one is due any moment."

"Has Sylvia gone into labour?"

"I don't know who it is, but I best go."

When she reached the second floor, the bell stopped ringing. Sister Bernard stood on the landing holding the bell, hardly able to contain her excitement. "Sylvia's had a baby girl. Another little one is on the way. How we never guessed."

"Sylvia Dawes?"

The Matron frowned. "Did I say Dawes?"

"No, but perhaps we need to be clearer with each other and the girls. Changing their names solves nothing, except to confuse and alienate everybody."

"Sister, what's wrong?"

"I'm tired...tired of it all." She brushed past Sister Bernard and went to a birthing room.

Kim lay on the bed, a sheet pulled up to her neck. Sister Gregory waited for her to ask to see her baby as a Sister carried the last born crying out of the room. But Kim said nothing, seemed dazed and unable to speak.

Sister Gregory stepped beside the bed. "How do you feel?"

"Like God has his vengeance."

"I'll call your mother."

Kim nodded, her pale and blank gaze following the Sister carrying away her baby, before she rolled over and faced the wall. "How could I have two and no one know?"

"They're premature and very small."

"Will they be all right?"

"I think so."

"Are they identical?"

Sister Gregory widened her eyes to stop tears falling and glanced at the open door. *Say nothing, but it's time for truth. Enough lies.* "A boy and a girl."

Another Sister walked into the room, reached for Kim's arm, and gave her a needle. "This will settle you and help you sleep."

"Which was born first?" Kim asked.

"The girl," Sister Gregory said.

"Best to forget," the other sister said. "Relax and allow the needle to take affect."

"Put Mary and Robert, after my parents, on their birth certificates."

Sister Gregory walked slowly to the door, couldn't get words out for a long moment. "Rest and I or the Matron will bring the birth registration forms for you to sign."

The other Sister patted Kim on the arm. "It's over now. No need to bother yourself anymore. It's all finished."

Melbourne, 1992 _____ *Kim*

KIM DIDN'T know how to respond to the letter, how to explain the failure and the worthlessness she felt for allowing Angela to be taken. There was a sunny break in the sky, but scattered clouds hinted of late showers. Typical of Melbourne. The ever-changing weather matched her feelings, from wanting to cry, to crying, to laughing at being forced to admit her shame, her secret, her failure to profound relief that life could go full circle, and the closure she never dared imagine might be possible.

She wondered how many of her neighbours already knew about the letter, if shame showed on her face, if her face always showed that she wasn't the one she tried so hard to be. A loving mother and wife. In truth, an outcast, a tart, who didn't deserve to keep her first children.

She allowed herself to imagine for the briefest of moments being an unwed mother raising her babies, but she couldn't. The only images were of strangers loving her babies—faceless babies. There had never been an image, a photograph to cherish, only a distant cry that never faded. Yet, she had never stopped wondering where her babies were—if they were crying. If they were sick. If they were safe—and Kim prayed every night, loving parents cared for her babies.

Kim now had a husband who loved her and a daughter she adored. But...her husband never knew the real her. She never allowed him close enough. She never trusted him with her secret, feared he would turn away disgusted. She had always kept that part of her inside, never allowed him to touch it, reach it, share it. But it had always been there—a little tremor inside that never disappeared. There had always been a distance between them, a great secret separating them.

She still felt that tremor full of searing pain she couldn't escape, frightened and alone—trapped in that moment of long ago. It was madness. A moment she had feared not for herself, but a desperate horror when her firstborn breathed air. It was a place, a memory, she was afraid to fully see—to allow—to fully remember. Even now, even after the letter, even after almost twenty-six years, she didn't know how to tell her husband or admit to her daughter the truth, or how horrible her deceit really had been—could not tell them all of it. *Maybe they don't need to know there were two babies*...maybe she could continue to pretend none of it happened, *leave it in the past*...leave it all where she was told it belonged.

Phil's Ute, ladder on top, moved into the driveway. He jumped out in shorts and t-shirt and those big work boots as if it wasn't winter. He was built like a big bear with dark curly hair, huggable, and all man—all happy, confident. No mincing words with him.

Kim considered moving the letter from the table, but then she'd always be trapped—never be free of her lies. He came into the room, threw his keys onto the table and without a word, only a cheeky grin, walked to her.

He hugged her, and his hand slipped to the small of her back to press her tighter. "I saw Christine down the shop with a couple of friends...she's happy—and we're alone." He put his hands to the sides of her face to hold her where he wanted her, and she knew if he kept touching her, he'd make her mouth open, and make her eyes close, and she'd escape into his kiss and everything else and not want to reveal the letter—would lose her courage to ever reveal it. *She's happy*...Phil said that. *Christine's happy.* A thought from long ago crept in...a thought about her babies' future happiness. *Let me die with that knowledge.*

"Phil, no," she murmured against his lips, and turned her face away, her body wanting to hold him tighter, afraid he might never hold her again, but her mind told her not now. *Now's the time to tell him everything.* "I'm sorry, but I—" She stepped back and shut her eyes to stop the trembling in her voice. "I have something important to tell you."

"I'm important...." He kissed her neck. "Christine's not coming home till later."

She put her hands on his shoulders and gently pushed him away. But his arms stayed around her waist, his eyes still mischievous, and she struggled to gather her thoughts. "When I...." She moved away—his eyes now studying her. "I received a letter today."

He crossed his arms and leaned against the sink. "And...?"

Kim looked away from the husband she had lied to for the past twenty-six years. "Remember when we first met, how I...feared...it took so long to allow—for us to get close?"

"You get a letter from Andrew?"

Kim shook her head. "But I...just before I met you—I stayed in an unwed mother's home."

A crease spread between his brows. "You fell pregnant to Andrew?"

She nodded.

He pointed to the letter on the table. "This kid has contacted you...?"

"Through an adoption agency...she's mine."

He frowned, searching for words, and she expected anger to strain his voice, but sadness, disappointment lurked in his tone. "At times...I did think you were hiding something from me.... I don't know what you want me to say."

She moved toward him. "I tried so many times to tell you...and...."

"You never trusted me in all these years...."

"That wasn't it."

"I thought I knew you...but...." He brushed past her and picked up the keys off the table. "I'm not hungry...won't be back for dinner."

SISTER GREGORY sat in the recreation room at dawn, reading the letter, while everybody else prayed. It was from him. From Vietnam. Sylvia's young man. It was written two weeks before, his handwriting almost illegible—rushed. He was also capable of seduction—his letter filled with as much angst and pain and lust as Sylvia's letter written to him. She reread some of his sentences again and again, a little part inside each time breaking, understanding why Sylvia held on to her Tommy.

I can't remove you from my mind since that last night. Innocent. Trusting. Beautiful. Mine. The feel of you. The warmth of your body. The taste of you. The feel of your stomach, the feel of our baby moving inside of you.

I came to the hospital just after I got my brown envelope, but the Matron called the coppers. Got a hiding and they kept me locked up for two days. I tried then to call the hospital, but they wouldn't let me speak to you. I spoke to my sister, but she wanted to adopt our baby, was only interested in helping that way.

Since I've been in this hell hole, I'm scared half the time, not sure if the thought of death or what might happen back there with you is worse. Each time I think about us, you alone, me here, and the thought our baby will be ripped away from us forever, I could shoot myself for not having the sense to leave you alone. I refused to come to Vietnam, didn't care if everyone thought me a coward, but a warrant office told me if I didn't come they'd lock me up for two years, which wasn't going to do either one of us any good.

I know I can't expect you to wait for me, but...

Sister Gregory tried to push away what the smudge on the letter meant. It was as if a tear fell, his finger wiped it away, and it smudged over his words *I will forever love you*. He said he was fighting in the jungle, trapped in a bunker, machine gun fire just missing his head, while it rained a torrent for days.

Now with the letter in her pocket, she placed a folder on Mother Terrance's desk. "You might be interested in this. It's evidence that child and mother suffer long term effects from separation."

"Sit. Sister Bernard told me you're concerned for a waiting girl who tried to kill herself."

"It was a broken spoon she accidentally cut herself on while removing nails in her window, and it was I who gave and suggested she take a sleeping pill."

"It's out of our hands. The donation provided to the hospital for Sylvia's baby has been applied to the completion of the new dormitory."

"Sylvia, after she's signed the papers, has a year to appeal in court before the adoption is made legal."

"I know that." Mother Terrance stood. "But Sylvia Dawes does not. I would think a Sister who devoted her life to the cause of the little ones, wouldn't tell her."

Stop it, stop this lying, all of you, all of us. "It's policy that these girls receive counselling before they sign the adoption papers."

Mother Terrance raised her voice, louder than Sister Gregory ever heard before, "Policy is not law! And it isn't our place to provide counselling services for these—."

"I only meant...."

"Please don't interrupt. It's the job of the Catholic Welfare Department."

"I understand that."

"I'm sorry, Sister, but I'm lost with where you're going with this. What do you expect us to do? Our role is simple, and you're complicating matters. If we let the girl walk out of the gate with her child, she has nowhere to go." She met Sister Gregory's stare. "She has no idea of what is in store for her outside our gates, should she take her child."

"I think they all have a little idea."

"Most of them are only children who need adult guidance."

"Our guidance isn't helping one waiting girl."

"And…?"

"I wonder…if perhaps we should give the girl some news of her young man?"

"What purpose could that serve? Now that he hasn't turned up to meet her, her feelings will fade."

"Maybe they'll fester and make her so ill, she will eventually do something silly—and lose her baby, her life, our donation."

"I understand she is in a room with nothing but a bed and four walls with a novice watching her, and if she does somehow manage to attempt to harm herself again, that will only make it easier to take the child."

Sister Gregory stood very still. "She's been moved back to her room. She isn't going to harm herself, never was, but what if her young man should try to remove her from here?"

"He's been deployed to Vietnam months ago."

"Then we have nothing to fear."

"It will give the girl false hope. In two years, he will have forgotten all about her. Besides, you have implied she is unstable."

"She's unstable because she feels he deserted her."

"The reality is, he has."

"What if he didn't want to go, wouldn't have gone if he could have found a way to stay? What if he came here to tell her, but we turned him over to the police? Servants of God that we are."

"That's irrelevant, and I'm not sure why we're discussing it. We both know the best place for the child to go, regardless whether the father stayed or left. The girl can't cope with the pressure of pregnancy, let alone the pressure and responsibility of raising a child on her own. None of them can, not even those who come from affluent families. And I don't like your tone, what you're insinuating."

Sister Gregory thought about taking the letter out of her habit, then silently prayed to God to forgive her for not doing so. "I don't believe the girl had any intention of hurting herself or the child, that's why she has been placed back in the dormitory."

"Your point?"

"We have assisted other single girls."

"They had nowhere to go. They fell through the cracks of a system in place to protect them by removing their children at birth. They stayed under the welfare radar, who had they known would have removed their children and placed them in institutions. Sylvia has a home she can return to."

Sister Gregory's heart beat so loudly, she imagined her ribcage vibrated. "As far as I'm aware they live in a caravan, at least for the few months before her admission, and she can only return without her child."

"Society does not and will not condone unwed pregnancy. It's evident by them bringing their daughters to us."

"Not all their daughters relinquish their children willingly. Sylvia is one of them, and others are coerced and bullied. By not allowing her to keep her child, we are not only contravening our own manuals of adoption practice, but also the protection clause of the adoption and children's act."

"Sister, tell me why you think all these girls come to us?"

"I'd always thought illegitimacy was a consequence of immorality and...."

"Had always thought.... What's changed?"

"I've looked through the girls' records, every one of them that came through our gate for the past twenty years. They come from all classes, not only the poor or from broken homes."

"Polices in place are in the best interest of their children, and provide for the unwed mother to return to their lives unscathed by the shame and guilt that would otherwise be present, and ensure the stability of family and society as a whole." Mother Terrance rubbed the back of her neck as if it would wipe the tension from her face. "If illegitimacy is not controlled, it will have a detrimental effect on the stability of society and the sanctity of married life."

Sister Gregory heard the lecture, had heard it many time, but it had lost its force, its credibility. "There must be something we can do?"

Mother Terrance considered the question and shook her head. "Things are best left exactly the way they are. Ignorance is a wonderful thing. This child is due any day. Any further stress may put at risk both mother and child." Mother Terrance stood for a long moment, then sat and a deep silence fell on the room, before she finally looked up at Sister Gregory. "Let it rest. She's a young girl who fell in love at the wrong time in her life. The country has thousands of them."

*

For the first time Sister Gregory noticed a gloom, or was it a suffocating air in the dormitory—an air caused by all the restrictions? Despite the Pope's recommendations and numerous meetings within the Order, changes only trickled through to the Sisters of St Anthony. She thought of the words Pope John XXIII had said. *It's time to open the windows of the Church and let in some fresh air.*

She sat in her chair. *Why do you stay? Because you can leave any day.* Vatican II gave all the sisters impunity, the right to leave if they chose, but it didn't remove the shame attached to leaving the Order. If she left the Order, she would leave with what she came with. Nothing, apart from a few articles of clothing that no longer fit. Her vow of obedience, a vow to listen to the voice of God, even now nagged at her. The voice of God mingled in. *Why leave now? Where would you go? What would you do?*

She had sought the sanctuary of the convent to escape all the pain paralysing her after her mother died, thought locking out the rest of the world and spending it with women who loved God more than life itself would ease her pain and transfer God's love to others, to the needy. But only Sister Anthony seemed that way.

Mary, Mother of Jesus, give me strength to stay…to see my way.

She wanted an answer from the Lord loud and clear that all would be all right, and when none came, she went to the showers, no longer able to stand her habit, or her veil, sweat dripping over her entire body. She stripped off her habit, ripped the veil off, her

174

shoes and stockings. Then she stood under the cold running water in her chemise, so she couldn't see her own body.

The beautiful music she'd heard in Sylvia's room played in her mind—a man pining for a lover who he hadn't seen in a long, lonely time. He hungered for his lover's touch. *Needed her touch. Needed her love.* She thought back to her own small and white hand on the gate and the postman's large and tanned hand beside it. She stepped out of that last barrier so her skin could feel the water, stepped out of the chemise, allowed her skin to soak under the water and her body to feel the wicked and sensual touch of soap against her flesh. *Leave the Order now! You're only thirty-two. Leave while a part of you is still alive.*

She'd seen hundreds of women giving birth and couldn't push away the memory of their legs thrown apart in release of their children, those same open thighs having moved in rhythm against a man's naked body born in the image of Christ. Her body, the one married to Christ, looked no different from any woman she'd seen in childbirth. It was full and lush. She couldn't deny as she ran the soap across her breasts, then toward her stomach, her body had desires. *I crave the touch of your lips...one more kiss.*

Kissing the Polish boy, all those years ago...kissing slowly, thoroughly—the noises they made, the lingering, caressing motion of their hands, the supple movements of their hips and thighs pressing against the other, as they blended and melted together consumed her.

She threw the soap onto the floor and raised her face to the spraying water, until she shivered. Then like Eve, she felt naked and ashamed. She pulled the chemise over her shivering wet body, daring not to let her naked fingers touch her own flesh, grabbed her towel, patted herself dry, then put on her stockings and habit. The Chinese proverb flashed through. *To understand a mother's love, bear your own children.* She held her veil and ran her fingers through her hair. It was a little longer, growing, but still spiky, and she knew grey would soon start. She put on her veil, knelt on the tiles with arms outstretched, then prayed. *Hail Mary full of Grace....*

KIM POURED two lemonades and sat them on the table. The silent house was about to get noisy. Christine walked into the room, but Kim could not say a word, only study her fifteen-year-old daughter, study her more closely than on any day since her birth.

"Hi, Mum." Christine walked straight to the table and gulped down the lemonade. "What's for dinner?"

"Steak and veggies."

"Where's Dad?"

"He's gone out for a bit."

"What's up? You're looking at me strange."

Kim, sitting at the table, lowered her gaze. She never thought they would have this conversation, though sometimes, over the years, she thought of what she might say if this day came. She often thought about telling her husband and daughter more about the life she once led, the person she really was, but she never found the words, the right moment to reveal the shame or the guilt—and she was terrified.

"I fell pregnant before I married your father."

Christine stepped closer and whispered, "You lost your baby?"

Kim held her daughter's hand. "I gave away...."

"It wasn't Dad's?"

"Before I met your father." Kim picked up the letter off the table and handed it to her daughter.

Christine opened the envelope cautiously, her stare alternating between her fingers unfolding the letter and her mother. The photograph fell out, but she caught it. She inspected the picture for the longest moment, then slowly placed it on the table and read the letter. Tears filled her eyes as she placed the letter beside the photograph. She walked to the biscuit tin and grabbed another one. "Well, this is a little like being told the opposite of Santa doesn't exist. I've always wanted a sister and, like some strange dream, I suddenly have one. Does Dad know?"

Kim nodded.

"But he hasn't always, has he? I can tell by your face."

"I told him today—for the first time…after the letter arrived."

"So what does he think?"

"I'm concerned about what you think. Come and sit."

"Well, you're full of secrets. No wonder they call it the swinging sixties." Christine stood there trying to make her fifteen-year old self look all smart and grown up. A crease formed between her brows, like her father, and Kim saw her daughter's forming, swelling feelings, a mix of threat and hurt and wonder about this sudden change in their family. She moved to the table and glanced at the photo. "Why didn't you name her?"

"I did."

"Then why's she saying that?"

Kim searched for an answer and said only loudly enough to be heard, "I don't know."

Christine studied the photograph. "How old is she?"

"Twenty-six this year."

"She's pretty…looks like you."

"You're pretty too, and people say you look like me."

Christine pushed the photograph away. "No, not like her."

Kim patted her lap. "You're not too old…."

Her daughter's eyes watered, and she sat on her mother's lap. Kim wrapped her arms around her waist, held her tightly, and kissed her cheek. "You'll always be my baby."

"What will happen now?" She picked up the photograph and ran her finger just as Kim had done over the film's surface. "When can we meet her?"

"We can't just meet. I'll have to write back."

"Can I meet her?"

"It will be up to her…where we go from here."

"Why contact us if she doesn't want to meet us?"

"To find answers…decide if she wants to meet."

"No wonder you keep giving me lectures about sex."

"I don't lecture you at all."

"Some of my friends are already doing it."

"Because you can, doesn't mean you should." Kim held her tighter. "And the whole point about me talking to you about sex is so that the same thing doesn't happen to you…so you're prepared and protected from unwanted pregnancy and diseases before getting close to someone. Nan never spoke to me about sex when she was alive, never."

"Did she know?"

"Of course she knew."

That seemed to surprise Christine, and she stood and placed the photo back on the table. "So she forced you to give away your own baby?"

"It isn't as cut and dry as that."

"Well, she either did or didn't force you."

"Back then, Nan went…we went to church twice a week."

"What's church got to do with anything?"

Kim looked away from her daughter's accusing eyes, and her voice lowered. "It's still considered a sin if unwed, if you're Catholic."

"Since when is new life a sin?"

"Not new life, but if unmarried the act that created it."

"Act? Now you're speaking like Nan used to."

"I felt I was very bad for having sex. Dirty. And giving up my baby was my punishment."

"Oh, Mum, that's…." Christine kissed her mother's cheek and hugged her…and Kim tried to get the words out to tell her daughter, there was more than one baby…*you also have a brother*…she said to herself, but maybe that secret didn't need to be revealed…maybe one day, but right now, it just seemed too hard…too draining, too confronting…and Kim held her daughter tightly.

"LET ME up. Please, let me up."

Sister Gregory heard the voice from down the hall. *That's Sylvia.*

"You're not going anywhere," Sister Dominic said. "Stay there."

There was a delay, then Sylvia shouted, "What are you doing?"

Am I the only one, Lord, who can hear? The whimpering in the birthing room became a shout. *Oh, Lord, are you listening?* As usual, no one in the hallway even glanced at the door enclosing Sylvia in a birthing room. None of the nuns or novices said a word. *So much for change for the new Vatican edicts.*

Sister Gregory rushed toward the room, looking at her watch to time the contractions, but didn't get a chance to count three seconds, when Sylvia's rumble of a groan slowly built up to a high pitch of agony. Sister Gregory stood quite still, didn't move a muscle, Sylvia's terror building in her own chest, until Sylvia let out a cry—almost of relief.

Sister Gregory opened the door. Sister Dominic and another Sister held Sylvia down on the bed. "You need to stay here."

A contraction bent Sylvia, and she convulsed and vomited.

"This is to stop," Sister Gregory said. "Can't you see she's suffering enough? Let the girl move." She rushed to Sylvia's side. "Breathe with the pain."

Sylvia tried to cooperate, but Sister Gregory imagined the agony of it all made concentration impossible. Sylvia whimpered, her eyes pleading for mercy. Her lips opened and closed, gasping for breath, trying to ease the pain.

"We're going to die, aren't we?" Sylvia said.

"Your body's a temple for the Holy Ghost…you've shown no respect for it. This is God's punishment for sinning," Sister Dominic said. "Prayer is the best thing for relief."

Sister Gregory shot back, "No one is going to die."

"She needs to stay on the bed," Sister Dominic said. "I'm in charge of these wards."

"This isn't a torture chamber, and I'm second in charge of how this hospital runs," Sister Gregory shouted. "Give her the gas. Clean up this mess. Do it now."

"I don't want gas. They tried to give me a needle…." Another spasm seized Sylvia's body. "You're trying to kill me."

Sister Gregory smoothed the damp hair from Sylvia's forehead. "Don't be silly. It won't hurt you or the baby." She pulled the gas mask toward Sylvia. "Listen to me. You must relax. Otherwise you will not be able to bear the pain."

Another contraction ripped through Sylvia and with it another out-flowing of vomit.

"Something is wrong." Sister Gregory edged Sylvia away from where she'd been sick. "She's in too much pain for first stage labour."

"Go and find Dr Dennison," Sister Dominic told the other Sister. "Otherwise get the Matron to call a Doctor from St Peter's."

Sister Gregory trembled and shouted at Sister Dominic, "Sister can stay with me. You find Dr Dennison." She held the gas mask over Sylvia's face. "You need to lie back…let me examine you to see where the baby is situated. Trust me…please. I've done this many times." As Sylvia tried to cooperate between contractions, Sister Gregory looked to heaven and prayed to St Margaret for Sylvia to have a safe birth.

SYLVIA WOKE to the sound of babies crying and her stomach aching, in a hospital bed surrounded by a white flimsy curtain. She could hardly move. Her stomach and breasts were bandaged tightly. A tube was between her legs. *My Baby's gone.* She gasped. The big intake of breath made her stomach hurt more, and she only moaned. *It's over.*

Oh, that evil Sister. That horrible pain, and them, oh them holding me down. Then Sister Gregory, then the doctor, then—*sign the paper. Sign them now. You've run out of time.* Then nothing. *Only a baby's cry,* then in and out of dreams, blinding lights, a flashlight, shadows everywhere, no faces, no names, no more baby's cry—*not my baby's cry.* Only the memory of it.

Through a small gap in the curtain, she couldn't look away from the young mother in the bed beside her, nightgown unbuttoned at the chest, feeding her tiny baby sucking on her nipple. Sylvia didn't resent the sight, but ached for what she didn't have—a maddening urge to hold her baby. *The room's full of women feeding their babies.*

The breastfeeding woman near Sylvia cried while cradling and feeding her baby. Sylvia wanted to move, offer comfort, but the woman's tears dissolved into a smile. *She cries for all she has, for the wonder and miracle of her baby in her arms*—the tears releasing and accepting the magic of it all.

"Excuse me." Sylvia leaned toward the woman and held the curtain away. "Your baby is beautiful. Do you know what I had?"

The woman smiled. "No, love. Sorry."

"Do you know when I came into this room?"

The woman shook her head, not taking her eyes off her child.

"Am I still at St Josephs?"

The woman frowned. "Where else would you be?"

Sylvia let the curtain fall back in place, only the small gap allowing her to glimpse the woman. She must also be a part of the conspiracy. Everyone was going to be silent, pretend it never happened. That her baby didn't exist. Footsteps crossed the floor, and Sylvia knew straight away who it was. They weren't measured and paced, but rushed and hurried—a scuttle.

Sister Bernard pulled part of the curtain aside and smiled. "It's wonderful to see you awake. I have someone who I'm sure you'd like to see. A Sister will be here soon to remove the catheter, and we'll see if you can move around a little bit."

Someone stood beside Sister Bernard, their shadow behind the curtain. *Oh, my God. You have my baby.* "What did I have? Is it a boy or girl? Oh, thank you for bringing my baby to me."

"There's no need to trouble yourself over that. Concentrate on your recovery. The little one will be looked after," Sister Bernard said.

"What's wrong with my baby? Why are you stopping me from seeing my baby?"

"That isn't possible." Sister Bernard lowered her voice. "Now that you've signed the adoption papers."

"I never signed anything."

"You did last night. You'll have to accept it."

"You can't do this," Sylvia said, then shouted, "I want to see my baby. Oh God, has it died?"

Her mother pulled the curtain aside, while wiping away tears running down her cheeks. "You have to stop this. If you see the child it will haunt you forever."

"The papers are signed. Move on," Sister Bernard said.

"I never signed anything. It's my baby, *my baby*. Please help me keep my baby."

Her mother tried to keep her voice down, but it wavered, "You listen to me. What you did was wrong. It will be looked after by someone who can care for it. You must forget it."

"Mum, I beg you, let me keep my baby." Sylvia studied her mother, her figure as slim as it was at three months pregnant. "What happened to your baby?"

Her mother's eyes narrowed. "Here's not the place...."

You've had an abortion. "Just because you didn't want yours...."

Her mother leaned in close and whispered, "How dare you. I miscarried." As if she were afraid she would strike Sylvia, she folded her arms across her breasts. "Because you have lost your faith doesn't mean I've lost mine."

"Why aren't you and Dad together? Wasn't the baby Dad's?"

"I'll leave you alone." Sister Bernard closed the curtain and walked away.

"Of course the baby was your father's. We're back together." Her mother lowered her voice. "I was told if I had any more children I could die. Your father told the priest and asked if we could use birth control. When the priest told your father no, that we must let God's will be, your father never went back to church.... I told him I was using birth control. But I wasn't. I couldn't."

"You risked your life for another chid? Dad left because you wanted another child?"

"Your father was angry with me...I'd lied about taking the Pill and put my life at risk. Not that I owe you an explanation. I'm an adult."

"Is that why you put me here, because you thought you might die?"

"If something happens to me, you'll never be able to look after it...it broke my heart to leave you here, and it breaks my heart to see you now."

"Oh, Mum, I'm so sorry about your baby. I'm so sorry for letting you down."

Her mother kissed Sylvia's forehead. "You haven't let me down."

Sylvia grabbed her mother around the neck and held her close. "I love you...so sorry about your baby."

"Remember what Nan used to say?" Her mother whispered into her ear. "Only good girls get into trouble. Nothing will ever make me stop loving you."

"But my baby's alive."

"I know your heart is breaking."

Sylvia pulled away. "What if I can't have anymore children?"

"That's not going to happen."

"It's happening to you."

"Sylvia, I'm older."

"When the Beaumont children went missing and the dead girls were found at Wanda Beach, you went on and on about how their parents, their mothers must be nervous wrecks, must have their hearts torn to bits not knowing where their children were."

"Please...."

"You even stopped Leanne playing outside...was afraid someone would take her—yet you expect me to give my baby to strangers.... I'll be like the dead girls' parents...never see my child. I can't believe you wanted me to give Tommy's sister my baby."

Her mother bowed her head. "I don't know what you're talking about. I've never spoken to Tommy's sister since she married." When she raised her eyes and met Sylvia's, confusion spread over her face. "What's Tommy's sister got to do with this?"

"She told me you knew she was going to try to trick me into giving her my baby."

Her mother sat on the side of the bed and patted Sylvia's forehead. "You're worrying me. You're not making sense. I haven't spoken to Tommy's sister."

Sylvia pushed her mother's hand away and cried. *You're all trying to drive me insane.* "Why won't someone tell me if it's a boy or girl?" Then Sylvia shouted, "I trusted you, and you betrayed me."

In an instant, a Sister grabbed Sylvia's arm and jabbed her with a needle...*in and out of sleep...in and out of sleep. Another needle. In and out of sleep. Shadows, strangers, in and out of the room—and in the distance that baby's cry. My baby's crying.*

SISTER GREGORY tossed the files aside, shuffled paper all night, but achieved nothing as if the alphabet escaped her, and now the sun would soon rise. *She's a young girl who has fallen in love at the wrong time in her life. The country has thousands of them.* Mother Terrance's statement was true and could have referred to the thousands of young girls and women who became nuns. Sister Alexander realised she preferred the love of a real flesh and blood groom in the form of a young doctor. Sixteen other Sisters of St Anthony around the country applied to the Pope so they could also leave the Order.

She wondered why Sylvia's spirit stirred her so much. *I lack the same spirit—like some lovers, we are opposites.* She wondered if her mother had lived, would she have given her only daughter to the convent. She wondered if she had a daughter, if she would so easily be able to give up that daughter. *Impossible to know...*

Mother Terrance was right. The country was filled with young unmarried girls and young women in love. The world was falling apart on the outside. Its buildings, its transport, its people, their policies, their failures, descending on St Anthony like an enemy army testing how long a fort can hold.

Why try to save one defiant teenager? Why try to save someone when there is no guarantee any of it will help? Despite all the evidence pointing to obvious heartbreak between mother and child if separated, there was no way Sylvia could survive above the poverty line and keep her child without support from family and friends. But he said in his letter, Sylvia's young lover, that he would help...send all his pay to her.

The sun still hadn't risen when she went to Sylvia's room and motioned for the novice to leave. Sylvia lay awake in the dim light from the bedside lamp, watching her step closer. There were other beds in this room, but no other girls. The others still waited for their turn to give birth. But there were windows here—the stars now disappearing and the light of day about to seep through the darkness.

"You look different with just the veil...prettier."

"I'm still the same person, just not covered as much."

"I don't understand why I can't see my baby once."

"It's best if you don't see the child." She didn't believe the words, felt her own heart break at saying them.

"How long have I been in here?"

"Seven days."

"Do they already have my baby?"

"Not yet."

"I looked at my chart at the end of the bed. What's *BFA* mean?"

"Baby for adoption."

Sylvia sunk back into her pillow—the colour draining from her face as if trapped in a whirl of confusion. "I don't remember signing anything. And *BFA* is dated on the chart before I even came to this room. Those records start from when I first came to the hospital."

"By staying with us, we understand that you intend to relinquish your child."

"I said that first day I didn't want to lose my baby."

"But you signed the papers yesterday, don't you remember?"

"How could I remember anything? I've been drugged out of my mind for days. The Matron told me I signed them the night my baby was born." Then she cried. "I'm a failure. My signature under *relinquish* proves I'm a failure, wasn't even worthy of keeping my own baby. I don't have anything to live for."

"You have the rest of your life."

"That day in the shower you said you could help me.... That there was a way."

"There's nothing I can do about the child, but let me help you

186

up. I want to show you something."

"My baby?"

"Something else."

"I'm staying here."

Sister Gregory kneeled so her face was at the same level of Sylvia's and whispered, "Trust me, please. We can't speak here." She stood and reached out her hand. "Come."

Sylvia held her hand, but when she stood her legs buckled. "Oh, the pain in my stomach."

"It's because you've only been going from your bed to the toilet. You need to walk a little further. Grab a pillow and hold it against your stomach. When you stand your insides will feel as if they're falling out, but they're held in place by stitches. Come, take my hand. Stand straight, and try not to lean forward. Don't look down... focus on the wall... I'm holding you."

As they stepped into the chapel yard, the first rays of light broke through darkness, and Sister Gregory pointed to the sky. "What do you see?"

"The sun breaking through clouds."

"But what do you really see...what do you feel?"

"I don't understand."

"Have a close look."

"That it's the start of a new day."

"That's true, but I see and feel something else also. I see God's work. Each time I see something so beautiful, I have my breath taken away. I'm in awe. It evokes something greater, a wonder that is timeless. That there is something more to this world...something beyond the here and now. Something beyond us."

"God deserted me. He hasn't listened to anything I've said. I feel as though I've gone insane."

"Nothing will separate you from God's love. He knows we're weak." She lowered her voice. "You're not insane. An insane person thinks they're sane."

"I don't understand why God took my mother's baby away from her. She wasn't weak and kept her faith. And if God knows I'm weak, why would He expect me to give away my baby? I don't understand why it was wrong for me to love Tommy, or to want to keep my baby. Isn't that what it's all about? Love?"

"Love should be consummated in the confines of marriage."

"I know something has happened to him."

"He never deserted you."

Sylvia turned grey. "He's dead?"

"I don't know if he's dead, but how were you going to meet if he's in Vietnam?" Sister Gregory handed her Tommy's letter. "What made you think he was going to be at the station?"

"I tried to tell you and Sister Bernard that day, his sister wrote to me, pretending to be him, so she could get our baby. I don't believe he'd do or want such a thing, then again, he told me he wasn't going to Vietnam…maybe I should have let his sister have our baby…least then…"

"Read the letter."

Sylvia's face took on the look of terror, but the expected tears never came only a moan when she finished reading as if it were the last sound she would make before she died. "Now there's nothing to stop you taking our baby."

Sister Gregory said nothing. What could she say? The girl was right.

Sylvia's face reddened, going over Tommy's words again, and her eyes widened like the night she went to throw the chair at the window. "How dare you all." She almost choked on her next words, fear and anger spurting the words from her lips. "Why not allow him to see me…tell me—let me friggin' know what was happening? Who made Sister Bernard God?"

"I understand your anger."

"How dare you…you understand nothing."

"I don't agree with all that happens here."

"You don't have feelings—none of you do."

"I can see you're hurting…."

"I feel as if I've died."

"If you embrace God, you might be surprised at how strong His love is for us—that every moment of our lives has a purpose for the benefit of us all."

"A part of me is amputated. Gone."

"If you seek God in the midst of your pain, He will help you face whatever He has planned for you."

Sylvia turned to walk away, back to her bed, slowly, shuffling. "Damn God. Damn you all. You all had me convinced Tommy didn't love me."

"Sylvia, you've done the right thing. Tommy's gone for at least two years. Forget it. Move on."

The pale and blank expression on Sylvia's face said she couldn't forget him, couldn't brush aside his words. *I haven't forgotten you. I'll never stop thinking about you. I've loved you since we were kids.* "I thought nothing would rip us apart."

"He hasn't stopped loving you...."

Sylvia frowned, searched for words, anger straining her voice. "You all made him go—he didn't want to go...why weren't we allowed to say goodbye?"

"I'm sorry...."

"Our baby is gone, and I'll never be able to face him now our baby's gone." She wiped away tears rolling down her cheek. "He wouldn't have left if he didn't really want to."

"The other option would have been to risk jail."

"Kim told me they aren't forced to go."

"How did you meet Tommy?"

"His family lived next door to us for years. Dad left just after Christmas and Mum couldn't afford the rent, so we moved into a caravan park. Tommy and my brother were mates, and we hung out together since we were little. He was a like a big brother. We used to horse around. Then one day, something changed. I suddenly thought he was a good sort, and I started to avoid him."

"I imagine it hard to avoid someone living next door."

Sylvia nodded. "One of my girlfriends came over a couple of years ago and went, wow! Who is he? He was walking to his car, and I said oh, that's just Tommy. That started it. I got jealous of her eyeing him, but before that he was just Tommy."

"So you've known each other a long time?"

"Since I was five. When my brother joined the army, it was only the two of us left. Everywhere I went, Tommy was there—the pool, the bowling alley, the river. Somehow, one day we kissed. We'd been swimming all day in the river, playing around with a group of friends, and we ended up alone, kissed. That's all we did for so long, only kissed, for months and months, and it became agonising. This wanting to be closer. It was just unbearable want...need. It was unbearable being together because we couldn't get close enough and unbearable being apart."

"Your mother and father allowed this to develop?"

"Not in the way it did. Mum started to question me about him, but I kept denying it...kept saying we were just friends, like we'd always been and that she was being stupid."

"I see."

"You think I'm stupid too?"

"I'm not judging you, Sylvia, but listening."

"The thing is, we couldn't stop. We tried. He told me I was too young for him, and he put his name down for National Service, and we didn't' speak for a month, and I felt like I was going to die. I couldn't eat or sleep. I felt sick all the time...we couldn't keep away from each other—we tried so hard."

"Life changes and we can't stop the effect it has on us. We all grow, but it doesn't lessen how we felt in the past. Those moments will always stay precious...you feel very sad now, one day these painful days will end. There's an old saying that it's better to have loved and lost than to have never loved."

"I want to see my baby. Let me see my baby and say goodbye... Please...don't deny me a moment to see my baby."

*

"Sylvia Dawes is asking to see her baby."

Sister Bernard sat behind her desk, and fiddled with a pen. "You know the hospital's policy."

"Evidence supports the mother resigns herself better to the choices she's made regarding adoption if she can look and hold the child a least for a few moments."

"There isn't any point in her seeing the child."

"Perhaps in this case it would be for the best."

"The best way for her to rejoin society is for her to forget the baby exists."

Sister Gregory sat opposite the Matron. "Do you really believe they ever forget?"

"I'm your supervisor. I represent the voice of God. My will is God's will."

"Mother Terrance is now Mother Superior."

Sister Bernard placed the pen calmly on the desk. "So it has come to this?"

"I've always admired you."

"Admire and like are two different things."

"Not in this instance."

"You're well aware praise means little to me...." Sister Bernard stepped to the window and lowered her voice. "I don't dictate what society demands. It doesn't matter what I think should happen, only that I assist these girls to rejoin society. I'm doing what I can to fulfil that need." Her voice trembled. "I've heard the whispers...that I'm cruel, but I'll tell you why I do it."

"There's no need."

"Indeed there is. I see your compassion for the waiting girls—can tell you feel I've none."

"That's not what I...."

Sister Bernard held up her hand. "Please...I've worked with unmarried mothers my entire life...in homes I've seen unwed girls breast feed their babies for six months, then leave. Some babies stayed two or three years before being transferred to Government institutions...the little ones whose mothers visited them occasionally, stood day after day, holding the gate rails waiting for Mummy to return. Some of those children stayed in Government homes until they were young adults."

"Some of these girls merely want to say goodbye...to have one moment with their children, to have something, a memory, an image of their flesh and blood to take away with them."

"If they see their babies they will fall in love with them, then there will be no way the girls will allow their child being adopted. Their children will end up in foster care or in institutions, then they will be too old for adoption. Infertile couples want babies, not toddlers and little children. The country is full of welfare and foundling homes full of neglected children."

Sister Gregory bowed her head. All sisters were drawn to the Order to care for the little ones, and care for them they did, for over a hundred years, but was it God's will to part them from their mothers? Newspaper article after article ran through her mind, and three words kept flashing in. *Adopt Unwanted Children.* Sylvia's child was wanted as was Kim's and so many of the other girls. "Why was Sylvia placed in a room with married women who breastfed their children?"

Sister Bernard leaned forward. "Sister Dominic said there was nowhere else for her to go."

"Sister Dominic needs reminding that we are sisters of mercy and compassion, and I will have a report on your desk this afternoon recommending she be transferred into a role not allowing her to punish those who had sex outside matrimony."

"This young girl's predicament, none of them, is Sister Dominic's fault."

"She's ignorant and cruel. The spiritual search for God is an individual choice. Sister Dominic should not be in a position to use her own beliefs against any of these girls."

"Why does your heart weigh so heavily because of this girl?"

"It's not just Sylvia…. I've been thinking of leaving….perhaps I've made a mistake." As soon as the words escaped, she saw her own surprise mirrored in the redness of the Matron's face.

"Oh—no—no! That's only the temptation of the devil. If you're unhappy here, I'll move you somewhere else. I mean…I'll suggest to Mother Terrance to move you to another vocation of your choice…. You could return to teaching in schools…. Surely this isn't all because of one girl?"

I'm not sure why.

"From a young girl you took to heart the invitation of Jesus to follow him. I witnessed your transformation. You've always had a great yearning to grow in a deep relationship with God. Remember, living life in common with people of like minds, living close to God and serving the needs of others was a path you chose with no doubts."

"I came here a child."

"It was God's will, not ours you chose. Have you given up seeking God? Are you no longer eager for the Work of God...for all things that will humble you?"

"I think I've been mimicking what is expected of me."

"Vatican II has given us so many more opportunities. Do you have no family at all that you could visit?"

Sister Gregory bowed her head. No one missed her. There was no one to miss, only memories fading and drifting in and out. "I have nowhere to go, can't imagine any other life. But there is a place Sylvia could go with her baby."

"It's out of our hands. The papers have been signed." Then the words struck the Matron. "It isn't possible for every girl who refuses to acknowledge their wrongs to go to St Joseph's House in the convent."

"There's room."

"And what of the donation already made to the convent? You're aware as much as I am that the world works in a certain way. No one gives anything to anyone for nothing, not even to the Church. They know Sylvia's child was born. When it is delivered to them in two weeks, they have promised to double their donation."

"What if the child didn't live?"

"Pray to God that doesn't happen."

"Everything is in the Lord's hands. If that were to happen, then what of the donation already spent?"

"I won't speculate...won't go there. The child is healthy."

"What if Sylvia finds out her rights when she walks out of here and demands her baby? Procedures provided by the Minister of Child Welfare states the child must be protected from unnecessary separation from his own family...that there should be no attempts to persuade the natural parents to place the child."

"For thousands of families we've been a centre of care, compassion and new beginnings." Sister Bernard raised her voice. "She's already relinquished all rights to the child and even if she didn't the adoption act is clear. A mother's consent can be dispensed with if it's deemed to be in the child's best interest."

"The document isn't supposed to be signed until five days after the birth, and Sylvia has another year to revoke her consent."

"No court will give the child to a girl who attempted suicide."

"It was an accident." An unexpected threat, like a beguiling snake, came into Sister Gregory's voice, and it surprised her but it was too late to turn back. "It wouldn't help if the media believed a girl in our care attempted suicide."

"I see that our conversation has descended into blackmail."

"Not at all. But what will happen if Sylvia convinces the media, we treated her badly? She's up to that, and we both know it."

"Well! You appear to have an answer for most things, except for what we and the child gain if we let an unstable girl keep her child."

"You asked me recently to speak honestly, and I didn't. I thought of letting Sylvia escape, wondered what was the worst that could happened to her if she met her lover and they clung together and refused to be separated."

"They are separated…."

"Why didn't you tell me that day it was Sylvia's Tommy?"

The Matron flinched. "How do you know who that man was?"

Sister Gregory thought about Tommy's letter. "I just do."

"You want to speak honestly?"

"You didn't trust me…."

"I was wondering if you were losing sight of our aims."

"Perhaps that was the start of this…dissatisfaction with what we do…the cold reality that our kindness and service to these girls is misaimed…. Do you really believe Sylvia is unstable?"

The Matron sighed. "I assume we are speaking in confidence."

"I would like to speak as not only sisters but as women."

"It's clear some of these girls suffer great anxiety over the loss of their children…a resistance to doing what needs to be done to ensure their little ones live a better life."

Sister Gregory told Sister Bernard a solution that could keep all parties happy. The Matron took off her glasses and rubbed the corner of her eye. "Thousands of parents have chosen our hospital facilities to house their daughters during a shameful period of their lives. What you're suggesting, if it ever leaked out, would ruin our reputation not only with parents but also within the adoption industry.... I don't' think I'll be a part of it." She put on her glasses and smiled in a way that showed she was not concerned. "There isn't a girl who stayed with us, including Sylvia, despite her defiance at times, who would let the whole world know their shameful secret. We've done everything we can do to ensure she makes the right choice and worthy parents receive a child that will thrive in a loving marriage."

Sister Gregory considered telling the Matron about Tommy's letter, *but no, not yet.* "One day...one of the waiting girls might feel it's everyone else's shame and secret they're hiding?"

Sister Bernard took in the words and frowned. "I've never underestimated your ability, but you're not the Matron of this hospital or Mother Superior yet."

"Didn't the Vatican Council suggest individual thought be embraced, not suppressed?"

"You're playing with words."

"The Pope's words—perhaps we should be more concerned with the girls who don't want to keep their children."

"Why do you suddenly think love is enough to overcome poverty, being shamed, shunned and excluded?"

"Love conquers all...doubt it, but a Chinese proverb bothers me greatly."

"Such as?"

"To understand a mother's love, bear your own children."

_____ *Sylvia*

THE CRIBS were lined up along the corridor. The pink, blue, and yellow baby blankets created a rainbow effect. *It's going to be all right. Keep on walking. If anyone tries to stop you, scream the place down.* Sister Gregory stood beside a crib, in front of a window, rocking in her arms a crying baby snugly wrapped in a yellow blanket. She shook her head at Sylvia so slightly, Sylvia wondered if she imagined the motion. But the warning, or was it sadness in the Sister's eyes, couldn't be mistaken.

Sylvia stopped a few feet away—the power to move her legs—gone. She strained to hear the other babies crying. The baby in Sister Gregory's arms cried the loudest, yet it could have been crying from miles away like the other babies sounded, but this baby's cry was different.

"Sylvia, I told you it would be best if you didn't come."

"Is that my baby?"

"Yes…you've done a wonderful thing. The little one will want for nothing."

"Is it a boy or a girl?"

"Don't do this to yourself. You need to forget all this happened."

Why do I hurt so badly if I've done a wonderful thing? Why, if I've done the right thing is everyone telling me to forget it? "Is it a boy or a girl?"

"Girl."

"She's stopped crying."

Sister Gregory nodded again, so slightly only a magnifying glass would notice.

If I don't see her face, just once, I won't have anything at all.

Not even the memory of her face. Only her cries. Sylvia stepped closer, her arms empty, aching. The silence coming from her baby louder than the cries from the other children. "Why was she crying?"

"Healthy babies cry. You need not worry. Her parents will love her."

I love her. "Can I look at her?"

Instead of a little shake of her head, there was another minute nod. Sister Gregory bent slightly at the knees to give Sylvia a view of her baby's face. "She's a beautiful little girl."

Her baby looked back, just a glimpse, but a knowing glimpse, her lashes thick and dark like his. *Mine. Oh, God, mine. A part of him. Gorgeous eyes just like him.* A small bundle of contented innocence who would never know how much she wanted to keep her. *Your daddy wanted to keep you too.* "Can she see me?"

"You're probably shadows to her. Her eyes are yet to adjust to light."

"She's so tiny…frail." She resisted the urge to search for her daughter's hands and feet hidden in the blanket, until she couldn't fight it anymore and reached frantically, needing to touch her own flesh and blood and found her baby's tiny fingers and held them gently—let the warm little fingers wrap around one of her own. "Can I give her a kiss?"

Another little nod. "Then you must go."

"Can I name her?"

"In your heart. The adoptive parents won't know the name you put on her birth certificate."

Sylvia leaned trembling toward her baby, the scent of her child—a warm, sweet, sleepy smell. *Margaret's your name.* "I called you Margaret," she whispered. "May St Margaret give you strength to slay all the devils you'll come across."

Their scent mixed with talcum powder filling her senses, taking away all thought except the smell of her child and the tiny fingers gripping her own. Her lips touched the warm cheek, and the softness against her lips made her sigh so lightly, for she wanted this moment to be only theirs. *You're beautiful. Just like him.*

You're mine. Ours. The most beautiful thing I've ever seen. I'm sorry, but you'll be fine. I'm doing this because I love you, but I swear I'll find you one day. "Somehow, I'll find you." And for those few seconds everything was as it should be. *Goodbye, for now, my little one.*

###

Sister Gregory cradled the baby close to her breasts and watched Sylvia walk away. The young girl's head twitched as if she considered turning back, but Sylvia continued along the hallway, her pace quickening. *God bless you, and may He help you bear each cross in your future.* She hugged the now crying baby, Sylvia's baby, close to her chest. "Shush, now little one. It will be all right."

But as she sat in the rocking chair, then paced the room cradling the baby, she cried, knowing the baby had sensed, had felt the bond with its mother and now felt abandonment, but surely it was impossible to grieve so young. *You can't miss something you've never had.* Unlike all the other times, she cried not only for the mother but also for the baby in her arms.

PHIL HATED Kim smoking in bed, but he wasn't here. It had been the longest day of her life, and he wasn't here. In all the years they had been married, he hadn't missed too many dinners. Tonight Kim ate dinner alone with their daughter Christine. Not that Kim ate much. Then Christine went around to a friend's house, staying for the night.

Kim climbed into bed. Not sure what she would say when Phil came home, if he came home. After Christine left, she put the letter back on the table, read it a few more times, studied the woman in the photograph, every inch of her. It was impossible to deny that she must be that child Kim had pushed so far away from her memory, had almost convinced herself that none of it had happened, that she'd really been set free and made pure again.

Time had turned it into a dream, an impossible dream to come to terms with. Time helped her shove the memories away, helped her to not know on what day her twins were born, not remember the date or the time, only a horrible haze—images and voices flashing—so little of it real.

The light from Phil's headlights flashed down the driveway, hitting their window, and the heaviness in her chest lightened. But he didn't come into the room, just turned the kitchen and lounge room lights on. She wondered if he'd sleep on the lounge. She'd been told never to reveal what had happened, reveal her shame. They were right all the time, all of them—what she'd done was unforgivable, made her a bad person, unworthy of Phil or any good man.

She moved then, pulled the covers off. *Go and talk to him.* But she didn't have to. He came and stood in the doorway. "I'm sorry I didn't come home earlier."

She let the words sink in and breathed so much easier. "I should have told you." She cleared her throat, knowing what she had to say, praying he wouldn't leave the house for good. "Angela was a twin...my other child was a boy."

He sat on the side of the bed. "I just read the letter."

Mouth dry, she fought the urge to touch his face, the curls of his hair. "I can't believe it. It's unforgivable...what they convinced us to do...is...my children will never forgive me...not totally."

His warm hands cupped her face, and he leaned to kiss her—featherlike kisses over her face. "It's going to be okay. We'll be all right. I was just being a jerk. It doesn't make any difference to me."

"I'm sorry...so sorry," she murmured against his lips. "I never had the words to explain...still don't."

His lips gently teased her mouth open. "It's all okay...I understand..." She closed her eyes and wrapped her arms around his neck, pulling him closer—and he was all she breathed, all she felt.

The kiss ended slowly, her lips leaving his reluctantly, lingering for one more kiss. "I love you."

An inch away from her lips, he whispered, "I was jealous...."

She held his hand, brought it to her lips and placed a kiss on his fingers. "No need."

"You've been given a second chance."

"They told me this would never happen. That it had to remain a secret. She doesn't know me...hates me."

"She's confused...trying to find answers. Come here. It happened a long time ago...look at me." He tilted her face to him. "You're being too hard on yourself."

"I felt selfish for wanting to keep them...."

"You've been a great Mum."

No, no. I haven't, not to them. I wanted it all to go away. "They must have made a mistake."

"She is the spit of you at the same age."

"I wonder how many girls they told it was to remain a secret. I wonder how many have spent all these years thinking it a mistake they can forget—a past that didn't deserve mentioning...or remembering."

"How many girls stayed where you did?"

"I don't remember...perhaps a dozen or so, no more, must have been more. The place was horrible, our rooms like cells, and the whole place smelt like disinfectant."

"Did you make friends with any of the girls?"

"We were told to keep to ourselves, oh, but I do remember one girl...."

"Did she keep her child?"

"I don't know—she wanted to." She looked into her husbands eyes. "But—most of us wanted—everything to be different."

SISTER GREGORY instantly knew who she was meant to meet in the reception area. Only one middle-aged couple looked anxiously around the room—the woman's eyes large and wide—her lashes thick and dark—*like Sylvia's Tommy's eyes...like their little girl's eyes. Beautiful eyes.* She walked straight toward the couple. "Mr and Mrs Smith."

The couple stood, and the woman held Sister Gregory's hand. "Thank you for meeting us."

"I'll get the Matron, Sister Bernard, to speak with you."

"No, please," the woman said, "Sylvia said to speak to you."

"Sylvia Dawes wrote to you."

Mrs Smith nodded. "A few months back."

"I'm sorry...but it isn't my place."

The husband stared straight into Sister Gregory's eyes. "For our son, for them all, please...."

Sister Gregory looked around the room. No one seemed to take any notice of her and she nodded. "Follow me, but I only have a few moments."

She walked ahead of them, silent, but fearing what was to come and her response to it. She opened her office door and motioned for them to sit in the chairs at her desk.

"We've done a great injustice to Sylvia," the mother said, "and our unborn grandchild, and our son, and we want to fix it."

Sister Gregory sat behind her desk, taking in the words. "Sylvia has had the baby. I'm not sure what there is to fix."

The mother leaned forward. "What did she have?"

"A girl."

"Oh, my," the mother said. "Is the baby healthy?"

"She's beautiful."

"Can we see Sylvia and the child?"

"Sylvia's still recovering...had a hard time during the birth."

"We initially gave permission for our son to marry Sylvia...," the mother said, then reached into her bag and pulled out a handkerchief, wiped her eyes, and motioned for the father to finish.

Mr Smith looked at his clasped hands. "But her parents convinced us they were too young. I had a friend—a warrant copper...threaten to lock Tom up if he didn't go to Vietnam." He patted his wife's hand, but she moved it away, gave him a steely gaze. "We...I thought if we kept them apart, the baby would go to someone who really wanted a child, and then they could move on with their lives."

"We shouldn't have forced him to go...them apart," the mother said. "It should have been his choice. He didn't want to leave Sylvia and their child, and we've heard rumours the war over there with our boy has intensified."

Sister Gregory crossed her heart. "My prayers are with you. I will pray for your son."

The mother wiped her eyes. "My son begged us not to allow their baby to be taken from Sylvia."

"Sylvia said your daughter wanted to adopt the child."

"That wasn't what Tom wanted."

"But your son is in Vietnam. How would Sylvia survive by herself?"

"We don't have the space, room in our little flat, but we can help financially a little."

Sister Gregory rubbed her brow. "The child has already been promised to a couple."

"It's our grandchild," the mother said. "If Tom doesn't come back to us...the child will be all we have of him."

"I'm sorry...I'm not sure there's anything I can do—but pray for his safety."

_____ *Sylvia*

SYLVIA COULDN'T see the children across the road, only the trees blowing in the wind. The construction of some tall buildings in the distance was complete, the shining glass of the multi-storey buildings reflecting the sun. The view to the distant suburbs was clear. *Margaret, where will you live? I hope they love you as much as I do. I hope you love them.*

She didn't turn when she heard the footsteps, slow and precise. "Thank you for letting me see my baby."

"The Lord can feel your pain." Sister Gregory pulled a handkerchief out of her pocket. "Take it."

"Don't preach to me about the Lord...."

"I have something to ask you."

"My baby isn't enough."

"What will you do when you leave here?" Sister Gregory moved away from the window and sat on the bed. "What are your plans?"

"Find a job, so I don't have to live with my parents. The caravan's too small anyway. It can't ever be the same for us again."

"They're back together?"

Sylvia nodded.

"That must be a relief."

"Makes no difference to me."

"You don't mean that."

Sylvia blew her nose and sat beside the Sister. "I'm glad they're back together, but I don't feel like myself anymore."

"You need to think about the future...what you will do with your life. You need to concentrate not on what you can't have, but on what you can."

"I wish I finished school."

"To teach."

"Dad always said I didn't need an education, and after all this I feel really stupid."

"These days young women can have careers of their own. Some choose work over love and others combine work and family if they have a supportive partner. What if I spoke to your father?"

"He's a stubborn ox."

"I might try anyway, if you don't mind. I would like to help. I've tried to help since you first came, and I won't stop until you walk through the gate."

"Well, I'm leaving tomorrow."

"What time is your mother coming?"

"Don't know."

"Try to keep your faith."

"Oh, you're going to try to help me keep my baby...I can see it in your eyes."

"I'm not sure I can deliver miracles."

"Then what are you talking about?"

"What will you do without Tommy?"

"There isn't much I can do."

"I mean in the sense...." Sister Gregory's face blushed. "Two years is a long time to wait for Tommy."

"I won't be able to face him, after he wrote to say he would send me every cent he earned to help me keep our baby."

"Men who see war up close, sometimes never returned the way they left...sometimes their minds or bodies or both are shattered."

"I feel bad enough.... What about all the young mothers married to soldiers? They are no better off."

"I'm trying to make you see the reality of your predicament and wondering how you will escape returning here."

Sylvia suddenly felt more frightened than she thought possible, her mind going in directions she didn't want to go. "Why does everyone think because I've had...loved Tommy, I've turned into a tart?"

"I think I was wrong to tell you love wasn't lust. Passion is normal...normal when someone cares for another person." She glanced at the door and whispered, "Should your Tommy come back to you, or you find yourself in love with another man, please consider speaking to these people." Sister Gregory reached into her pocket and pulled out a piece of paper. "It has the address of a Family Planning Clinic. They can assist in such matters. They care nothing of religious beliefs."

"You and everybody else have told me sex was wrong outside marriage." Sylvia bowed her head. "My mum thinks contraception is a sin. She risked dieing, rather than use it. That's why Dad left."

"I also believe it wrong...but it's obvious many people don't. It's not my job to force my beliefs onto you."

Sylvia took the piece of paper. "You sound like you've lost your belief."

"Perhaps..." Sister Gregory stepped to the door. "But I'll keep praying it returns."

"…HEAVY AUSTRALIAN casualties and eighteen killed in Long Tan, Vietnam."

Sister Gregory usually found great interest listening to the ABC News, being connected to the outside world, and a pleasure listening to some of the music. The words just announced caused her to stop. She closed her eyes. *Oh, dear Lord, please keep the rest of our boys safe.* None of the wounded or deceased names were announced.

She switched off the radio, a recent addition now Silent Time wasn't necessary. She sat at her desk and prayed for all the families who must be suffering and lingered over her words while praying for Sylvia and Tommy. *Hear their prayers to be together again.*

She finished praying, crossed herself, and stared at the picture of Pope Paul VI—the first reigning Pope to catch a plane, and the first Pope to leave Italy in over a century. He urged all Catholics for the first six months of this year to study and accept the decisions of the Vatican council and apply them in spiritual renewal. Most sisters hoped women would have a part in the world equal to men and not just as their servants. But he had opened a can of worms, maybe of serpents. He gave Catholics freedom from some ancient rituals they were previously expected to perform, but denied them the right to choose when to have children.

Sadly, the Pope wanted to move into a new world as far as he felt necessary—and Sister Gregory couldn't help wonder how many would leave the Church. The world they lived in was not the ancient world, the world of the Bible. She didn't feel like staying and promoting the word of God, when doing so clearly put so many women at a disadvantage and left them at the mercy of their partners.

Some waiting girls and married women asked when they would be cut open so their babies could be born. Despite the power of the media and current magazines to educate, and the Church's intention to catch up with the rest of the world, she had a deep feeling, nothing was going to change, not soon enough. She rested her elbows on the desk and her chin in her palm.

The door slowly opened. "Did you hear me knocking?" Mother Terrance asked.

Sister Gregory stood. "…daydreaming."

"I've just left the married women's ward. We've taken fatalities in Vietnam. I had a call from a Commander. A woman in the ward lost her husband in the fighting. I've just told her the news. She's terribly distressed."

"Do you want me to stay with her?"

"That's not why I'm here…sit, please…I've been speaking to the Matron."

Sister Gregory took a big breath, closed her eyes, slowed down her thoughts, and prayed to God to give her the strength to be honest and blurted out, "I think it would best if I left the Order."

"How long have you been considering this?"

Sister Gregory swallowed and begged for tears not to fall. "Maybe…from the first day, forever."

"You seemed fine until you came into contact with the day to day running of the hospital and involved with one girl in particular, or is this because of Sister Dominic? I've read your report to the Matron."

Sister Gregory stared at the Pope again—not sure what to say or how much to say.

Mother Terrance leaned forward. "I've spoken to Sister Dominic and also the medical students. Sister Dominic told them the girl's child was in the breech position and that Doctor Dennison was required immediately. When the girl heard this, she went to run from the room—that's when they held her down on the bed."

"It wasn't clear on the day what was happening…except the girl was distressed and in pain not normally associated with first stages of labour—since when do we hold down girls in pain?"

"…that was excessive."

"Every word out of Sister Dominic was not only sanctimonious but cruel. The girl was terrified."

"I have spoken to Sister Dominic about holding the girl down, but really, I don't think she realised the full extent of pain her actions or words caused."

Sister Gregory raised her voice. "I overhead a waiting girl the other day who stayed at King Street Hospital for her first child, telling another girl how the staff there tied both her hands to a bed-head to hold her down, despite her pleas to let her move around during labour. Sister Dominic spent a month there last year. Torture seems to suit her."

Mother Terrance closed her eyes and pinched the bridge of her nose. "I hear you… Sister Dominic is overworked…hasn't taken a day off for almost three years. I will insist she take some time off for respite in a convent in the country."

"That would be best."

"Now, we have that resolved, what's really bothering you?"

Sister Gregory didn't say anything for a long moment, wasn't sure if she could manage the implications her words might have, until she couldn't hold back any longer. "Sylvia Dawes' plight has made me question all we do—everything inside of me.…"

Mother Terrance rested her clasped hands on the desk. "Her plight is no different from any other girl here for the last thirty years." She looked down at her hands. "…And your personal plight is one we all have from time to time."

"Except she has voiced her wants more than others."

"The others have sense and move on…realise what they've done wrong and surrender themselves to the consequences."

"The consequences are so severe…how could they ever really move on?"

"We can't predict the future for any of these girls, but what we do know is that adopting out their children gives them the opportunity to embrace the world as if their body was as pure as they were born, and gives their children the opportunity to be raised by two loving parents."

"Sylvia claims she never signed the papers."

"A claim I've checked. Doctor Dennison was in the room when the papers were signed."

"Dr Dennison is the Matron's brother."

"You're stepping into dangerous territory...." Mother Terrance's hands broke apart, and she placed a palm firmly on the desk. "Don't beat around bush. Get on with it."

"Our practice is to solicit the signature on admission and..."

"Sister Bernard said they were signed on the sixth day...after the birth."

"Well! They weren't."

Mother Terrance frowned and her hand wavered just above the desk. "Sister Bernard said—," she leaned forward, "why wasn't this practise mentioned in your report to me?"

"I thought they were known to you."

"Well, you're wrong, very wrong." Mother Terrance slapped the desk and raised her voice. "Legislation forms Law! Isn't something to play with at whim."

"I only became aware we made them sign long before the five days on the day Sylvia arrived. Sister Bernard tried to get the girl to sign the papers that day in her office."

"Are you aware of other times?"

"I've always processed the forms as they arrive in my office...dates all looked fine."

"Perhaps this is a one off case?"

"I don't think so...."

Mother Terrance sighed. "Sister Bernard would have the best intentions on her mind...but perhaps deviated in this Sylvia's case."

"I told Sister Bernard there is a way for Sylvia to keep her child and the donation to the hospital. Another waiting girl had twins, and she and Sylvia resemble each other in build and colouring."

"But how does Sylvia support herself if she keeps the child?"

"There's room at St Anthony's Cottage in the convent grounds, and a vacancy in the hospital kitchen, plus government provides a little funding for these girls…she also has support from the child's paternal grandparents. They want to keep their grandchild."

"How do you know all this? How do you know she won't end up back here in the next few months?"

"They came in and told me so. She's in love with the father of the child. He with her, still."

"She is young. Two years are a long time for anyone their age to survive without companionship from the opposite sex. She'll be fair game for any man who shows her an interest."

"I think she might be a little wiser for this experience."

"If one was offered help, they'd all expect it. Those places at St Anthony's Cottage are for girls who don't have anywhere to go. Sylvia has a home she can return to."

"Sylvia can't return to her family with the child. They live in a caravan, and by what the Matron said, Sylvia's relationship with her mother is hanging by a thread."

"Working in the hospital is hard. She's young enough to be able to pursue a career, something she won't be able to do with a child. Allowing the girl to keep the child while unmarried will only cause the child to grow up being ridiculed."

"The father of the child will send money to Sylvia until he returns."

"How do you know this? The young man is in Vietnam."

Sister Gregory thought about the Pope's picture on the wall and imagined him frowning at her disobedience. "He wrote to the girl."

"Now I understand…."

"She deserved to know why he never met her. Deserved to know that he tried, but Sister Bernard had him arrested…the girl deserved to know he hadn't forgotten her, and his intention is to be reunited together with their child."

"Vietnam widows will rise, Sister. We don't know if he is caught up in the current battle and isn't dead already. He may never return and even if he does, this girl will still not be old enough to marry without her parent's permission. If they haven't given it now, I fail to see why they will then. Perhaps the boy is of a nature they think their daughter would be best to be rid of?"

"The young man had the courage to stand up and say he didn't want to go to Vietnam, that he wanted to stay with Sylvia, had the courage to come by here and tell her until we called the police on him and never told her. If he's got the courage to do that and now fight for his country, if Sylvia loses their child, he may find a solicitor to fight their cause."

"It wasn't long ago that a judge refused to give a young woman back her child after she signed the adoption papers. The woman appealed only a few months after signing the consent forms. This was a twenty three-year-old woman."

"In that case, consent was given when she was quiet capable of appreciating what she was doing. Not under the influence of medication, not where the date is all wrong."

"There isn't any evidence Sylvia didn't sign the papers when the Matron said."

Sister Gregory's voice wavered. "You said a bit ago, don't beat around the bush. Well, here goes straight at you, at us. Sylvia didn't sign the papers. I was there. Months ago, I gave Sister Bernard a letter in Sylvia's handwriting, with Sylvia's signature at the end.... Sylvia told me the day after her baby was born, the Matron told her that she signed them the night before. She never did any of that. She was too drugged to mark an X on the signature line. Our Sister Bernard is a liar and forger. And...I'm ashamed I did nothing about it sooner."

"Have you told the Matron your thoughts?"

"Not in so many words."

"Her response...?"

"None of these girls will let the whole world know their shameful secret."

"If this leaked to the media, our reputation will be destroyed."

"Then let Sylvia keep her baby."

"Were these twins identical?"

"A boy and a girl."

"The couple adopting Sylvia's child have already seen a picture of Sylvia."

"The girls look alike. We could still file the correct documentation in relation to mother and child, so if something should ever happen and the records are opened, the file contains the correct identification of mother.... But I've never understood why the adopting parents know these girls' addresses and sometimes what they look like, when the girls aren't provided any information about the people that will raise their children."

"This is for the child's protection, so the mother doesn't come looking for the child." Mother Terrance shook her head for the longest moment, then looked down at her clasped hands. "Of those who do keep their children, even those we've already helped at the Mother House, some lose the child anyway in a year or two to the welfare when they realise they can't look after them. The children are too old to be adopted."

"It's not all of them. Shouldn't it be their decision if they keep or adopt their children? Shouldn't they be allowed to try, if they want? How many men these days walk out when they find out their wives are pregnant? How many just walk out, period? Being married will not ensure a child is raised with both parents either."

"And there are many men who raise their children, when their wives leave the matrimonial bed and home."

"Not all because the mother is a bad woman...by law she can't take those children from the father."

"When is Sylvia leaving the hospital?"

"Her mother is coming later today."

"I think it's all a little too late now. Perhaps we'll just ride out whatever storm may come of it. Sylvia is not the first teenager to want to keep her child, and I'm sure although Sister Bernard's choices were misguided, they were well intended." She looked into Sister Gregory's eyes. "But what are we going to do with you? I don't want you to leave."

_____ *Sylvia*

SYLVIA WALKED toward the reception area, hoping and imaging that somehow she would leave with Margaret. *It's over. All finished.* One day, somehow, she would meet her baby again. Surely, God would realise how wrong it was. Margaret would probably grow to look more like him—have his height, his walk, his lips. *She has your eyes.*

Margaret. If they ever did meet again in years to come, she would have to speak the name strangers gave her daughter, thinking how strange to say this name of the woman, her daughter, her baby. The woman would recognise Sylvia, laugh and cry at the same time, and Sylvia would take Margaret in her arms and close her own eyes. Their scent would mix, filling her senses, taking away all thought except the warmth coming from the body she held.

Sylvia would forever remember one moment in time, which had been theirs—the scent of talcum powder, the tiny fingers gripping her own, the warmth and softness of her daughter's cheek against her lips. *Shhh...It's okay. It'll be all right* she'd say to a stranger—her daughter. For those few seconds everything would be as it always should have been. In that daydream, that wish, it was as if everything in the universe had been returned, gone full circle—her aching arms, her bones, her legs, her heart, returned to where they belonged.

But that reality wasn't possible. They would never see each other again. In the reception area, a woman sat beside her young daughter, and Sister Bernard spoke to Sister Gregory near the desk. Sister Bernard smiled at Sylvia.

"Where's my mother?"

"She's waiting for you at the gate."

"I want to say goodbye to the other Sylvia, Kim."

"She had twins and needs rest. She'll be staying a little longer."

"Well! That should make your day. An extra soul you can play God with."

Sister Gregory gently took hold of Sylvia's arm. "I'll escort you to the gate."

"I shouldn't have trusted you—"

The Matron clenched her teeth. "Don't cause a scene here...."

Sylvia couldn't read anything in Sister Gregory's expression. It was stone cold, no softness in her eyes. "...I thought..."

Sister Gregory led her to the hallway. "Silence. Please come."

Sylvia gripped her suit case handle. "You tricked me...you betrayed me too."

"The gate needs to be unlocked," Sister Gregory said. "Please, don't say anything else and leave now."

Sylvia walked toward the frosted glass doors, past the paintings of St Margaret and had the impulse to throw her suitcase through the glass but instead opened the doors. She walked toward the gate, knowing once she walked through it, her baby would be lost forever.

"You should have a sign on the gate," Sylvia said. "Entrance to Hell, Sanctimonious House."

"I admire your spirit," Sister Gregory said. "Whatever happens, don't lose it."

Sylvia looked sideways at Sister Gregory, but the woman focused on the ground, appearing not to want to reach the gate either. No old nun pruned or sang. She was dead like Sylvia. But it would all be all right. Sylvia would get over it. She wasn't really hurting. She couldn't even cry. It proved they were right. It was going to be easy for her to forget about it—as if it never happened. Once she stepped through the gate, she could go back to her own world. No one would know the difference.

Two novices walked around the grounds. Sylvia knew she would never forget the smell of lavender or ammonia, or the crunching sound that came from the nuns walking over the gravel at night—but somehow, she couldn't remember signing the adoption papers. It was like being two people. One person, or a part of her was left in the hospital—remembering little things—images and feelings burned into her mind. The other person walking toward the gate burying the memories—would never be able to speak of what happened here.

It was a secret. Something never to be spoken of. The matron was right. She didn't deserve her child—didn't fight enough—didn't care enough—and at times wished she wasn't pregnant and the whole mess would disappear. She would never let anyone know the shame she felt for being pregnant, about allowing her baby to be taken. That was one more thing she would keep hidden deep inside with her daughter's name.

The little children shouted and laughed in the street, and Sister Gregory mumbled, "Some people don't deserve children." Sister Gregory glanced sideways at Sylvia. "Their mother was told the road is unsafe, but still her children play outside."

Sylvia wanted one more view of her baby, one more glimpse, but Margaret wasn't being held in front of the window. No Sister was cradling her baby so she could say goodbye one more time. *Margaret's somewhere, but where? Is she crying? Who's comforting her?*

The closer Sylvia stepped to the gate, the gut wrenching sense of loss deepened…and she knew it would never leave. They had lied to her. She would never stop wanting what they took from her. But with each step closer to the gate, a fog surrounded her. Numbness spread through her legs and mind. The gate seemed miles away, her baby's cry ringing in her ears, the scent of talcum powder seemed to be in the breeze. *I'll never forget you. I swear I'll never stop loving you or wanting to know where you are. I'll find you if I'm ever given a chance.*

"Where's my mother?" Sylvia asked.

"She's waiting somewhere else," Sister Gregory replied.

"I don't understand."

"I've been speaking to the Sisters of St Anthony's

Congregational Leader, Mother Terrance. I've told her about you."

"I thought they were Mother Superiors."

"The world is changing and so is her title. We have a proposition for you. You can live at St Anthony's Cottage at the back of the Mother House with your baby, if you're prepared to work in the hospital."

She didn't hear right—*with your baby*—*must be another lie, another trap. Oh, God.* "I don't want to be a nun."

"That's clear by our conversations." Sister Gregory laughed. "You're not being forced into a convent, but being offered housing and employment and advice on Government subsidies you're entitled to until your Tommy returns."

"You told me I couldn't survive without my parents help."

"With a little of their help, the baby's father, and grandparents, plus us, at least for the interim we can keep you together."

What am I missing, what is wrong in this dream? "My mother said she wouldn't have anything to do with me if I kept the baby, that I'd be out on the street."

"Your mother is waiting in the bus with her granddaughter. She wants to see where you'll be staying, so she can visit. She told me that your father and she are going to find a house, so you can all live together until Tommy returns."

Sylvia noticed the sky. It was clear, a brilliant blue autumn day, without any wind—the hint of spring in the air. She thought of taking off her shoes and running over the lawn, instead she searched the dormitory windows. "But I thought my baby was gone?"

"Mothers have thirty days to revoke a signature."

"Why didn't you tell me this before…while I packed or something?"

"I was only told of Mother Terrance's decision twenty minutes ago, after she spoke to your mother. I was forbidden to tell you. We couldn't let the other girls know where you're going."

"I can't believe what you're saying. I don't understand why you're doing this after everything you said…everything Sister Bernard said."

"I've never had children…can only imagine the loss that would stay with a mother forcefully separated from her child. I believe, as do some of us, it would be long term. We can offer you some security while you're with us. Hopefully, by the time you choose to leave, your world is a different place."

A waiting girl looked through the glass, from the window, from *that* room, Sylvia spent six months in. She wondered how much that girl would fight, would resist, or maybe like most, she'd resign herself and her child to their fate believing all would be forgotten, could remain a secret, and their shame buried forever when they signed the adoption papers. "What about all the other girls?"

"We each have our own crosses to bear."

KIM WALKED toward the hospital gate beside her mother, hoping it was all only a nightmare—one that would end soon. She could hear her babies cry that day in that birthing room—see herself look away as the sisters carried her babies toward the door...first one, then the other, then nothing...*only a haze—in and out of sleep.*

Kim's mother wrapped her arm around her waist. "It's going to be all right."

Kim nodded, her arms aching, her legs heavy. One part of her didn't want to walk through the gate, climb into the taxi waiting on the curb, then fly away to her old world—but the other part wanted a plane to carry her to the other side of the world, right now, as far away as she could go and never return. They were right. She couldn't escape fast enough. She'd forget all this once she stepped through the gate...*the gates of Hell.* No one would know she was a failure. That she had a secret. She didn't fight enough to keep her children and would never speak of them. She would never let anyone know the shame she felt for falling pregnant. *I'm so sorry... I love you both...I've done the right thing. They've all said it's the right thing. You'll both be better off without me.*

A nun released the chain on the gate, providing a clear path to that waiting taxi.

Just go...just keep walking. Don't stop. Just get in the cab...you'll be home soon. Don't look back. Don't look at those windows, that building...at the girls watching you leave.

A car sped down the road.

It'll only take a couple of steps onto the road...and it can be over.

"Lovey," Kim's mother said, "I'll get in the other side. You get in here."

Kim slid into the back seat. The little girl and boy were playing in their front yard, laughing and giggling, their mother watching from their terrace balcony.

Dear God, keep my babies happy...keep them safe. Let me die with that knowledge.

KIM STOOD and imagined everyone around her would notice the tremble in every nerve. She looked at all the young women's faces, searched for those brown eyes. *She isn't coming. She's changed her mind.* Relief brushed over her, that she might not have to visit that deep and dark place inside, that she might not have to allow it to all burst out, to relive all that pain of her children being taken from her. But somehow she knew if Angela didn't show up, a deep sadness, emptiness, would stay with her forever that they might never stand one time face to face—never connect at least for a moment in their lifetime.

###

Angela saw her. *The woman in the picture.* She was petite, and although Angela was taller, it was the first time she'd seen a stranger and didn't feel like an oddity, out of place. The woman was attractive, and her clothes spotless, the creases in her shirt and pleats down the front of her pants perfect. Angela didn't step forward, didn't want to intrude on observing, watching this woman nervously fidget.

Maybe she didn't need to meet her now, maybe this was all she needed—to see this woman she'd dreamed about forever, at a distance...she was safe watching this woman who she hoped with all her heart one day she'd meet face to face, and she realised that she was thoroughly enchanted by this stranger—afraid to move an inch in case the woman disappeared and it was all a cruel illusion, afraid this stranger didn't want to find her.

This woman didn't even care enough to give her a name. The nuns of St Anthony named her, and the adopted parents kept the name in gratitude to the staff at the hospital. But she felt out of place in that family, her adoptive family, as if something was missing. She didn't belong anywhere…felt out of place her whole life. Oh, but her adoptive mother loved her, and she loved that woman—was grateful for her unconditional love, her kindness.

Angela wanted to walk away, felt torn about her adoptive mother sitting home alone, wasn't sure she could manage the pain and the tears rising in her eyes. *You've seen her. You owe her nothing.* The woman's searching gaze met Angela's. Angela had never looked into another woman's eyes and seen herself. Then the woman's lips trembled.

They stood in a vacuum just staring at each other, unable to move, unable to speak, just wanting this moment not to disappear. Angela finally belonged somewhere, to someone, and in that instant she looked across at this stranger and realised what she'd spent years searching for. *Peace. A connection. My mother…my other mother…my real mother.*

Angela appeared taller than Kim expected. *She has his height, his walk, his lips. She looks like him. But her eyes. Oh, my God. Mine.*

"Angela," Kim said, thinking how strange it felt to say the name of this woman, her daughter, her baby, and suddenly the woman laughed and cried at the same time, and Kim wrapped her arms around her daughter. Then it came back—the sound of Angela's cry, the sight of the sisters scuttling away with her babies, the helplessness and uselessness, and an outright horror for what was happening, what she was allowing to happen. She clung to Angela tighter, afraid to let go, afraid this would be the only time they would ever be as it should be. "My Mary, my baby Mary. It's all right. It's going to be all right." Kim closed her eyes and their scent mixed, filling her senses, taking away all thought except the warmth coming from the woman's body. And for those few seconds everything was as it should be.

The woman pulled back. "It's just such a shock to see you...I never thought I'd find you."

Kim nodded, speechless, unable to find words. *Here you are. My baby.* "I was told I would never see you again."

"You named me, Mary?"

"After my mum."

"There was no name on my birth certificate. I thought you mustn't have wanted...."

"They told me it wasn't my place, but your mother and father's...."

"I feel as though I'm betraying my mother for being here. She's so upset."

She has been betrayed. We've all been betrayed. "Your mum will always be your mother—no one can replace what's she's done. What of your dad?"

Angela looked away. "They didn't stay together. Separated when I was one."

"Do you still have contact with him?"

Angela shook her head. "I think they broke up because they couldn't have their own children. I think it was Mum...she seems so ashamed sometimes that she couldn't have me. She said the greatest wish she's ever had was to somehow change fate so that I came out of her body."

"Did she remarry?"

Angela shook her head. "I think he broke her heart."

Kim felt numb. Sister Gregory had told her that *every child deserves a father.* And Kim had believed that...thought that was the only way to raise a child.

Kim's attention turned to taking in the vision that was her daughter, what this young woman was saying, the reality this person she'd dreamed about was really sitting in front of her, and she floundered for words, for something sensible to say. "How long have you known?"

"Somehow I've always known, felt a longing and lonely as long as I can remember. I didn't understand, and when I was about fourteen I asked Mum if I was adopted, but she said don't be silly. I never felt as if I was like anyone in my family apart from my brother. Then Mum and I had an argument one night... I was a brat—screamed at Mum that I wished I had another mother." Angela wiped away tears. "That's when she told me, a week later, but I'd die if I could take back what I'd said to her."

"She knows you love her."

"I love her more than anything." Angela looked away then fidgeted with the spoon on the table.

"She must be feeling very anxious for you today.…"

"She said if you love something, you let it go...she said...it's not about her. It's about me."

"I'm grateful for all she has done for you." Kim searched for something else to say, something of substance, suddenly lost with the realty a great unknown space separated them. "So you have one brother?"

Angela nodded, but sat quietly, and it was as if the closeness they gained started to disappear and widen between them. "Do you know who my father is?"

Kim nodded and opened her handbag. She knew where the image of him was, but she didn't want to pull it straight out, didn't want their time to end and nervously fumbled with the photograph. "We were engaged to be married...when.…"

Angela eyes widened and she seemed to blow out a little breath of air, considered her words, not sure what to say. "I know things were different back then.…I don't mean to make you feel bad."

Kim tried to clear her throat, felt a thickness she didn't think she would be able to remove, and swallowed. "I thought he was gorgeous. You look like him." She pushed the photograph toward Angela.

Angela picked up the photograph and studied it. "But he didn't want us?"

"He wanted me to have an abortion...I couldn't bear the thought...knew someone would think you were a joy as I much I felt you were...would want and care for you." Then the *us* struck Kim. "You know about Robert?"

"If you mean Philip, yes. He doesn't want to know you. There is a letter on his file."

"You've spoken to him?"

Angela nodded. "He's happy with his life."

"He said that? I mean he is...? His parents took good care of him...." The realisation of what Angela said hit Kim and she held back tears. "Robert was raised with you."

Angela nodded. "They were meant to adopt another woman's child, but that fell through, so they took us both. He said he hopes you knowing that will make you happy, that it will be enough to know our mother raised us well."

Kim rubbed her brow, then looked down at her hands, feeling inadequate as she did the months after her twin's birth. "I will always be eternally grateful you both had a loving mother."

"I thank you for that."

It was with those words *I thank you for that*, and Angela's earnest look that showed Kim the strength of the bond between Angela and her adoptive mother, and Kim bowed her head, closed her eyes, but couldn't' stop the tears. "I'm sorry. I promised myself I wouldn't do this."

Angela leaned over the table, and Kim could tell her daughter was crying when she said, "So did I."

They embraced then, and hugged again, the most awkward of hugs, somehow over the middle of the table, and with their faces next to each other the years and the unknown disappeared, with a desire to be as close as they could, almost like lovers, they hugged and kissed, their tears mingling.

"I'm so sorry for the pain you're feeling," Kim whispered into her daughter's ear. "I'm so sorry."

Angela allowed herself to be kissed and cuddled, until their tears subsided, and they returned to opposite sides of the tables like strangers afraid of anyone seeing their closeness. After a moment, Angela said, "Don't be sorry...I'm not unhappy."

Kim sat silent, inadequate, could only take all of this stranger in, the woman her baby had become, and noticed her own hands on Angela, and searched through her bag and pulled out another photograph and handed it to Angela. "My husband, and... other daughter. Christine's fifteen."

Angela studied the picture, frowning just as Christine had. "She looks as tall as me."

Kim nodded and reached out her hand. "We all have the same hands...same as my mum's."

"Did they know about me?"

"Only my mum knew...but they want, if you ever want...to meet."

"A friend of mine was adopted," Angela said, a searching, a questioning look meeting Kim's. "When she found her biological mother, her mother said she was treated badly, was forced to give up her baby."

Kim looked down at the tablecloth...ashamed, ashamed she'd been convinced she wasn't worthy to keep her children. "I wasn't treated badly—would have kept you both had I known how. At the time I believed God was choosing parents for my children...that God would only choose the best parents...married parents."

Sydney, October, 1966 _____ *Sylvia*

HE ARRIVED home from Long Tan, Vietnam. But his best mate never came home alive. Eighteen of them never came home. At first he was only a bit of colour material, one part of a mass of khaki, until Sylvia stepped closer to the tape barrier and saw him marching.

The soldiers marched into the distance, their slouch hats looped to the side, marching not only to the drum's beat but an internal rhythm to keep their strides in perfect alignment—their stares focused on an unknown horizon—on their memories, their mates, were what they marched in time for.

Not a protester in sight, but a woman ducked under the tape barrier, ran toward the soldiers leading the march, so quickly Sylvia didn't realise what the woman held. He turned his face slightly, his eyes toward the woman, flinched, then red splattered as if a silent bullet struck his chest—blood red all over his uniform and an instant when confusion and disbelief silenced the closest crowds. People ran toward him. Sylvia ran toward him. *Why the soldiers? Why not the politicians who sent him there...? Took him away?* But the soldiers marched on. Sylvia's brother marched on. It was red paint thrown at the soldiers, but nothing would stop them marching for the fallen—for Tommy and all the others.

KIM STOOD at the window, waiting and wondering how it would all go. She remembered Sister Bernard's words. *It will remain a secret, and no one need know.* Now Kim wanted the whole world to know she had another daughter and son and what had happened. She thought of Sister Gregory then. *This isn't a choice I can make, but something you need to think about really hard. You need to make that decision.* But Kim realised now, she had never made a decision, had gone along with the flow, and everything flowed deeply out of her grasp and control.

Angela's little red sedan pulled up outside her house. Angela looked in her review mirror, then hopped out of the car, carrying a little black bag. At the same moment, Phil and Christine drove into their driveway. Kim stood and watched...afraid to move. The two girls came face to face, standing a few metres apart. They were both the same height—same colour hair, same eyes. Phil didn't miss a beat, walked over to Angela, took her hand, leaned in briefly, hugged her and kissed her cheek. He stepped back and introduced Christine.

Kim could see the awkwardness in both girls, both not knowing what to do, both staring at the other, taking all of the other in. Christine bit down on her bottom lip, then made a hesitant step forward, and they fell into each other's arms and embraced as if long lost friends afraid to part. Kim relished that moment—her two daughters, sisters hugging each other. But Kim couldn't stop secretly wishing she could hug Angela as a baby—had felt that connection years ago. That would always be a secret. Kim knew she needed that moment that would never happen and that Angela needed it too.

Regret would never leave the pit of Kim's stomach. She hadn't realised until she'd met Angela how much you could miss someone, yet still function—it was only now she could acknowledge that loss—now that she had her baby back again and as grateful as she was for the chance to get to know Angela, that numbness still existed deep inside over her son who didn't care to know her.

Christine and Angela turned their faces to Kim that moment, still hugging. They wiped away tears and smiled the largest smiles. *I have a sister. Oh, I have a sister.*

We have a part of us back...me back.

Historical Note

All the characters in *Unforgivable* are fictitious, including the religious order of the Sisters of St Anthony and my St Joseph's Hospital. Between the 1940s and 1970s, many unwed mothers stayed in hospitals or homes run by the Catholic Church until the birth of their babies.

During this period some sources estimate that 150,000 Australian women relinquished their children to adoption. This figure per capita was higher than any other country for the same period.

Following the enquiry into what is known as the *Stolen Generation* regarding the forced removal of children from Australian Aborigines and Torres Straight Island descent by Australian government agencies and Christian Missions, came a different enquiry regarding the removing of unmarried mothers' children.

In 2002, after many years of women claiming they were forced and coerced into giving up their illegitimate children, sometimes without their consent, the Australian government opened an enquiry named *Relinquishing the Past*. The enquiry invited Australian women who were unmarried and pregnant during the period to submit evidence.

The enquiry found evidence supporting women's claims of pillows or sheeting used to stop them seeing their new born children, restraints in some cases, the use of medication to subdued the women into signing the papers, as well as denying some women the right to hold their newborn children and also to name them. The rights of fathers who did want to support their children and unmarried girlfriends were often denied. Other women were only allowed to hold their children for a few moments, after they signed the adoption papers.

One of the clearest things to come out of the report was that almost every woman's story was the same, where systematic subversive methods of coercion or force and bullying happened Australia-wide with only small variables in treatment depending on the homes or hospitals where they waited for the birth of their children.

But most of these practices were in keeping with social attitudes, available financial support and social work knowledge and beliefs of the time. Some practices, such as removing the baby immediately following the birth to prevent bonding, were believed at the time to be in the best interest of the mothers for their emotional and mental health.

The belief that married couples were better suited than single mothers to bring up children, was a reflection of the era's societal attitudes towards illegitimacy and the extremely limited social and financial support available to single mothers.

The pressure on single mothers during this period was enormous, with evidence found in newspapers, including advice columns, *Letters to the Editor,* advocating for single women to give up their children for adoption by couples.

Perhaps one of the most surprising things out of the enquiry was that only one unmarried and pregnant woman came forward who had kept her child in this period. Kate Howarth's, bestselling and moving memoir, *Ten Hail Marys*, tells the tale of a young woman who fought and succeeded in keeping her child from adoption, while also highlighting some controversial laws and social policies of the times.

During the inquiry, the Sisters of St Joseph submitted evidence some women did keep their children and were provided accommodation within their convents and worked in St Margaret's Hospital in Sydney.

In January 2012, The Royal Women's Hospital in Melbourne submitted an independent report to the Senate Standing Committee on *Community Affairs Inquiry into the Commonwealth Contribution to Former Forced Adoption Policies and Practices* and in their press release, stated 45% of single women admitted to their hospital between 1945 and 1976 relinquished their children.

Later in 2012, the Australian Government apologised to women who were forced to relinquish their children, for their role and contribution to former forced adoption policies and procedures.

A Woman Transported

"A Woman Transported is a grand sweeping story that takes the reader from the slums of London to the untamed splendour of Australia. I really enjoyed the details and complexities of the story and characters. Definitely a worth while read."
Heather Gregson Author of *Dog of War*

Isabel is faced with only one choice — fight her way out of the rookery of St Giles with her wit and beauty and somehow follow the ship that sent her mother to the sunburned convict land of Australia, or else die too young after a short life of wretchedness.

At the height of the convict transportation to Australia, an unseen boundary separates the poor from the rich. Isabel's stunning beauty and strong will attract the attention of a wealthy man, but the upper classes have their own secrets, secrets entwined with hers. Daily, she has learned hard lessons on the mean streets of London, but they can't teach her fast enough about the treachery of the wealthy. She must navigate both the gardens of the upper class and back alleys of the downtrodden in two continents. And she will, or die trying to find her mother.

www.ingramcontent.com/pod-product-compliance
Lightning Source LLC
Chambersburg PA
CBHW020604180626
46810CB00007B/2642